THE INN KEEPER

LUISA BUEHLER

TORONTO • NEW YORK • LONDON
AMSTERDAM • PARIS • SYDNEY • HAMBURG
STOCKHOLM • ATHENS • TOKYO • MILAN
MADRID • WARSAW • BUDAPEST • AUCKLAND

It never happens without the extraordinary
support and encouragement from Gerry and Kit.
Thank you six times over.

Recycling programs
for this product may
not exist in your area.

The Inn Keeper

A Worldwide Mystery/November 2014

First published by Echelon Press.

ISBN-13: 978-0-373-26921-1

Copyright © 2009 by Luisa Buehler

Printed in U.S.A.

Acknowledgments

As with each of the books I write, the research becomes the fuel for the engine of the story. With this book the research became a journey for me. What started with a cursory review of slavery developed into a need to know more about the people who ran for freedom and the people who honored their God-given right to be free.

I'm grateful to the authors who have written on the subject, especially Glennette Tilley Turner, author of *The Underground Railroad in Illinois*. I would also like to thank Harriett Gillem Robinet for her invaluable insight on this topic.

I appreciate the evening I spent at Augie Aleksy's bookstore, Centuries and Sleuths, grateful to the people who sat around with me, Augie; his wife, Tracy; story manager Lynda Fitzgerald; and customers Bill and Pam. They listened while I fleshed out the premise and plot of *The Inn Keeper* and they tipped me to a resource I hadn't uncovered.

Thank you to Kelley Meagher, historian, Book Mouse employee and new friend, who took me to Ottawa, Illinois, and showed me confirmed *stations* on the Underground Railroad.

In my own "backyard" I marveled at the presentation of *Journey on the Underground Railroad* at Graue Mill. As a participant, my heart raced while we pretended to be runaways creeping stealthily, moving through the night ahead of the dogs and their cruel masters. In an unguarded, unreasonable moment, I felt fear, then hope that I'd make it. I can only hope that the tone of my story conveys a tiny bit of their reality.

"Follow the Drinking Gourd" to freedom. Could coded directions within a song encourage slaves to escape north? Look for the quilt a flutter on the rail. Follow the patterns to safety. Could anything be more precious than freedom? Could anyone be more despised than a Judas who traded on trust to collect his silver?

ONE

"IT'S GETTING SO it feels weird taking a shower at home. I haven't turned the spigot in the brownstone for ages." My sister-in-law stood in the kitchen doorway, her skin gleaming from hot water and no makeup. "You've been lovely to let us camp in whenever the spirit moves us."

"No thanks required, Hannah. We're thrilled to have you and Connor." I settled my nephew in the baby swing and started it rocking. "Especially Connor."

Hannah smiled fondly at her son before catching sight of the tray sitting on the kitchen counter. "Good heavens, Grace. Who are you feeding? Please tell me you've company coming."

"No, it's just us tonight. I thought we'd evaluate a bottle or two of a new wine Harry bought. I wanted us to have enough food to curb the effects of the alcohol."

Hannah shook her head. "My brother used to tell us how your entire family cooked for the holidays, preparing several main dishes and all the accompanying ones. 'Massive quantities of food,' he'd say." She waggled her finger at me. "You can't make a snack for less than twenty people, can you?"

I might have taken offense if she hadn't spoken the truth. Her cornflower blue eyes, identical to her brother's, sparkled beneath similar dark blonde brows. I always marveled at how the same strong features could bring such charming beauty to one face and sexy strength to another.

I'd been reminded of the resemblance on a daily basis.

With the onset of Hannah's newest plan to remodel a house in our compound, I'd seen her more often than usual. The prospect of my sister-in-law and nephew living in the house where Harry's ex-lover and mother of his son, Will, had once lived pleased me beyond words. The fact that Hannah's life partner and my best friend Karen hadn't embraced the move, and was in fact rehabbing an old boardinghouse in Oak Park, worried Harry and me.

Hannah fiddled with the wine bottle I'd set on the counter. I took it from her hands, deftly sprung the cork, and poured a generous amount of wine into two glasses.

"Let's sit in the nook."

Hannah slid onto the old church bench her grandfather had refinished after it had been damaged in a fire at the family church in Arundel, England. A perfect match for the trestle table, Harry had sent for it when we built our home in Pine Marsh. I watched as Hannah's fingers traced the pattern of the carved roses on one arm of the bench. I wondered if she regretted relinquishing the family heirloom now that she and Karen were settling into a home.

That thought led to another, but I hesitated to voice it. Instead, I placed the over-laden tray on the table and passed a small plate and fork to Hannah. Connor's timely *coo* suggested he might want a nibble of something. My sister-in-law popped up from the bench.

"Hullo, little one. I didn't forget about you."

Hannah pulled a container from the fridge and removed the cover, exposing an assortment of baby biscuits. She held one out and Connor's little fingers wrapped around the treat. He immediately "nummed" the tasty biscuit.

Seeing his delight, I said, "My uncle Jimmy grins like that when he doesn't put in his teeth, except he usually dunks his biscotti to soften it."

"Maybe when Connor's older he can dunk them in tea."

"Yeah, cause Uncle Jimmy dunks his in his homemade wine. *Vino* and crumpets."

"Well, yes, as long as he holds out his pinky." Hannah acted out her words.

I sat across from her and held up my glass. "To the wacky blending of our distinctly different cultures, *salud*."

"Cheers," Hannah responded. We clinked glasses and each of us took a sip.

"Mmmm. My brother does know his wines."

"I don't know. It's a little dry for my taste."

Hannah wrinkled her nose and smiled. "Your taste is bean related."

"Strange you should say that. I was just thinking about brewing a pot of Cinnamon Nut Swirl for later." I sensed the timing was good to voice my earlier thought. "Hannah, it's been great having you and Connor stay with us while you supervise the remodeling. I'm a little confused about the outcome, though. Karen is rehabbing the boardinghouse into a B&B. Are you going to live in Pine Marsh and hire someone to run the place? Or, are you remodeling the house here to sell and pay off the B&B while remaining in the brownstone? Harry says I shouldn't be nosey, but honestly, I can't figure it out."

Hannah's face momentarily reflected a shadow of sorrow. She mustered a "lips only" smile and reached across the table to pat my hand.

"A fair bit of 'yes' to most of your questions. Karen and I are thinking about separating for a time to figure things out. We've discovered some major differences in our feelings about habitat and parenting. We're not sure about our future."

My heart thudded in my chest and I felt a pinch of tears at the back of my eyes. "You two are great together. It's probably the stress of the babies and the rehab plans.

Maybe you should put the projects on hold and work on whatever you're struggling with now. You two love each other, don't you?"

Hannah's wry smile tugged at me.

"Of course we do. But that's not always enough." She rolled the wineglass stem between her fingers. "Gracie, I want to raise the kids out here with space and horses and nature. Karen wants to raise them in the brownstone with early enrollment in a posh preschool in another brownstone, a brick and mortar environment with the occasional field trip to somewhere green."

Hannah's eyes darkened with what I could only assume was a reaction to numerous conversations on this subject with Karen. I could also assume that her description of the situation was a tad biased, as Karen's would be. I watched her take a healthy sip of her wine.

"I want the kids to take riding lessons to gain confidence and poise. She wants them in karate to learn self-defense. I want to hyphenate their names 'Kramer-Marsden'. She wants Clare Kramer and Connor Marsden for insurance and legal reasons."

I hadn't heard that one before. It did sound odd to separate siblings by different last names, but then it happened all the time with remarriages or no marriages. There seemed to be something deeper, but I didn't know if I should probe. All at once I felt a prick of guilt at listening to my sister-in-law's side and not my best friend's. Hannah settled it for me.

"I apologize for going on about our issues. I should be going. Connor and I need to pick up a few things on our way home. There's nothing happening here until Monday. Why don't you and Harry and Will pop over tomorrow afternoon? You can see the progress on the B&B. Karen says the contractor has discovered sub flooring and a dirt cellar, which could make a perfect natural wine cellar."

Her eyes gleamed the happy blue I'd come to associate with a contented Marsden. Maybe separate projects would help them come to terms with their relationship. They say "absence makes the heart grow fonder", but my cynical friends always added, "of someone else". Could that be it? Was there someone else for one of them?

"Grace?"

I pulled my thoughts back to our conversation. Hannah waited for an answer to a question I'd missed. I shrugged my shoulders and smiled, but that only bought a frown from my sister-in-law.

"You don't know, or you're not sure?"

"I, uh, I'm sorry. I missed the question."

"No matter," Hannah said with a sigh. "We've had too many. Let's enjoy this marvelous repast you've prepared. We'll talk about this again before I leave."

I smiled my appreciation and filled my plate with small delights. Hannah refilled our glasses, which made me suspect Harry would be driving his sister back to Oak Park. We munched in quiet companionship.

Connor had gummed his biscuit and sat smiling at Elmo, my cat, who had surreptitiously licked the crumbs from the floor and the baby's fingers. My perfect feline stretched prepared to reach up to Connor's inviting biscuit-speckled lips.

"No, Elmo."

Elmo stood his ground, one paw on the swing moving to and fro with the baby, as though he were pushing it.

"Elmo, you have your own food. No."

Connor shrieked and reached out with chubby hands when the cat finally turned away.

"Mean, nasty Auntie Grace." Harry stood in the doorway. He walked over to Connor, picked him up, and snuggled him nose to nose. "Hello, my little chap. Won't they let you play with puss? These hens having a peck at you?"

I rolled my eyes at Harry's extravagant use of English colloquialisms. I'd accused him in the past of trying to make the children bilingual, but he'd simply ignored me. He didn't ignore me now, though. Tucking Connor under his arm like a football, he greeted first me, then Hannah with kisses.

"I'm absolutely famished," he said, pointing to the tray. "Would you put some of everything on a plate for me whilst I bond with my nephew?"

Hannah brought another glass to the table and filled it almost level. I shrugged mentally. Maybe no one would be driving to Oak Park tonight.

"Harry, I love this wine." Hannah emptied the last of it into her glass. "Hope you have more."

I piled the small plate with two of everything for Harry and pushed the large tray toward Hannah. "You'd better eat if you're going to drink another bottle."

Harry smiled at his sister. "Does seem like a bit much for a teetotaler like yourself, Hanns. Something bothering you?"

I saw her shoulders twitch. As much as I wanted to stay, I knew the conversation would flow more freely between brother and sister without me there. I murmured an excuse and picked up my plate and wineglass. I looked back at them from the doorway leading to the mudroom. Twin blonde heads dipped closer.

Elmo curled around my legs, perhaps understanding he needed to leave as well. I glanced down at him with a smile.

"C'mon, Elmo. Let's go find your sibs."

Elmo lived indoors with access to the outside. His

siblings, Patches and Trey, were barn cats content to hunker down in the straw in one of the stalls housing our two horses. I ate the last morsel on my plate and placed it and my wineglass on a shelf in the mudroom before filling my pockets with feline and equine treats. If we were headed for the barn I had to be ready for four hungry mouths.

"Let's go find those kitty cats," I said as I reached down and scratched Elmo's back. An agreeable *meow* sealed the plan.

The sound of a car door slamming drew me around the corner of the house. Walter Stahl, Harry's long time friend and odd jobs man, greeted me. "Ah, Missus Grace. I am hurrying to find Mr. Harry."

"He's inside with Hannah."

"Gut, gut. I am wanting her also."

Walter's speech pattern splintered with anxiety. He'd emigrated from Germany fifteen years ago but his accent remained thick. His demeanor made me nervous. "Is anything wrong?

"Ya. I am telling Mr. Harry."

Walter's loyalty to Harry was legend in our family. I released the breath I'd been holding and motioned Walter to follow me. We entered the house through the mudroom and crossed into the kitchen.

Harry and Hannah stopped talking. My husband glanced first at me and then at Walter. Like I had, Harry must have sensed trouble when he saw the older man's face. He immediately rose from his chair.

"What is it?"

Walter ducked his head toward Hannah. "I'm coming to say about Gertrude's house. She call me little time ago. The men who vas moving old floor find trouble. Police there now. Karen and Gertrude are only there with baby."

"Slow down," Harry said, frowning. "What trouble?"

Walter took a deep breath. "Under floor, they find someone dead."

TWO

My HEART TIGHTENED and the room tilted under my feet.

"Grab her!"

Walter reacted with a speed belying his size and age. He held me upright in his strong arms for the few seconds it took Harry to reach me and guide me to the bench.

"I am saying too fast. Please, Missus Grace, I am sorry." Walter's face twisted in concern.

"Darling, what is it?" Harry kept his arm around me. "Here, sit. Put your head down."

"I'm all right. I don't know, just got woozy for a second there. Maybe too much Shiraz." I wondered myself at my reaction. During the last two years my path had collided with the energy of too many old bones and tragic secrets. I had no desire to hear more about this discovery. "Really, I'm fine. I was on my way to the barn when Walter arrived. I think I'll take April out for a spin."

My smile fooled no one. Walter and Hannah stared at me with identical furrowed foreheads. Harry squeezed my shoulders, then turned to Walter.

"I'm staying in this evening. Perhaps you could drive Hannah and the little chap to Oak Park. I'm sure if the police are involved, Inspector Kramer will be on the scene. He should lend whatever support Karen may need, and you'll be there for Gertrude." Harry released me and rubbed his hands together. "All right then, everyone has someone." He brushed my cheek with his fingers.

Walter's brow creased with questions but he remained

silent. He nodded once and turned to Hannah. "I am waiting in auto for when you ready. Soon, I am hoping?"

Hannah's widened eyes sought Harry. Her head tilted
slightly. "Of course, Walter. We're ready now. Can we take
my van? I've the baby's seat in there and I need the van
over the weekend."

"Ya, ist gut. Gertrude vil kommen back mit me to pick
up auto."

With logistics settled, the three of them left, Hannah
promising to apprise us of the situation. I sat quietly while
Harry busied himself brewing tea, his English answer to
most crises. I would have bet the house that he would have
flown out of here with Walter, thrilled to rush into some
sort of investigation. Instead he stayed.

"I'm really okay. I mean, if you feel you have to go."

Harry's shoulders stiffened and he turned to me slowly.
"If I felt I had to go, I would have gone." His eyes bore
into mine.

I wondered if he meant it or if he thought he needed
to keep an eye on me. Long forgotten memories of my
Dad and Aunt Mary telling me to "Stay with your mother
when she gets upset, keep her company," played through
my head. I didn't understand until later about the manic-
depressive demon my mother fought. Did Harry wonder
about my demons?

"I really was going to saddle up." I stood and began to
clear wineglasses from the table.

"Sit down, Gracie. Please?" His voice carried no pa-
tronizing tone. "Don't shut me out." He took the glasses
from my hands and set them in the sink. His hands sought
mine and he brought them up to his lips. "I meant what I
said on the island. I would be inconsolable without you."
He slowly kissed each knuckle, all the while staring into
my eyes and willing me to stay. I'd almost died during a

vacation to Christian Island when Harry hadn't been with me. I had no intention of leaving now. Still holding my hands, he nudged my chin up. I stretched to meet his lips.

A trio of meows broke the spell and we whirled to find the kittens atop the table licking the olives and sniffing the cheese assortment.

"No!" The word exploded from Harry. Three furry culprits hit the ground running and scampered from the kitchen. Elmo slowed at the door and pleaded for understanding.

"Bad cat, Elmo," Harry growled. "You live here; you should know better."

So much for understanding. Elmo turned tail and raced to catch up to his less conflicted sibs.

"I must have left the door ajar when Walter arrived," I said apologetically.

The corner of Harry's mouth lifted slightly. He pointed to the trail of scattered olives. We burst into laughter.

"Remember Arlo?" I asked through a fit of giggles. Arlo was the wayward tomcat that belonged to Harry's parents. On our last visit, Arlo had devoured our picnic lunch in the few minutes it had been left unattended.

Harry nodded. "I recall we lost all the olives that day, too." We laughed harder, enjoying the remembered good time and relaxing in the warmth of shared experiences. I slipped my arms around my husband's waist and leaned into his strong chest. Harry's six-foot stature provided perfect hugging height. His lips pressed against the top of my head and I snuggled in closer. He whispered a delightful suggestion in my ear, then nipped my lobe. I lifted my arms to encircle his neck and pressed against him, turning my face to deal with his strong mouth.

"Hmm. I love the way you feel against me." Harry's arms tightened around me.

This close, there was no doubt how he felt about me.
My body quivered with anticipation. Alone, alive, and so
ready. The events of the last two years had tested our resolve to stay together, strained our relationship with family, and put our lives at risk. During that time Harry had
never firmly chosen me over the crisis *du jour*. Tonight
he had, and for that alone he would be rewarded big-time.
I smiled before I realized kissing lips don't do smiles. He
pulled back slightly.

"What's so funny? Honestly, Gracie, this is hardly the
time to chuckle."

"Everything is wonderful. Did I give permission to remove those lips from my proximity? Get back here." My
lips puckered in blatant invitation and I batted my eyes for
good measure. I started to grin, amused by my own antics.

"Hold still. How can I kiss you with all that movement?"

Harry's lips locked onto mine and wiped the smile off
my face. He shifted in preparation to lift me into his arms.
No simple sweep since I'd never been a featherweight and
ten years of marriage had shifted my center of gravity. The
romance of a pencil-thin waif carried off to the *letto matri-
monile* gave way to the reality of a sturdy thirty-something
me fearful our impending romp might land my husband
in traction. In the second before lift-off, I squirmed and
threw off his attempt.

"What's wrong?" Harry's blue eyes searched my face.
"Grace?"

I couldn't tell him I thought I was too heavy for him to
lift me, didn't want him to ever realize that. The picture
of him bowlegged under my weight tugged at my mind.

"I need to clean up the kitchen. They might come back
and eat more. Or mice, we'll get mice."

Harry's face reflected confusion. "Who gives a teat if
they eat it. It's the cats' now anyway. And we don't have

mice. If this isn't what you had in mind," Harry shrugged, "you only need tell me."

He grabbed a paper towel and picked up the errant olives, dabbed at the floor with the towel, then tossed it in the garbage can. Carrying the can to the table, he tipped the tray until the cheese and peppers slid into the receptacle. Then he pulled the plastic liner from the can and angrily twirled the top into a knot.

"Finished. I'll drop this in the garage on my way out."

Harry's calm tone chilled me. I'd hurt him.

"Where are you going?" I feared the answer.

"Oak Park. No need to wait up."

With those few cutting words he left.

I stepped toward the door, but he'd already closed it none too gently. I heard the overhead door riding up the track and knew he'd be gone in a minute. *Move, dammit, move. Catch him. Not now. No.* I squeezed my eyes shut against the tears and followed the pattern in my head. *Turn to the right, turn to the left. Turn to the right, turn to the left.* My obsessive-compulsive behavior disrupted my life at times of stress and anxiety, like now.

I finished my pattern and rushed to the garage. The overhead door rested firmly against the concrete. Harry was gone. No use to chase after him. I needed to think.

My number one cobweb clearing exercise was a brisk ride atop April Shower, my Tennessee Walker. I strode into the mudroom and grabbed my jacket from a peg.

I'll feel better after a ride. Oak Park, he said. Will he be visiting Lily, or checking on a dead body?

THREE

APRIL WHINNIED BEFORE I opened the door. She stretched her head across the top of her stall begging for a nose tickle and treat. I offered her baby carrots in my palm. She gently snuffled them into her mouth. She knew my empty hand would provide another treat, and she pushed her velvet nose into my palm.

"There's my pretty girl. Such a good girl."

An impatient snort cut short my praise. Cash Cow pawed the floor sending straw shards around his stall.

"Okay, okay. You're a good horsey too."

I placed an apple half on the tips of my fingers and arched them down as soon as Cash grabbed the treat. My hand/his mouth coordination still left a lot to be desired.

"Sorry, Cash, but it's just the girls today."

I filled his treat tray with a few tasty morsels as a token of consolation for not taking him out. He was an exciting, powerful horse and I enjoyed riding him when I felt vibrant and in control. April was my pal, my comfort, less fattening than chocolate, less judgmental than friends and totally capable of keeping a secret. I swear she senses my demeanor when I walk into the barn. She can tell which one of them I'll choose. She knew she was the one today.

I led her out of the barn and mounted quickly, feeling guilty as Cash's whinnies filled the late afternoon calm.

"Sorry, big guy. I promise, I'm next."

A low *giddy-up* and we picked our way beyond the privet hedge, through the band of woods that separated

Pine Marsh from the golf course, across the horse trail that runs behind the ninth hole, and finally to the undeveloped meadow.

April's gait, which is less than perfect for her breed, almost got her destroyed by her previous owner. I, maybe better than some, understood the pain of imperfection, or "less than" status. Her lopsided movement doesn't bother me a jot. When we reached the meadow and I cued her to run, her gallop was as good as the best. Her ears laid back, she lengthened her stride and ran for the sheer joy of it.

When I met Harry I knew I'd found the person who would care not a jot for my imperfection and who would encourage me to find my stride. I wasn't in danger of being "destroyed" but my obsessive-compulsive issues had scared off more than one suitor.

I gently reined in April. We were approaching a slope that climbed to a small hill. It wasn't safe to run full tilt on this ground. April picked her way to the top of the hill and stopped to munch grass. I leaned forward and laid my head along her neck, absentmindedly twirling my finger in her mane. My heart ached for the way my life with Harry had been two years ago, before the restless spirits of old bones had begun to intrude on my life and my sanity.

Lost in thought, I crouched lower on April, letting my arms hang down on either side of her neck. I swayed easily with her body movement as she wandered about the hill choosing tasty bits of greenery to chew. Just as I was beginning to relax, a cool breeze slipped up the back of my jacket. I shivered and quickly straightened in the saddle.

"Let's go, girl. Can't stay out here all day."

I'd lost track of time. The short spring day was almost over, shadows moving in where sunshine had been moments before. I couldn't run April through the meadow in low light; it was too dangerous for her. I knew it would be dark when we returned to the barn. Nevertheless, we took the ride home at a slower pace.

I didn't like riding through the woods at night, but there was literally no way around it. Pine Marsh abutted the golf course. The property line separating the two was blurry at best and blended eventually into a patch of marshland. Either we galloped across the golf course to the entrance or we went through the woods at the back of the properties.

"C'mon, April, we're almost home this way."

My horse tossed her head and side stepped onto the mulched path. Her nervous behavior came directly from my body language. I'd gripped her with my thighs without giving her a knee signal, and I'd held the reins too tightly for her tender mouth. She knew to be upset, just not why.

The thick hardwoods gave no easy egress for the waning light, allowing only slivers of illumination to penetrate. I concentrated on slow deep breaths, exhaling long streams of air to dispel my nervousness. My brain clamored for the pattern. April felt the release and calmed down. While I breathed in and out to the pace of an internal urge, my companion found the trail and brought us home. Once there, she halted and waited for me to dismount. I *had* to perform my breathing pattern six more times. April stood still, her ears pricked forward as if she understood my strange behavior. With my last long cleansing breath, she stepped closer to the barn.

I swung down and lifted the latch on the barn door. The light switch activated as we stepped inside. Cash snorted his welcome and I heard a trio of meows from somewhere in the straw. I removed April's bridle, hung it on the peg outside her stall, and repositioned the lead on her halter.

"Here, baby girl. Sorry I tugged at you."

She gently picked the small carrots from my hand. I tickled her nose and kissed her cheek, then proceeded to remove her saddle and pad. I brushed down her back and withers, lifted each hoof to remove stray bits of debris, and filled her snack tray with horse chow nuggets. Then I added fresh water to her bucket and turned her into her stall.

Cash pawed for attention. "Okay, you big baby." I dumped some chow in his tray and his needs were met. So he didn't think there was such a thing as a free lunch, I held back the sugary treat he preferred and made him earn it. I'd been teaching him simple hand signals—parlor tricks. When you don't have a job and you don't have kids, you do what you can to have something to show for your days.

On cue Cash nodded "yes", shook "no", and tossed his head from side to side. I gave him his treat and kissed him good-night. "Elmo, are you staying or coming with me?" An orange kitty stumbled out from behind an empty water bucket. "All right then, let's go." His sibs preferred the freedom of the barn and no other felines appeared. "You two keep the mouse population in check," I called over my shoulder. I heard an affirming meow.

I latched the door behind me and gathered Elmo in my arms. "I know it's early, too early to go to bed. Well, for me, that is. You'll probably be curled up in two minutes. Wish I could sleep away the hard days, the long ones when I feel this way."

I understood that wish. I'd seen my mother succumb to a manic depressive malaise that kept her in bed while the rest of the world worked their lives to the best of their ability. I'd come to understand she'd done the best she could, but I knew I had to do better.

I put Elmo down in the mudroom, hung my jacket on a peg, kicked off my shoes in a practiced arc to the boot mat, and pulled off dirty socks. Collapsing on the bench, I

crossed my arms against my chest. The mudroom seemed
colder than the house, but it wasn't temperature that chilled
me. My husband, best friend, and probably by now some
of my nosey family were at the boardinghouse.

*Harry wanted to be with me tonight and I pushed him
away. Why can't I get it right? Am I in some kind of self-
destruct mode like Mom?*

"It's apparent I have to be where they are because they
aren't going to accommodate me."

Elmo meowed his agreement as I slipped on the still
warm socks and inspected the jumble of shoes and boots
for a cleaner, more presentable pair. I needed a quick wash
up and my purse. The bright bathroom lights exaggerated
the dark circles under my violet eyes. I brushed my hair
straight back off my face and behind my ears. My shorter
hairstyle still took some getting used to. I hadn't decided
if I'd keep my thick sable-brown hair at this more manageable length; it made me look like a bubblehead. I could lose
the extra weight. I could let my hair grow. Maybe both?

Old habits die hard. My OCD forced me to take my
time checking doors and turning off lights. Mercifully, I
flipped off the last switch and felt no urge to fiddle with it.

"Elmo, I filled your water bowl. I won't be too late."

Like you care, I thought as the garage door rode up the
rails. *As long as your bowls are topped off you wouldn't
mind when I got home, if I got home. Okay, Gracie, now
you're obsessing. Turn on the car and get going.*

Good advice from the part of me that paid attention
during therapy. I drove swiftly through Pine Marsh, glancing in my rearview mirror several times before reaching the highway. The steady hum of Interstate-88 under
my tires provided a quiet backdrop to my thoughts, half-
formed ideas that pushed and shoved at each other until

my brain sorted and shelved them in a cerebral Dewey decimal system.

I sailed through the Hillside Strangler, the nickname for the local traffic bottleneck, and exited I-290 at Des Plaines Avenue. I weaved my way through the side streets of Forest Park into Oak Park, eventually reaching Gertrude's old boardinghouse. Several cars, two squads, and the coroner's vehicle choked the street on each side.

Light spilled from the first floor windows of the charming two-story, turn-of-the-century home. Unable to maintain the place on her own, Gertrude had applied for Landmark status and the financial assistance that accompanied it. When her application was denied, she sold the house to Hannah and Karen. Since purchasing it, they'd begun the renovation that would ultimately result in *Brit's Haven*, an upscale B&B marketed to visiting Englishmen. The plan was to give Brits an exclusive Chicago-Style experience. The rest of the family wasn't sure what that meant.

I parked well away from the crowded area and walked slowly toward the house. I nodded to a couple standing at the end of their front walk.

"Hi. Hope you don't mind if I park here. My friends own that house and I want to find out what happened."

"No, that's fine," the woman said with a smile. "We were wondering the same thing. Did someone get hurt?"

"Sandra, I told you: the ambulance is for hurt, the coroner's van is for dead." The man grinned at me. "I mean, that makes sense, doesn't it?"

"Bill, you're as subtle as a brick." The woman's blue eyes held deep affection for her husband. She linked her arm through his. "I'm sure we'll find out later. C'mon, we're due at the Flynns' at 7:30."

I nodded and walked on. The next house had no inquisitive owners at the curb, and I crossed to the crowded side of the block. Karen Kramer, my best friend since college, stood with her back to me, feet set wide apart, arms wrapped around her chest. Her closed posture made me call out rather than tap her on the shoulder.

"Karen?" She whirled around, stepping off balance but recovering quickly. I reached out to steady her arm. "Nice recovery. I would have landed on my butt if I did that. Didn't mean to startle you."

"Thank God you didn't touch me or I'd be in the top branches of that tree." Karen smiled up at the hundred-foot-tall tree in the front yard. "Well, maybe not the top branches."

I hugged her, then rubbed her arms. "Where's your coat? You're like one big icicle." I wrapped my arms around her again. My 5'4" height couldn't cover all of her willowy 5'10" stature, but from her elbows down I was on it. I released her and unzipped my jacket. "Here, I'm wearing long sleeves."

Karen dove into my still-warm jacket and grinned at her exposed forearms. "Three-quarter-length pea coats. It's all the rage. Thanks, Gracie. I didn't realize how cold I was. This whole thing has thrown me for a loop. The guys are in there watching the removal."

"Did you see the body? I mean, do they know who it is?"

My friend's expression turned cautious. "I thought Walter told you."

"He did," I said, frowning. "He said 'someone dead' was in the sub-cellar."

"Not a body, Grace. A skeleton." Karen whispered the last words. "Old bones."

FOUR

I SWALLOWED QUICKLY, then clenched my jaws against the bile that rose unbidden in my throat. I shouldn't have come.

"Grace, you okay? I'm sorry, I thought you knew. Gertrude and I are getting ready to leave and take the kids home. Hannah's staying. You know her. Always hoping for 'contact' from beyond." Karen rolled her eyes, but the grin that usually accompanied discussion of Hannah's "beyond the grave" obsession flashed false across my friends tight lips. "Anyway, we're going. Come with us."

An evening with my normal two-feet-on-the-ground pal and her two adorable babies sounded great about now.

"I'll meet you there."

"Meet who where?"

Ric Kramer's voice startled me. Karen's brother walked toward us at a brisk pace I'd never have thought possible six months ago. He'd been injured in an explosion caused by a nutcase firing a mortar shell into my house. He still used one cane, this one shiny black wood with a pewter knob top. Those in his close circle surmised he didn't really need a cane but enjoyed them as a prop. I think he fancied himself Bat Masterson. The theme song from the old television show began playing in my head. *Back when the West was very young.*

"Grace?"

I tilted my head to see him more clearly. His dark eyes were so familiar with that quick crinkle around the edges when he smiled.

"It's good to see you. I heard about the island; happy to see for myself that you're okay." Ric lifted his hand and brushed the back of his fingers against my jaw line, then tugged on the ends of my hair. "Nice to see you didn't have to go shorter," he said, referring to the last encounter I'd had with recently uncovered bones, an encounter that ended with a bob haircut to even out my singed hair. His strong white teeth flashed a smile that most women would die to receive. "Where are you going?"

"She's coming back to the house with Gertrude and me," said Karen. "We don't need to hang around here."

"Does Marsden know you're here?" Ric rarely referred to Harry by his Christian name preferring to keep a distance between him and the man he insists is all wrong for me. There had been a time, a set of circumstances during which I thought I would have a life with Ric. We'd moved well beyond that, but even though strong feelings fade, they don't disappear.

I shook my head. "Got as far as Karen and decided I shouldn't have come." I reached up and put my hand on Karen's shoulder. "Thanks for the invite but I think I'm going to head home. Coming here was a bad idea and I should go before anyone else…"

"Gracie! Over here, Gracie!" My brother Marty and my Dad waved from the front porch of the boardinghouse.

"…sees me." I shrugged. "Oh well, guess I'm here for awhile."

Karen leaned in for a hug. "If you change your mind, we'll be there."

I walked across the front lawn; Ric fell in step with me. "It really is great to see you, Grace." His eyes sought mine but I kept focused on the front porch. He reached for my hand. "Grace, I have information I need for you to know. Can you meet—"

"Jan's here too," I blurted out, stopping him in mid-question. My father's lady friend (what else do you call your dad's squeeze?) Jan Pauli waved at me. I lifted my hand in response.

"Grace, can you meet me—"

"Gracie, honey, what are you doing here?" My dad stepped between Ric and me and engulfed me in a bear hug. Ric knew when he was beat; he veered off toward the side of the house and the yellow plastic tape that separated the bystanders from the professionals. I saw him lift the tape and ducked under.

"Harry said you didn't feel well. Everything okay?" My dad let go and waited to gauge the honesty of my answer by the color of my eyes. A physiological quirk turned my violet-hued eyes pansy purple during times of anxiety or excitement.

"I felt a little odd when Walter told us about the discovery. But after I took April out and got some fresh air, I got curious and well, um, here I am." I hoped the semi-truth would keep my eyes pastel.

"Fresh air, that's what you need. Harry told us you've been holed up in your room for hours writing again. Honey, I know you feel you went dry with the kids' series, but they were best sellers. You're still cashing those checks aren't you?"

My dad's attempt to put my writing career in perspective embarrassed me. I'd lost my publisher over a year ago when I couldn't deliver a contracted book. The joy of writing had been sucked out of me by cruel events beyond my control. I'd only recently taken up my pen again. This time I wasn't writing for children. My next book would attempt to document how the restless spirits of old bones have reached out to me. I really wanted to know why it happened. And part of why I came here was to see if it would happen again. I knew I'd have to get closer than the front porch to do that.

I shrugged and smiled. "You know me, Dad. Can't not write." I hugged him and whispered, "I love you. Thanks for loving me." I let go and glanced towards the boarding-house. "How are you and Jan doing?" It had taken awhile for me to accept that my father was attracted to someone other than my mom. It had been almost six years since she died and Jan was the first woman he'd taken an interest in. Being the only girl amongst four brothers, I had been and continue to be the apple of his eye. *Now there's a "tamata" in the bowl.* I grinned recalling my Uncle Jimmy's slang term for women.

Dad put his arm around my shoulders and led me toward the porch. "We're doing great. There's something I want to talk to you about." His voice dipped to a whisper.

"Hi, Jan." I pulled away from my father and walked quickly to the stairs. I moved up one step, she moved down one, and our quick hug spanned the difference.

"Hi, Grace. Harry said you didn't—"

I waved off her concern. "Temporary blahs. I'm fine. How did you two hear about this? Did Walter ride through your neighborhood too?"

Jan nodded. "Yeah, shouting 'one if by land.' When Gertrude called him about the discovery he was at the house teaching your dad how to make strudel in exchange for Nonna Santa's calzone recipe."

I nodded and smiled. Part of me cringed to hear "the house" and "Nonna Santa" slide from her tongue like she'd been part of us forever. I squeezed my eyes shut and pictured my mom.

"Grace, are you all right?"

"What's wrong?" My dad's voice blared across the few feet between us.

"I don't know," Jan said. "We were talking and she suddenly closed her eyes." The thin tremor in her voice pleaded for reassurance.

What *was* wrong? My eyes weren't squinched tightly shut, but they weren't open either. I stood perfectly still.

"I'm fine. Just resting my eyes." Truth was, I needed to finish counting to twenty by two's, and they kept interrupting me. My obsessive-compulsive disorder complicated my life at the oddest times…*eighteen, twenty. Finished.* Two pairs of eyes stared at me. I smiled weakly. "Sorry. Had to pull over and park my brain for a minute."

"Where's that husband of yours? You need to go home and park your butt."

"No. Don't bother him. I'm going to head over to Karen's and catch up with her. Let Harry and Hannah enjoy their time together." My sister-in-law, who was as sensitive to the "spirit world" as a fence post, never gave up on the hope that she'd connect to the other side. The other side could stay put as far as I was concerned.

I said good-night to my dad and Jan and retraced my steps to my car. I caught movement out of the corner of my eye. A black man stood near the far side of the house staring across the lawn towards the activity. His ragged clothes hung on a too-thin frame. His head snapped around as though he'd heard something behind him. The fear on his face when he turned was unmistakable. I tensed and peered into the darkness surrounding him, ready to shout for help. When I glanced back in his direction, the man had melted into the shadows.

Please God, make him real. Make him a homeless person seeking refuge for the night.

Maybe that was the answer—a homeless person who'd been living in the abandoned house before the construction had returned to see if he could chance one more night under a roof. Or was he a soulless person returning to see who'd found his remains? I shuddered at the thought.

FIVE

INSIDE MY CAR the thought of some spectral being checking out who found his earthly remains seemed silly. I laid my arms across the steering wheel and leaned my forehead on my wrists.

Geez, Grace don't go looking for them.

Them? What them? I just saw.

Saw what? Do you want this to happen?

Are you cra...

Hey, we agreed never to use the "c" word.

A rap on the window startled me and I pushed down on the horn. Ric jumped back from the window as several heads turned in my direction. One particular blond head came bobbing toward me at a fast pace. I opened the door and slowly swung my legs out. Maybe I could sit and avoid total contact with anyone.

Harry reached the driver's side. "What's wrong? What's going on? Kramer, why the bloody hell can't you leave her alone?"

This wasn't going to end any better than it started.

"Leave her alone?" Ric glared at Harry. "I didn't do anything. I rapped on the window because she had her head down on her hands. I thought she might be sick."

I knew he rapped on the window because he had something he wanted to tell me and because he wanted me to meet him somewhere.

"She's not ill; leave her the hell alone." Harry's voice rose in exasperation.

"You're the one who told us she wasn't feeling well. I acted on your cue. You can't have it both ways, Marsden."

"I can have it any way I damn well please." Harry stepped closer to Ric.

Ric glanced at me. "I have an investigation to continue, but I will call later to check on you." He turned to Harry. "I'm not playing whatever you think you're dealing." He turned away and strode back to the house.

"What are you doing here?" Harry asked. "You obviously wanted nothing to do with me. I know you didn't come because of the bones. What or who drew you to the house?" He glanced at Ric's retreating figure. "Perhaps someone you knew would be here."

His tone left no question. He thought I'd turned away from him because of Ric. How stupid could a man get?

"I came because I realized I didn't want to be alone. In hindsight, alone would have been a better place." I swung my legs under the wheel and leaned out to grab the door handle.

Harry stepped forward to block the door. He crouched in the opening and extended his hand to me.

"Gracie, I'm sorry. I had no right to go off like that. I didn't want to come here. I felt angry—no, confused—that you rebuffed me. I should have stayed. Gracie, our relationship shouldn't be this difficult after all these years."

He held my left hand and waited for me to respond. I leaned against the headrest and turned my chin to the right to loosen tight muscles.

That's when I saw him again—the man in the ragged clothing. He stood between the police tape and the house staring straight at me. The hairs on my neck scraped against the headrest. I jerked my hand from Harry's grasp and gripped the wheel.

"Gracie, what is it? What's wrong?"

I kept my eyes focused on the wheel and pointed with my right hand. "Someone at the side of the house. Not police. Black man." The sentences squeezed out from behind clenched jaws.

Harry rushed into the street. I turned my head hoping to watch my husband confront the man I'd seen. Harry hesitated, glancing back at me before crossing the street and walking the length of the tape. He stopped and spoke briefly to a policeman. There'd be no confrontation.

I pulled the door closed and started the engine. I needed to get away. It was happening again. People that only I could see. Thoughts not mine yet running through my brain.

Harry swung back towards the car, but I'd already pulled away from the curb. I needed to think, to talk to the most non-judgmental person I knew. I glanced at the time; it was not too late to visit Elmhurst.

"HEY, COME ON IN. Slumming?"

Tracy's grin lit up my heart. I stepped into the hall feeling relief flood my tense spirit.

"Who's at the door?" Matthew's voice preceded his appearance. Tracy's oldest son slid around the corner in a practiced move and stopped short of barreling into his mom.

"Aunt Grace. Hey, it's Aunt Grace," he shouted over his shoulder. "You haven't visited in forever." He checked the front porch. "Is Will with you? Where's Uncle Harry?"

"Slow down with the questions already. Let her come in and sit down." Tracy led the way to the kitchen. "How about a cup of coffee? I have that Mocha Madness blend you like. Actually, I think you gave it to me so I'd have something here you liked."

"I'll grind the beans." The sweet voice of Tracy's younger son sounded from the doorway.

"No, you can't, Ben. You're too little. Right, Mom?"

"I'm not too little and you're not the boss of me." Benny made a good case. "Right, Mom?"

"No one needs to grind the beans because I'm going to have a glass of wine with your mom"—I waited a beat to let that sink in—"after I get a big hug from you guys."

"My hug is bigger," shouted Matthew as his slender nine-year-old arms encircled my waist. The boys were tall for their age. Tracy's 5'10" height left little doubt they'd get even taller.

Benny rushed toward me. "Mine is stronger."

He wrapped his arms around his brother's neck and part of my waist and squeezed with all his might. Matthew wheezed and struggled, then broke his brother's hold.

"Mom, he choked me." Matthew's dramatic afterthought cough sent us into laughter. He rubbed his neck. "No fair. He *did* choke me."

"Uh, uh," protested Ben. "I was just hugging hard and your neck got in the way."

I knew it was wrong to laugh but I couldn't help it. I ruffled Ben's hair and pulled his arms from around me.

"Next time, we'll draw straws to see who hugs first."

"Go back to whatever you were doing before Auntie Grace got here," said Tracy. "And do it quietly."

One thing I'd say for Tracy, she had control. Well, most of the time. Total control over two young boys would be like having Stepford Kids.

"I really can make you coffee or I can pour you a glass of pink wine from a box. Pick your pleasure."

Tracy worked as an ER nurse at Elmhurst Memorial Hospital, but she never harped on the evils of burgers, tobacco, or alcohol. An acquaintance, a vegan, once chastised Tracy for not sounding the alarm about red meat. Tracy's reply, "If I did that and people stayed healthy, why, I'd be out of a job," caused most of us to spray our drinks through our noses. She'd then cut a particularly rare piece of prime rib and chewed it ever so slowly and with her mouth slightly open to further antagonize the vegan.

"Pink wine is perfect."

She filled two mismatched wineglasses to the brim and carried them to the table. I leaned forward to sip a little to be able to safely lift my glass. "How do you do that without spilling?"

"Years of pouring drinks at Fitz's Pub. Those guys wanted their glasses filled to the top and you'd best not spill on the way to the table. Never mind that after a few shots they spilled most of their drinks getting them to their mouths."

I lifted my glass. "To not a precious drop spilled."

"Cheers."

We clinked glasses.

"I love the surprise visit, but what's up?"

Tracy could read me like a book. "That obvious, huh?" She nodded.

"Everything seems at odds around me. Hannah and Karen are arguing about how to raise the twins. Harry's arguing with Lily about where to raise Will. Hannah is remodeling in Pine Marsh while Karen is rehabbing in Oak Park where they found a skeleton in the basement. My father keeps hinting at a big change, which has to be he's marrying Jan. And to top it off, Ric just cornered me to say he has urgent information for me."

I drained the wine and stared at the dregs that had escaped my gulp. Tracy must have sense my mood. She reached for my glass and carried it to the sink, then filled a mug with water and popped it in the microwave. She placed a small ceramic canister, a spoon, and a honey bottle in front of me. I lifted the lid and picked out a Lipton tea bag, then lowered it into the steaming mug she'd set before me.

"Let's go at this in order of importance." She lifted one finger. "Are you and Harry clear on how and where to raise Will?"

"He didn't ask my opinion. It's between him and Lily."

"Well, that's horse puckey."

My eyes widened. "Horse puckey?" I grinned from ear to ear.

Tracy reddened and waved her hand toward the rest of the house. "They've got ears that could pick up a bug farting on Mars."

A stifled giggle came from somewhere beyond the kitchen.

"I rest my case for horse puckey. Back to that decision process. Harry needs to consult you. Will is going to live with you full time, isn't he?"

"He's supposed to, which is why he's enrolled at Goodrich Elementary in our neck of the woods. Lately, Karen's been bending Lily's ear about this pre-K through 8 progressive academy in their area. Sort of like an Avery Coonly Academy, only in Oak Park. It's where she wants to send the twins when they are old enough for preschool."

"And Harry is fighting this?"

"Not the school; it's supposed to be fabulous. He wants Will in our environment, attending public schools and playing park district sports. He's a good soccer player and he loves scouts. Harry doesn't want to uproot him again."

"Makes perfect sense. Why is Lily not seeing this?"

"I think she sees it. But I think that relinquishing control over a child who was her total responsibility up until a year ago has her tied in knots."

"Sounds like a logical assumption. I guess you can't jump in until they sort it out." She raised a second finger. "Tell me about what Hannah is up to. Why is she remodeling in Pine Marsh? This affects me in a way you probably don't know about yet." Tracy refilled her wineglass before continuing. "William and I are partners with Karen and Hannah in the B&B."

She paused to let me comment. I only stared at her.

"Karen offered us the chance to join the venture. We're excited about the idea. William did an analysis of current facilities in the Oak Park area and found that Under the Ginkgo Tree does an excellent business. The focus on our target market is evolving. With plans for the B&B in hand, why is Hannah poking around Pine Marsh?"

"Good question. Frankly, I don't know." I stood up. "Thanks for the wine…and the tea." I took a final sip. "I should be getting back. Harry thinks I went home." I gave Tracy a quick hug. "Say good-night to the boys for me."

The night had grown colder and I remembered I'd given Karen my jacket. I shivered as I fumbled for my keys. I'd come for answers, but I was leaving with more questions. Why hadn't Karen mentioned her business arrangement with Tracy? Did Hannah know about it?

The ride home wasn't long enough to sort out much. One thing was clear to me, though. I knew I would go back to the boardinghouse, knew I wouldn't be able to stay away. The figure in the tattered clothes wouldn't let me.

SIX

HARRY'S CAR WASN'T in the garage and Walter's was gone. I didn't feel like figuring out who drove whom and where they were now. The day caught up with me. A long hot soak and a book in bed sounded perfect.

Elmo greeted me at the door purring and winding around my legs.

"You're going to trip me one of these days." I shuffled forward pulling my kitty magnet along. The kitchen appeared used and mildly abused. Dishes in the sink, crumbs on the table—I couldn't leave the room until I tidied up. I swept the crumbs onto the plastic lid from the olives and dumped everything in the garbage can. The kitchen appliances include a dishwasher that I rarely use. I like the sense of accomplishment hot, soapy water on dirty surfaces gives me. I slipped on latex gloves and enjoyed the soothing task of suds, rinse, repeat. My brain needed time to unwind; it ordered a pattern. Suds, rinse, repeat, squeak. Each piece of glassware, each piece of crockery had to have the suds, rinse, repeat, squeak pattern.

I used to have to do this without gloves repeating the pattern until my hands squeaked. Now I force myself to wear them anytime I do any kitchen wash-up.

Suds, rinse, repeat, squeak. Suds, rinse, repeat, squeak.

At some point during the pattern my mind relaxed and a quiet feeling settled on me, the sense of calm I strive to achieve. My friends and family didn't understand that feeling of having all your insides fit together seamlessly like a jigsaw puzzle without forced edges. Except there's always a seam that works its way up a little and gets snagged.

I rinsed the soap from the sink and pulled off my gloves. A quick pass with the dust buster under the table and baby swing and the kitchen emerged presentable if you didn't scrutinize. I'd lost my cleaning lady when she started dating my dad. It felt too weird having Jan cleaning my house by day while smooching my father at night.

I heard the garage door opening and felt a seam lifting.

Harry and Will entered the kitchen laughing about some shared joke.

"No, really, Dad. He said he could feel the spirits. You know, like Aunt Hannah wishes she could."

The same fleeting expression of guilty embarrassment slipped across their faces before overly bright smiles appeared.

"Hello, darling. Look who the cat dragged in."

"Dad, that is so corny. Nobody says that." Will pushed his shoulder against Harry's arm. Father and son, the spitting images of each other caught in different dimensions. Will's white blond hair would eventually settle into a deeper shade, and Harry's cornflower blue eyes would carry forward into the next century.

"Lily's agent offered her a chance to shoot some footage at a celebrity bird-watchers event," said Harry. "She made arrangement with Hanns to keep Will for the night until I could fetch him but when she found out I was in Oak Park she brought him over. Great luck, eh, Will?" He ruffled the blond head.

"Geez, Dad! You're messing my hair. I'm not a baby. You do that to Connor's head."

"I just found out about you. It's like you're eight months old to me."

Harry reached for Will, but the boy stepped back, catching his foot on the leg of the baby swing. I grabbed his elbow and steadied him. He rolled his eyes at Harry. "Parents are weird. I'm going to my room."

Harry laughed. "I'll be up later to tuck you in."

"Daaa-d!" Will rushed up the stairs to the bedroom that held duplicates of all his belongings at Lily's apartment.

Harry rounded on me and pulled me up in a hug. "Gracie, I'm sorry. I shouldn't have left." He kissed the top of my head the same way he often kissed Connor.

"What is so bloody funny every time I kiss you?" He turned and held me by the shoulders.

I shook my head continued smiling. "Connor...you always kiss...top of his head," I sputtered between bursts of laughter.

Harry fumed a moment longer before his good humor returned. One corner of his mouth lifted, then the other. He folded me into his arms, my head tucked nicely a few inches below his neck.

I pulled back a little to talk. "We never did have dinner. Are you hungry? What about Will?"

"I could go with a bit of something." He released me and headed for the fridge. "Hmm, not too much at the ready in here. We could order from Papa Passero's. The drivers have figured out how to find us."

"No doubt because of the big tip you give them."

"Gracie, we've no street lamps, no proper signage here. It's a bugger to find us." He opened the drawer with the menus. "They've a vegetarian pizza that Hanns says is good. Maybe with a large spinach salad. We could add some extras."

Harry never ate burgers or fries or typical fast food items. Even with pizza it had to be healthy.

"Would you pop up and ask Will what he wants?"

Growing up in a family of five kids, no one ever asked

us what we wanted. We were thrilled when any type of carryout showed up. Being accustomed to home cooking, ordering out was a treat. I climbed the stairs to confer with my stepson.

HARRY STOOD AT the island jotting down his preferences. He kept his head down and asked. "Do you want a quarter anchovy? What does Will want?"

I leaned against the doorway until he stopped writing.

Giggles threatened to make my speech incoherent. "Will…wants…sliders." I burst into laughter and thoroughly enjoyed the pained expression on Harry's face. Had my food police husband met his match in his son?

"Those disgusting square pieces of questionable meat by-product?"

I laughed harder, barely able to nod my head in response. "Cheese. You can order cheese on them." More hoots of laughter.

Harry's face reflected horror at the possibility of sliders entering his home let alone his child's digestive tract.

The sound of the doorbell put dinner on hold. Ric Kramer stood on the porch.

"You've a nerve coming out here, Kramer," Harry said angrily. "What don't you savvy about 'leave her alone'?"

"I'm not here about Grace. At least not tonight. It's Gertrude. The police have brought her in for questioning and Walter's on the verge on being arrested for obstruction."

Harry opened the door wider. Ric walked past him and nodded at me. He knew his way around our house and walked into the kitchen. He pulled out a stool, hooked his cane on the counter, and leaned his elbows on the table. Ric Kramer still had drop-dead gorgeous appeal, even after a near death incident and subsequent rehab. His black hair gleamed more interesting shaded with gray at the temples and his face screamed sexy with the faint scarring under the jaw line.

I motioned to the coffeepot and he shook his head. "After the coroner removed the remains, the technicians went to work on the scene. The bones were found in a kind of cupboard built into a wall. The cupboard wasn't big, probably some kind of storage area. No identification was found."

"The police think Gertrude had something to do with this? Horses' arses, all of them if that's what they think."

I agreed with Harry, but I tried a different tack. "Do they just want information from Gertrude?"

Ric shrugged. "They need some kind of clue as to why her basement turned into a grave site for one person."

"Or more." Will stood in the doorway wide-eyed but calm.

SEVEN

Harry motioned him over. "What do you mean 'or more?'"

Will had a bit of hero worship for Inspector Kramer, which of course irritated Harry to no end. And Ric knew it. He put out his hand. "Hi, Will. Nice to see you again."

Will shook hands eagerly. "Hi, Uncle Ric. Nice to see you too."

The "uncle" bit killed Harry too, but since we'd instructed Will to call Karen "Aunt Karen", by default her brother would be 'Uncle Ric.'

"What's your take on this?"

Ric had a way of making everyone feel they had his undivided attention. At this point, Will had all of our attention after his bizarre comment.

"I saw one of those cupboards in a picture at Graue Mill. My scout troop went there to see the Civil War reenactors. In the basement of the mill they have pictures and stories about the Underground Railroad and how the slaves would escape by hiding in all sorts of places. People who didn't believe in slavery would hide the slaves until they could start on the next leg of their journey to Canada. Lisle and Downers Grove had safe houses called *rest stations*. The home of the mill owner, Graue, was a *station*."

"Son, that's interesting. But…"

Ric held up his hand to shush Harry. "Tell me about the picture of the cupboard, Will."

Harry's jaw muscles clenched, but he stayed quiet. Will's eyes shone with excitement.

"The cupboard was small. We drew out the measurements later to see how much room we'd have. You had to lie on your side to hide in there. Those slaves must not have been tall. You two wouldn't have fit, but Grace could have."

A chill snaked up my spine thinking of being trapped in that tiny space.

"Why do you think there could be more?"

Will gulped. "In the story it said people would build as many of these cupboards as they could to hide the escaped slaves. They were supposed to blend in like the regular wall."

Ric stood up quickly, knocking his cane to the floor. "I need to make a call. Thanks, sport," he added when Will retrieved the cane and handed it to him. He ruffled Will's hair and the boy seemed to grow an inch taller.

Harry glanced across the table at me with widened eyes in a "what just happened" look. I kept my lips firmly sealed. This was not the time to smile.

Ric hung up the phone. "I'd best get back there. Gertrude is going to need a lawyer, and Walter is going to need a handler."

"I'll take it from here." Harry picked up the receiver as Will and I walked Ric to the door.

"Thank you for coming by to tell us about Gertrude. A phone call would have been faster." I felt safe stating the facts since Will stood next to me.

"We serve and protect. You didn't seem yourself earlier. I figured I'd come by and wrap up the loose ends. And a good thing I did or I wouldn't have this information." Will beamed in delight as Ric reached out to shake his hand. "Will, my man, keep an eye on your stepmom, okay?"

Will nodded like a bobble head. Ric's grin ricocheted between strong, straight white teeth and deep brown eyes, creasing his skin with tiny lines that made the smile real. "Talk to you soon." He left before I could reply.

Harry called from the kitchen. "I'm going to pick up David. Until we know more, David can represent her, if she even needs representation. I'll keep a handle on Walter."

David Katernak was our business attorney. He had a great network of attorneys and could advise us on a criminal lawyer if one was needed. I hoped it wouldn't go that far. What could Gertrude possibly have to do with this tragedy?

Harry kissed me goodbye. "Don't wait up. I promise to wake you when I get in." He reached out for Will's head, hesitated, and lowered his hand. "You did a fine job explaining about the cupboard. I'm proud of how you helped this investigation. It may mean a lot to Gertrude."

"Thanks, Dad." Will's eyes widened in direct proportion to Harry's praise. For his part, Harry's face reflected his pleasure in having one-upped Ric. He smiled broadly as he opened the door to the garage.

"And Dad, don't worry about Grace. I'll keep an eye on her like Uncle Ric asked me to."

Another seam had lifted.

EIGHT

HARRY HAD SPENT hours with Walter while David sat with Gertrude. David had recognized that Gertrude's distress rendered her English a little confusing. He spoke German and tried to calm her by using her native tongue. In an about-face that he accidentally precipitated, Gertrude decided to speak only German and only to David.

As Harry explained the turn of events to me he couldn't help but chuckle at the three-ring circus he experienced at the Oak Park police department. The detectives were not amused and threatened David with obstruction of justice, stating he'd advised Gertrude to drop English.

"Oh my gosh, David wouldn't do that. He is so by the book," I had interrupted at one point.

"I know, but it seemed suspicious. He talks to her in German and the next thing anyone knows she won't speak English. What saved him was that one of the officers understands German. He vouched that David only told her to calm down and speak English slowly so the police could understand her. If that officer hadn't been in the room, David might be sleeping elsewhere tonight."

We'd fallen asleep around three o'clock only to have Will rap on our bedroom door at seven.

Harry's morning voice rasped, "Come! What's wrong?"

In an instant he was fully alert and tensed as if expecting trouble. Obviously, he wasn't used to kids waking earlier than their parents and wanting to share with them such necessary information as "We're out of Cheerios" or "Marty spilled the sugar bag on the floor and the cat is rolling in it." He'd get used to it, then miss it terribly in a few short years.

A small lump formed in my throat at the thought of all the time Harry had already missed in Will's life. The lump threatened to choke me as I thought of the children we'd never have, all that interrupted sleep we'd never experience. Our plan to adopt a child had stalled, then aborted, when Harry discovered he had a son he hadn't known about. It made sense—people adopted when they couldn't have their own children. He had his own.

"Dad, I forgot to tell you. I'm supposed to be at Mr. Rigg's house at eight o'clock. We're going through the supply shed to see what the troop has before we go shopping. I'm in charge of cooking next weekend. See." He waved a sheet of lined notebook paper at his father. "This is my menu and I have to check what we have."

Harry and I were now wide-awake, but in no position to pop out of bed with Will in the room. Harry accepted the sheet of paper and stared at the list. I leaned toward him and perused the items.

"Will, are you doing this for advancement?" I asked.

He nodded. "And part of the cooking badge."

"Check your handbook. You might need to list sizes of items and portions per item."

Will's mouth popped open. "I forgot. You're right. I have to tell Mr. Riggs."

"No problem. Go downstairs and check out the stuff in the kitchen. I see pancakes on the menu. Get the box and see how many pancakes you can make with how many cups. Figure out how many people will be camping, including the adults, and add up how much pancake mix you'll need. Can't help you on bacon—it's not allowed in the house." I made a face at Harry.

Will cracked up and rolled his eyes. "Thanks, Grace." He pulled the sheet from his dad's hand and tore out of the room. We heard him thump down the stairs.

Harry reached for me under the covers. "You are brilliant." He pulled me up against his warm body and lowered his mouth over mine. I enjoyed his slow kiss, then turned my face. He moved his lips to my neck plotting his course lower.

I pushed away. "Are you nuts? Don't start that now."

"Darling, you've brilliantly diverted him downstairs."

He just didn't know about the three-minute rule. We'd lost our window of time to get dressed.

"Harry, I mean it. Stop."

No warning except the gust of air current charging children draw around themselves and Will was back at Harry's side.

"Aren't you up yet?"

I turned my face away not wanting to answer why I was smiling.

"Grace, I can't find the box."

"It's in the lower cabinet to the left of the sink. I noticed you have soup for lunch one day. Cans of soup are in the pantry on the bottom shelf."

"Thanks. I have to be there at eight, Dad."

Harry nodded and watched his son rush through the door again. He turned to me. "How did you know?"

"Hey, your Druids got nothing on growing up with four siblings. My parents never got any sleep. Just remember the three-minute rule. That's all we've got. Don't dawdle."

"Yes, but he's been back. Surely he's set for a while."

I shook my head slid out from under the covers. "You'll learn."

I splashed water on my face, brushed my teeth, and threw on sweats and slippers. I met Will on the landing and purposely raised my voice. "He's moving slow this morning. Come on, let's make some pancakes. We've enough time."

Will had been thorough about using my foodstuffs for his calculations, but he was not concerned about cleaning up. The soup cans and pasta boxes were on the floor in the pantry and the pancake mix and peanut butter jar were on the counter. A bag of bread lay unopened on the island top.

"Is there a reason all this is out?"

"I'm waiting for Dad to check to make sure I did it right."

Will had never asked for my help with anything. He hadn't yet forgiven me for being the person his father chose to marry. In Will's opinion, if Harry and I were to divorce, then most assuredly Harry would wed Lily and they'd be a *real* family. If Harry had known about Lily's pregnancy, he would have married her. My biggest fear is that the lure of his son's deepest desire and Will's gorgeous and willing mother will pull him away from me. I have no child to share. I have no 5'10" willowy body to offer. I have no…

"Unless you could check it? I mean Dad's such a sleepyhead."

My heart lurched against my ribs. I nodded.

"What have we here?" Harry asked from the doorway. "Let's check this over and make certain of your provisions." He grinned and took the paper from Will's hand. "Let's start with the canned goods."

I turned away quickly to let Will off the hook and busied myself with making coffee. Tears pinched behind my eyes and I swallowed hard to regain control. I heard their happy prattle about portions for adults versus kids, and it hurt.

NINE

HARRY AND WILL left after devouring seconds on pancakes. I made whole-grain pancakes and cooked the veggie patties that masqueraded as sausage patties in our house. Will put away everything he'd taken out and even loaded the dishwasher with his and Harry's plates. I'd only nibbled at the messed up first pancake I'd made. I planned on eating cereal after they left.

I shook Cheerios into a bowl and carried them dry with my third coffee of the day to the breakfast nook. I turned on the bench seat to lean against the wall and pull my knees up. With the bowl propped between my stomach and legs I could munch cereal and sip coffee almost simultaneously.

After I settled in, the bird activity picked up. Harry had a laminated photo gallery of birds on the table next to a scorecard sheet meant to record bird sightings. He wanted anyone who sat here to take a moment to jot down birds sighted, the time, and which feeder they visited. Even Tracy's boys knew to pay attention and mark them down. Tracy keeps asking for the secret to his ability to get them to follow instructions. Everyone wanted to do Harry's bidding. He drew people to him, especially women. One English-accented sentence and they melt. I speak from experience.

A speckled sort of bird with a tufted head landed in the Dogwood. I reached for the photos, careful not to tip my bowl. The rap on the window startled my winged visitor and me. Lucky bird. He flew off while an overturned bowl of Cheerios ended up in my lap. I pulled my gaze from the mess I'd made and saw Ric Kramer's smiling face at the window. He motioned toward the back door.

I don't want to see him. I certainly don't want him to see me like this.

Why do you care?

Because women care about their appearance. What rock have you been living under?

It shouldn't matter. This is the nineties.

Yeah, well, I learned how to be a girl in the seventies.

I stopped arguing with myself when he rapped again. I nodded and motioned "one minute". He turned and walked toward the back of the house. I used the bowl as a scoop and rescued as many little *o*'s as possible. The others either fell to the floor or were crushed by my butt as I wiggled across the bench to stand up.

I pulled an old barn jacket around my shoulders and stepped into woolly clogs. Going to the door, I opened it with one hand while attempting to comb my hair with the other.

Geez, Louise. Why don't you pinch your cheeks and wet your lips?

Shut up. Not enough time.

Ric stepped into the mudroom bringing the scent of brisk air and Grey Flannel with him. I fought the urge to breathe deeply. He wore jeans, low-heeled boots, and a long-sleeved shirt under a down vest. His cane *du jour* was a knobby walking stick. *Robusto*, Nonna Santa would have said.

"Good morning. Hmm, all comfy and cozy in an 'I'm on my way to muck out a stall' sort of way."

"Would you like a coffee? I can clean stalls later."

Ric used his thumb to tilt my chin up. "Yes, I would

love a coffee," he smiled. "You are as gracious in grungies as in a gown. And as lovely, let me add."

I pushed his hand away before my eyes could betray me with a fast shift to purple, then twirled toward the door.

"This won't make it on the runway?"

Ric grabbed the collar of the jacket and it swung off my shoulders. I felt vulnerable especially since I'd thrown the sweats on over nothing else. I quickly stepped out the clogs.

"You know the way to the kitchen. Pour yourself a cup. I'll be right back."

I dashed up the back stairs to my bedroom. So much for gracious. My hands flew through the drawers selecting underwear, socks, sweater and jeans. Being the only girl with four brothers taught me the two-minute drill. "If you're not ready in two minutes, we're leaving," they'd shout at me, trying their best to leave me behind.

Even with the extra step of deodorant I could still do a two-minute set up. I came down the main staircase confident that I could face Ric on even terms when I had real clothes on.

He had filled the carafe and replaced the filter in the coffeemaker by the time I entered the kitchen. I pointed to the nook.

"You sit, I brew."

The last thing I wanted to see was "domestic Ric" puttering in my kitchen. The fewer images of him blending into my life the better.

"Never get in the way of a free meal is my motto," he said with a grin. He carried two cups to the nook, stopping to search the floor when he crunched on the fallen Cheerios. "Were these for Elmo?"

I shrugged. "They are now."

We laughed and whatever edginess I'd felt slipped away. "By the way," I said. "I offered coffee, not a meal."

This time his shoulders rose and fell. "I saw the box and the griddle and hoped the kitchen hadn't closed."

Geez, he's adorable when he grins.

Adorable, smorable. Don't feed him.

Okay, okay. Just stating a fact.

"If the lady has to think about it that long, I withdraw my request." He lifted his mug. "Cuppa' joe will have to do."

I laughed at his tough-guy persona and quickly scooped Mocha Madness into the basket. I leaned against the counter when I faced him.

"About last night…" I paused, waiting for Ric to wave off any explanation like they do in the movies. He waited, staring expectantly at me.

"Last night shouldn't have happened. I mean, I should have stayed home. I mean…"

Finally there came that permissive wave to stop stammering an explanation.

"Grace, I don't pretend to understand how you tick. I think you know how I feel about you, how I'll always feel about you. That's why I need to talk to you."

I turned my back and lifted the full carafe. I wanted to keep my back to him until the flush I felt rushing to my face simmered down below my collar.

I heard the garage door. Harry would see Ric's car parked at the curb. If Will was with him there'd be no scowls. If Will had stayed behind to work on his menu, the scene could get tense. I turned with what I hoped was a composed expression on my face. The door swung quickly, a Will sign, I prayed.

"Hi, Gra…Uncle Ric! Hi! I didn't know you were coming over. Check out my menu." Will waved a paper in Ric's direction while trying to slip off his shoes at the door. He rushed across the room to slide in next to Ric just as Harry entered. My husband's lips pushed against each other. I knew he hated the fact that Will admired Ric.

I lifted the pot and my eyebrows in inquiry. "Coffee?"

Will spoke over his shoulder. "Mr. Riggs said he's going to show me how to make campout coffee. He says it's the best stuff. Uncle Ric, did you ever have campout coffee?"

I feared he'd ask Ric to help him make it. The less Ric and Will spent time together, the better Harry would like it and the easier life would be.

I played the "bad cop". "It's not polite to rush in and interrupt an ongoing conversation."

Will's exuberance crumbled. Harry and Ric glanced at each other in confusion.

"Sorry," Will mumbled and got up.

"I'll give it a once over before I leave," Ric offered.

"Yeah, okay." Will's icy stare left no doubt that any ground I'd gained had been irretrievably lost. The silence that filled the room as he exited grew uncomfortable.

"Do you want this coffee or not?"

"Only if you serve it in a mug and not over my head," said Ric.

"Always have an answer, don't you?" My shrill tone startled me.

Where did that come from?

How about from your heart that's sad and your mind that's confused.

Let's throw in my soul that's under attack.

Okay.

Great. Now, you agree with me.

Harry took the carafe from my hand and placed it on the table in front of Ric. "Why are you here?"

Ric filled his mug, then slowly sipped his coffee while

gazing at me over the rim. "I was in the neighborhood. Nancy doesn't live far from here," he added by way of explanation.

Ric and Nancy Royal, a Lisle police officer, had been dating on and off for almost a year. Guess they were on again.

"Is there a shortcut to Oak Park through Pine Marsh?" Harry's rhetorical question increased the tension.

Ric must have realized how lame his excuse sounded. "I stopped by to let Will know that he was on the money about those cupboards. The techs went back in and found another skeleton. They found papers identifying the remains as Francis Downers, a woman who disappeared from Gertrude's boarding house forty years ago. She didn't go far."

Ric took another sip from his mug before rising from the table. "Thanks for the coffee, Grace. I guess my visit was a bad idea. I apologize for any inconvenience I've caused." He retrieved his walking stick. "I'm outta' here," he said as he headed for the mudroom. "Don't bother seeing me out. I know the way."

"I've had it with you, Kramer," Harry said as Ric brushed by him. "You know bloody too much about my house, my wife, my life." His anger dripped a chill on each syllable.

My stomach lurched at Harry's words. Ric had been responsible for saving Harry's life seven years ago. What could have been a lifelong friendship between two men never had a chance when Ric discovered his feelings for me.

Ric glanced back at me, but his dark eyes bore no expression I could read. He continued towards the mudroom.

Harry hadn't moved. His anger had blown the usual unflappable demeanor everyone expected from him. I stepped in front of him and put my hands lightly against his chest. A vein at his temple throbbed with the aftermath of his anger. I felt his heart pounding under my touch. The sound of the mudroom door closing released him. His arms circled me and I pressed my cheek against his chest. He kissed the top of my head.

We stood near the breakfast nook in full view of Ric when he walked around to the front. I had no idea if Harry saw Ric raise two fingers to his lips, then turn them toward me in goodbye. I closed my eyes and pressed closer to my husband.

"You reprimanded Will to stop him from interacting with Kramer," Harry whispered. "You did that for me."

I nodded against his chest.

"Darling, I appreciate what you did, but I can handle how Will feels about Kramer." A pleasant rumble sounded in my ear as Harry chuckled. "Maybe not after that outburst."

I turned my head. "I had no idea he was coming here. Last night he told me he had some information for me. I told him then I wouldn't meet him."

"No matter. I'll deal with Kramer. You have to straighten this out with Will. I love that you wanted to protect me even at the risk of alienating my son."

He kissed me gently and quickly. I hugged him before stepping back. "I'll be right back. Hold that thought."

"Remember, Gracie, he does like you."

"No problem. He's eleven. In two years he won't like either of us for about eight years," I pronounced solemnly remembering my brothers as surly, misunderstood teenagers.

Harry's face wore a bothered expression. "I've only just found him."

I patted his hand. "Yes, dear. You missed the gurgles and grins." We both had, but I wasn't going to think about that. I climbed the stairs, rehearsing my apology to Will on each step and tapped on his bedroom door.

"Will, can I talk to you for a minute?"

"I'm doing my homework."

I knew that wasn't a pressing reason for an eleven-year-old. I didn't blame him for not wanting to talk to me, but I couldn't let it go. I knew he'd spill to his mom, then she'd have one more tack to throw under Harry's tires. Although, we'd saved her last-minute trips and client visits several times, this weekend being an example. Given that, she might not be inclined to side with Will.

Fat chance.

Will must have thought I'd left. He opened the door and suddenly we stood nose to nose. We each jumped back a half step and put a hand up to our mouths. The split second reaction reminded me of a mirror image routine in a mime act. I burst out laughing. I don't think Will caught the inference, but he laughed too, his more the laugh of being startled and a little embarrassed.

I knew he wouldn't slam the door in my face. I stepped over the threshold but no farther.

"Will, I want to apologize for jumping on you for interrupting. I'm sorry I handled it that way." I waited for a response, dismissal, something. He stared at his feet. "That's all I wanted to say. I'll let you get back to your homework." I glanced at his desk devoid of any books, papers or folders. He face flushed with the attempted deceit. I turned to leave feeling I'd made as much peace as possible.

"Why didn't you want me to talk to Uncle Ric?"

It was my turn to turn pink. Is that what he thought?

"It's not that I didn't want you to talk to him. He and I had been in a conversation, and when you rushed in you really did interrupt..."

"Were you talking about leaving my Dad and marrying Uncle Ric?" His voice dropped to a whisper. I moved further into his room.

"Why would you ask that, Will. Did someone tell you that?" I suspected Lily at work with yet another nasty comment directed at or about me.

His glance never moved above my ankles.

"Will, I love your father and have no intention of leaving him."

He mumbled into the Yoda character on his shirt. "You used to love Uncle Ric. Why don't you still love him?"

I knew where he wanted this to go. Every kid wants his parents to stay together. A simple apology had turned into a gut-wrenching, soul-searching conversation.

"I know Uncle Ric still loves you. Mom said…" He stopped abruptly.

"Honey, it doesn't work that way. People aren't easy to figure out, and people in love are twice as hard to figure."

How much could I, should I, tell him. How to explain that years ago when British Intelligence left Harry and another agent in a South American prison, I turned to my best friend's brother for help? How could I tell him Ric called in every favor from his friends in Special Ops to work toward Harry's release? How could I relive the pain of being told that Harry had died in the escape attempt? And how could I tell him that Ric and I had fallen in love and planned a life together before I discovered Harry was alive?

Instead of speaking, I put my hand on his shoulder. The bony frame of a young boy soon to grow into his body trembled under my touch. He flung away from me and stood with his back to the door. He didn't hear his dad enter the room.

"Will, your mom is on the phone. She wants to talk to you."

Will rushed past his dad and thumped down the stairs to get to the call.

Harry put his arm around me. "Rough one?"

I nodded and smiled. "More than you know. Is Lily back?" I asked as he pulled me closer.

"Her event was a disappointment and she wants Will to spend the weekend with her after all. She has an art exhibit that she is judging and she wants Will with her."

"That sounds boring. Will wanted to go riding this weekend. And Devon promised to take him hiking and orienteering at Waterfall Glen next time he was here."

"This is her weekend, Grace. I can't trump her plans."

"It should be Will's choice. She can't have it all her way—*'take him when I'm busy, but drop your plans when I'm ready'*. It's not fair to Will or you."

I stopped ranting. The anguish on Harry's face told me he'd already had this conversation with Lily. I thought instead of how to cheer him.

"If you two saddle up now, you can get a nice ride in before he has to leave. We'll stop at Russell's Ribs for lunch. He loves that place."

"Great idea. I'll change, you tell Will. I'll meet you in the mud room."

I loved seeing the smile in his eyes and I rushed to find Will with the revised plan. Harry hadn't been able to ride for several years after his rescue. He had needed extensive rehab. In the last year he'd surprised me with Cash Cow, a companion for April and a mount for himself. He can't ride for long before his leg begins to ache, but he can ride long enough for a great dad/son outing.

I slowed my pace at the bottom of the stairs, not wanting to appear to be listening in on Will's conversation with his mother. I even detoured to use the bathroom to give him more phone time.

When I finally reached the kitchen, the phone was cradled and Will was nowhere to be seen. On a hunch I ran to the mudroom. Harry had bought Will a riding jacket to leave here. It was gone.

Harry's voice preceded him. "Let's take them through the woods at the ninth hole, then run them up to the meadow."

His cheerful words tugged at my heart. I saw him stop short in the doorway, the sight of my frantic purple eyes changing his tone from cheer to dread.

"What's wrong?"

TEN

"HE'S NOT HERE. His shoes and riding jacket are gone."

"Maybe he went out to the barn." Harry rushed to the door. "You know, to start saddling the horses."

"I didn't get a chance to tell him."

Someone rapped at the door. Harry yanked it open. Devin Atwater, our neighbors' son, stood in the doorway, his hand still raised.

"I came over to see if Will wanted to go hiking when I saw him take off on his bike. I called out to him but he flew past me. I thought I should tell you."

"Thanks, Devin."

Harry closed the door and faced me. "Maybe he's working off steam. You know, racing around the neighborhood."

I didn't know what to say. My brothers had all taken a shot at running away from home at some point because of some imagined grievance. With them it was more a safety valve. After riding for awhile they came back tired and hungry. Marty stayed away the longest time. I remember the growing panic as the hours stretched into the night.

"He's not all that familiar with this neighborhood, but he may know where some of his new friends live. Do you know their names? Do we have a school directory?"

Harry slammed his hand against the wall. "No, I don't know any of this. I should. What kind of parent am I? Why did he go? I'm going after him in the car. He can't have gone far."

"Harry, once he's out of the complex he could be riding to Green Trails or Summerhill or Woodridge Estates."

The phone rang. Harry rushed to answer.

"Hello?"

I knew by his expression it was about Will. Relief flooded his face.

"Thank you. I'll be there shortly." He listened a moment longer. "Yes, I see. Of course." He hung up the phone and braced his hands on the counter, his head lowered. He spoke slowly. "Will rode to his scoutmaster's house. He wants his mother to pick him up there." Harry's lips pressed together until his mouth was a thin line.

"Harry, he's reacting to everything happening around him. He doesn't know what to think."

"But why did he run off? We could have had more time together. We planned to do things. It's her fault his life is piecemeal. Why isn't he angry with her?"

I knew he didn't want my answers, knew whatever I said would be wrong. In that moment of his anguish I could only put my arms around him. He didn't move. We stood, my arms around him, his hands on the counter. I leaned my head against his back and tried to be calm and let my slow breathing permeate his body. The tightness around his shoulder loosened.

"He's okay and that's what matters. Call him tomorrow and ask him if he wants you to pick him up early and you can have your ride."

I felt him nod. This shared custody was taking its toll on Harry. He walked on eggshells around Lily's demands, fearful that she'd change the arrangement on a whim. Harry didn't have legal status as a custodial parent yet. He had rights as the biological father, but the legal system still regarded Lily as sole custodian.

It did appear that Lily had the best of both worlds—Will

when she wanted him, freedom to dash around the world when she wanted that. She had raised Will on her own for ten years, although we'd heard stories from Harry's son about several boarding schools and moves.

The phone rang again. I reached for it and answered with cheer I didn't feel.

"Don't you sound chipper," Karen said. "I'm calling to invite you and Harry over for snacks and stories."

"What kind of stories?" The little hairs on the back of my neck rose in response.

"You won't believe what's been happening. The city council thinks the boardinghouse might have landmark status since the discovery of the sub-cellar. That type of structure predates what was thought to be the original age of the building. And, we talked to a woman whose great aunt is visiting her and who used to live next door to the boardinghouse way back in the 1920s. She's coming over to talk about those times. And, I've saved the best for last. Unless Ric already told you?"

"About the other cupboards?"

"Yes, bizarre isn't it? Are you in?"

"Absolutely. Give us two hours." I hung up the phone and repeated the story to Harry. I saw the interest pique in his eyes. He must have seen the same in mine.

"Gracie, this could stir up trouble."

The line from the old slave song, *Nobody knows the trouble I've seen*...popped into my head. Who had I seen, and what had been his trouble?

ELEVEN

HARRY SHRUGGED AND shook his head. "We're in this, aren't we?"

I smiled and nodded. "Help me in the barn and we can leave sooner."

We cleaned out the stalls, fed and watered the horses, and tickled their noses while we promised them more rides and attention. April nodded her head and blew breath out the sides of her mouth, not a snort but more like a human *hmmph*.

Harry and I made great time and were on the road in less than an hour. He stopped by the scoutmaster's house to thank him and retrieve Will's bike. Paul Riggs walked with Harry to the back of the Jeep and spoke with him while Harry stowed the Huffy trail bike. I couldn't hear the conversation, but Harry seemed the better for it.

"Words of wisdom?" I asked when we pulled away.

"Hardly. He said he felt the same panic and confusion when one of his boys took off on him. Only difference was they were on a campout. Found him at the ranger station having a snack. Paul said the boy's mates were a tad irritated with him for disrupting the day."

"Really? Shortsighted of them. They could have counted it as an exercise for their Emergency Preparation badge."

"Spoken like a true scoutmaster's daughter." Harry caught up my hand and kissed it.

"And that would be for…?"

"For trying to protect my feelings earlier. You're quite

the lioness when one of your own is threatened. In the future, darling, choose Will over me. Today proves he needs it more than I do."

I felt the prick of rebuke under his gentle words. I shouldn't have championed Harry against a little boy. What didn't work right in my head? I swallowed hard and answered, "Okay, but don't come whining to me when we gang up on you."

I said it flippantly, remembering how as children we'd join forces with Mom against Dad to convince or connive. After the pleas and promises Dad would throw up his hands exclaiming, "How can I say no to all of you?" We'd cheer and climb all over him. I remember watching the expression that passed between my parents after one such occasion. They enjoyed it as much as we did. Could that be Harry and me?

We pulled up in front of the old three-story home on Grove and climbed the steps to the front porch. Karen pulled the door open before we knocked.

"Good timing. Must be the lure of a great story." Her dark eyes gleamed with mischief. She led the way to the back parlor. Hannah, Gertrude, Walter, and two women I'd never seen before sat in the comfortable chairs placed in a semi circle for conversational ease. Walter stood and offered me his chair. I knew to refuse would insult his sense of propriety.

"Thank you, Walter."

"*Ja*, I vas getting chairs from kitchen." He made good on his word and came back with three straight-back Shaker style chairs. Only Karen and Harry needed seating. The knock at the door explained the extra chair.

"Hello, everyone. Hope you didn't start without me." Ric Kramer moved to occupy the chair Walter had placed closest to me. Walter quickly inserted his burly girth between us, forcing Ric to sit elsewhere. As if choreographed, Walter leaned toward me mumbling something for show, then swung away as Harry smoothly moved into the space and sat down.

I leaned toward him. "Fred and Ginger would be proud."

A *"who me"* look slipped onto his face, but not before I saw the smirk at the corner of his mouth.

Karen began the introductions. The younger of the two women was Juliana Dodd, postmistress at the Eola post office. Her aunt, Josephine Hossack, was visiting from her home in Missouri.

Polite society mores indicated some general chitchat before we pounced on the real purpose of the gathering.

"We live in Pine Marsh," I said. "I didn't realize Eola had its own post office."

Juliana chuckled. "Most people don't. We like it that way." Her brown eyes reflected a wry sense of humor.

"Yes, quite the secret. I believe the 'hidden post office' is your doing." Harry smiled and I could sense that both women relaxed a little more. My husband's English accent and stunning smile had that affect on most women.

The elder woman leaned forward in her chair and pointed a thick finger at Harry.

"I like him. He's good lookin' and smart." She shifted her focus to Ric, moving her finger to designate him. "This one, he's good lookin' too, but he got the devil in him."

"Auntie!" Juliana's voice rose and she reached to pull the older woman's hand down.

"*Ist* nothing. We know *dat* already." Gertrude's matter of fact tone surprised everyone and turned the moment to one of laughter.

Josephine Hossack nodded at Gertrude, the only woman in the room anywhere close to her age. "She knows."

"Yes, Aunt Jo, she knows. But these people are more

interested in what *you* know." Juliana smiled at us. "My aunt is spending time in the area to do research on an interesting aspect of the Underground Railroad—the quilts used to signal safety to the slaves fleeing to freedom."

The elder woman nodded. "I have a collection of quilts and stories and pictures. My niece is helping me put it all together in a book about the quilts."

Juliana added, "It's a beautiful art form that shouldn't be lost. My aunt has collected wonderful examples and recollections from people who were children during that period. She lived next door for many years and wanted to visit the neighborhood again."

The elder woman kept nodding at Gertrude. "I remember you when you was just a bitty thing." Josephine passed a hand over her tightly curled grey hair and continued. "Always runnin' to the corner store for your mama, Mizzus Mathilda, weren't it?"

I'd never heard Gertrude's mother's name mentioned before. I guess I hadn't thought of Gertrude having a mother. She ducked her head in agreement.

"Your Clarisse was my best friend," added Josephine. "She'd always say to me, 'I'm the lucky one. I got this little *fräulein* wants to run my errands.' Yep, she always called you that 'cause she said she'd hear your mama's friends call you that way."

I hadn't understood when Karen said this woman lived next door. I thought of her as a homeowner, which would have been unusual in the 1930s.

"I came to be in Oak Park 'cause my great-granddaddy Julian came up the river only hours ahead of the plantation slave catchers. He was a boy when the owner told his momma he was selling her son 'cause he needed money. She scraped together some bits of food and wrapped a quilt she'd made and her faith in God around her child.

She told him to search for the 'drinking gourd' in the sky and follow the North Star. He made it to the river and couldn't find his way across. He knew the bridge would be watched. Through the kindness of a stranger, a white man who didn't hold with slavery, he got rowed across on a moonless night.

"Great-granddaddy got the fever and couldn't go on no further. Another stranger—they called them conductors—took him to a home just off the river in Ottawa. That family nursed him to health and done him another kindness. They paid for papers with his new name, Julian Hossack, so he could travel a mite safer. He came to a house in Maywood and made the acquaintance of a fine lady who'd started up this club for women to do good deeds for their community while the men yammered and argued."

Josephine paused to sip her tea. "Great-granddaddy never moved on. He'd been learning smithy work on the plantation and he applied to one of the blacksmiths in town and learned real good, so good that when his boss died unexpected, Julian Hossack bought the shop from the owner's wife. She was most willing; they'd had no children and she wanted to move back to her people in Ohio.

"My daddy was born in the back of that smithy. He learned to blacksmith from his daddy, and when he laid eyes on my momma when she was walking home from church, he stopped his work and walked out to say hello. My momma said to him how she didn't talk with strangers, especially them that didn't keep holy the Lord's Day. Well, he closed up right after she sashayed down the street and weren't never open on Sunday again.

"My momma didn't abide with fools or heathens. Not much longer, they got married. Little bit after, her momma came." She motioned toward Juliana, "Then came two boys, then me. Yes'm, I am the baby of the family born and raised next door. My sister married Mr. Dodd right as she turned sixteen. The boys went to work with daddy and took to sleeping in the smithy. You know men. They need their space. I stayed on with momma and learned how to keep house."

We were spellbound by her story. Her niece reacted like someone who'd heard it before but still enjoyed the story. I could tell by her face that she knew what came next.

"After momma passed I was lonesome for female company. Juliana's momma had moved over to the West side of Chicago where her husband had a fine job as doorman at the Palmer House hotel." Josephine turned to her niece. "You know your daddy turned heads wearing that blue overcoat with them gold braids. I'd of thought he was a general!

"Anyway, when the Klops family hired Clarisse, I was pleased as punch. I had a female companion who wasn't in no hurry to up and get married. Me and Clarisse had our days off together and we'd walk ourselves down to the picture show on Lake Street or over to the ice-cream shop for a cooling refreshment on them hot, dusty days. Sometimes we did both."

Josephine's genuine delight in recalling "the old days" brought a smile to everyone's face. She continued telling us about shared adventures and mishaps. Her affection for the family she served and her pride in that service wove itself through the stories.

"When Miz Gwenie 'bout busted herself open pleading and crying for a fancy new bedroom suite like in the magazines, Mr. Brooks he says—"

My involuntary gasp stopped her. Gwenie Brooks. Gwendolyn Brooks. This woman helped raise… She worked for…

Josephine chuckled at my surprise and shook her head.

"No ma'am, that Ms. Brooks did much more with herself than Miz Gwenie."

I blushed at my error.

"Auntie, you stop doing that." Juliana wagged a finger at the older women before addressing me. "She enjoys watching people jump to that conclusion."

I smiled. "Did I jump pretty high, Ms. Hossack?"

Josephine smiled and nodded. "I like her. Gotta' know it's okay to laugh at yourself when need be. Keeps the heart full." She waved her hand around the circle to bring us all back to her. "So Mr. Brooks he says, 'Miss Hossack,'—he always called me 'Miss Hossack'. Real gentleman he was—'would you be agreeable to accepting Gwenie's old bedroom suite and allowing me to refresh your room with paint and new wall coverings?'"

She sat back and turned her thoughts inward. After a moment she leaned forward. "And that's when Clarisse showed me the old chair in Frau Klops' cellar."

My spine straightened without a prompt from me. I knew to listen carefully.

"Clarisse told me Gertrude's family was building a new floor and all the things stored would be going to the alley for the junk man. Whatever the rags and iron man didn't take they would let the haulers remove. We sorted through the junk searchin' for treasures. Clarisse picked up a shiny blue box with little daisies painted all up over the cover and front. The hinge was missin' and the lid didn't set right. I saw a wooden crate filled with books, one of them a bible, and papers. I weren't after reading material.

"We saw one of them long skinny cupboards and wondered if forgotten treasurers might be inside. The wall panel that hid the cupboard was slid aside. There weren't nothin' in there but old air. We didn't know about the other cupboards 'cause we thought the wall was solid."

She shivered with the knowledge of what had been a few feet away from her in that cellar.

I jumped into the silence. "Was there any odor?"

I saw Karen roll her eyes and Hannah lean forward for the answer.

Josephine nodded. "Clarisse said that's one reason the family was sealing that section. Seems it smelled dank and moldy and no amount of sweet smells could cover it. Clarisse says on humid summer days or rainy spring days the smell be creeping up the stairs like something evil seeking out goodness to taint."

I shivered at her words, basic yet eloquent. I felt the folded napkin in my clasped hands and forced myself to relax my grip.

Her voice slowed. "Clarisse told me how her sister's boy came to visit for an afternoon and he played most the day in that cellar scooting around the castaways making up stories about adventures. He was a high-strung boy, and we always thought he was a little 'tetched.' He told his auntie he found a tunnel at the back of the cellar. He said pirates must have used the tunnel and he was certain he'd find buried pirate treasure. Clarisse was happy to see his mama come for him. Well, that boy, Jackson, he could not wait to come visitin' again so as to search the cellar for treasure.

"Next thing she knows, there's a new floor. That cellar was deep, even with the floor there was still room to stand up and raise your hand over your head." She shook her head. "I ain't never seen a cellar dug out that deep. I took the rocking chair and a pretty lamp for my bedside table. Clarisse took the box and another lamp. We didn't take any of cloth cause the smell had a hold on it. I don't rightly know if the rags and iron man even took the clothes and linens.

"That chair rocked my sisters' children, one of which is setting right there." Josephine smiled at Juliana. Her affection for her niece beamed in her raisin-brown eyes.

Hannah offered more tea. I appreciated the chance to let Josephine's story take hold in my mind. I tried to let that time period arrange the pieces of the story in my head, keeping care to avoid coloring the tale with modern ideas of my own. The men at this point seemed to lose interest. I'm sure Ric was only here in an official capacity in case Josephine Hossack had any relevant information. I know Harry and Walter planned to leave for a bit and return later for Gertrude and me.

Ric stood first. "Thank you for the opportunity to visit with you. It's been interesting." He shook hands with each woman. Josephine winked at him and I thought he'd drop his cane.

Walter and Harry murmured their thank-yous and good-byes, quickly shaking hands with the guests. Neither was accorded a wink.

Harry brushed my cheek with a kiss. "If it gets late and I'm not back, take the car. Walter can run me home."

The room seemed larger with the absence of the bulky men. The dainty settee and chairs filled the room proportionately again. Hannah filled my cup, then inclined her head towards the kitchen. I waited until she'd passed through the doorway before following her.

TWELVE

"I THOUGHT THEY'D never leave," Hannah said as she busied herself preparing another pot of tea. "I've got to tell someone or burst. You're not going to believe this."

I gripped my saucer, then relaxed fearing I'd snap the china. Instead I gritted my teeth at what I was certain would be an announcement of her separation from Karen.

"Have you swallowed something vile? Are you ill?"

I smiled around my clenched teeth and slowly relaxed. "I'm fine. What's your news?"

Hannah's eyes gleamed with excitement. She motioned me closer. "The two bodies weren't hidden in that cellar at the same time. They were placed there at least seventy years apart."

The hairs on my neck stirred. I rolled my neck to settle that feeling of impending doom. "Hannah, the autopsies aren't done. Who gave you that line?"

My sister-in-law believed herself to be a bona fide "sensitive", someone able to pick up vibrations from the dead. Either she believed that she had some sort of psychic encounter or someone who knew her had played a cruel joke.

"Did Ric tell you that?" I asked because he'd never approved of Hannah.

"Ric? Of course not. Why would he share with *me*?"

Her meaning scored home. I felt heat creeping up my neck and filling my collar.

"Who told you? I mean, how could they know until the autopsies were completed?"

Hannah smiled and cocked her head. "The shoe clip. It was part of Coco Chanel's Bijoux de Diamants exhibition in the early thirties."

"Where did you see it?" My heart rate quickened with the surge of curiosity that had cursed me all my life.

"Let's just say I've a friend in dead places."

My sense of foreboding deepened. The cup and saucer nearly slipped from my hands, saved by Hannah's quick grasp.

"I'm sorry, Grace. Didn't mean to upset you." She placed the china on the table. Hannah did seem contrite but also a tad disappointed in my reaction. I suspect she had hoped for a co-conspirator.

I shook my head. "Not upset. You caught me off guard. So, you know someone at the morgue?"

She nodded.

"That person showed you crime-scene photos?"

"Not of the cupboard; he wouldn't do that. Just the articles found in the cupboard. You know, to catalog them or some sort thing." Hannah waved her hand, dismissing her friend's breach of procedure.

"Were there any other items?" The question burst from my mouth before my minimal good sense could censor it. Hannah grinned; she no doubt sensed her lure had snagged a partner. She nodded.

"Hannah, are you brewing those tea leaves or reading them?" Karen teased from the doorway. "Oh no! I know you two. What's going on?"

The kettle whistled and Hannah rushed to fill the pot. "It should steep for a bit before it's ready. I'll bring it out directly. Karen, pass around the custard tarts and we'll fill it up one last time. I've only enough teacakes for one more round."

"Josephine loves them. She keeps calling them chewy

cookies." Karen left the kitchen smiling, knowing how aggravated Hannah became with the ubiquitous term when applied to teacakes, biscuits and scones.

"What else?" We had little time and I wanted to head off her predictable tirade.

"What else did he photograph? No other jewelry. Just an odd square bit that he thinks is metal. It would fit in that space." Hannah measured about two inches between her forefinger and thumb. "There's a depression or maybe a hole on one side." Hannah slid her hand into the side pocket of her leather bag. She removed an envelope, the interoffice type with the string fastener, and handed it to me. "Copies."

My instinct to reach for the offering blurred and stalled my hand in midreach. Chills rolled across my shoulders and down my arms straight through to my fingertips.

If you take it, you're involved.

Don't be silly. I'm not getting involved. They're only some pictures.

Pictures of things that belonged to the man you saw?

A man, that's right. Just a man, not a ghost.

I accepted the envelope.

"I'll load up the cookies, you bring out the…what's in the envelope?" Karen asked. She stepped into the kitchen carrying the empty tray.

My mind went blank. I stared at my best friend knowing that any second my quirky physiology would darken my violet eyes to purple and betray me.

Hannah chatted away, explaining the envelope's contents were additional thoughts on the remodel plan for the Pine Marsh residence. Karen's lack of interest in that area spread across her face like clouds rolling through a sunny sky. She busied herself setting out the remaining cakes and scones.

I retrieved my cup and left them alone, thankful to have avoided a confrontation with Karen, but amazed at Hannah's smooth lie. I knew she was lying but I couldn't spot the marker or "tell" that exposed her lies. I vowed to never play cards with her. Or for that matter, take her word as gospel.

"I wondered where you'd got yourself off to." Josephine smiled warmly. "I've been hearing tales about your abilities." Another smile.

Abilities? Oh, man! What had been said in my absence? I swallowed quickly, prepared to try a lie of my own.

"Miz Gertrude told us how you have a special way for"—Josephine lowered her voice—"folks that has passed this way before."

I fixed *Miz Gertrude* with a glare under which she had the good sense to squirm. Josephine continued. "My Juliana here won't ask because she don't believe."

Her niece rolled her eyes and put her arm on the older woman's arm. "Auntie Jo, these people are hoping to solve one mystery, not hear about another."

Another mystery? Good Lord. Maybe her reference had been to missing people. Odd way to say it.

"Child, you will not admit that someone's spirit is in that place. She might help them move on."

I stood abruptly. I knew my eyes gleamed purple; I'd felt the shift to panic as her words branded me some kind of freak. My hands balled to disguise the shaking I expected.

"I do not talk to dead people." My low voice overenunciated each word. My shoulders twitched and I feared tremors would follow.

Karen threw her arm around my shoulders. "Gracie only sees them, and only because she imagines what it must have been like for them. But they pay her no mind. What she excels at is obsessing over facts and ideas until she figures out what has happened. More of detecting skills than séance hokum."

I felt Karen's arm tighten in response to the shivers rolling across my shoulders. *An obsessive-compulsive detective as opposed to a nutcase. I could live with that.*

I have been living with that, all my life. Lost a couple of jobs and several friends because of it.

I relaxed. Karen gave me a parting squeeze and released me. I sat down and felt grateful for the solid seat.

"I don't want to see a single one of these cookies left," Karen grinned. "Or I'll have to box them up and send them home with you." She spoke directly to the older woman whose smile expanded to bursting.

Josephine clapped her hands in a girlish outburst. I could imagine her as a teenager responding the same way at the prospect of a new bedroom.

"Pass that tray this way. You put me to remembering Miz Trixie. She had the same spirit. Her sister, Miz Dolly, was the one with all the spunk. Clarisse would say when they was coming to visit, 'Here comes spirit and spunk', which was her way of saying trouble. Those two young things grew up wantin' for nothing and wantin' everything, if you know what I'm saying. Always arguing over who got to drive that fancy car their daddy bought them. They was only thirteen months apart. Most folks thought they was twins. Clarisse and me were only one or two years older than them two. Miz Trixie and Miz Dolly. I ain't thought of them in years."

Her reminiscing at a pause, I felt it would be a good time to leave. Her storytelling engaged me but my fear that she'd come at me again won the coin toss.

Hannah broke the silence with an offer no one could refuse. Not even me.

THIRTEEN

"HANNAH, SHOULD WE be down here? I mean, isn't it a crime scene or something?" Karen's logical question annoyed Hannah. Her face reflected pique.

"It's our house now, Gertrude's for years before. All three of the owners are in agreement."

"Two," muttered Karen.

"It's growing up with that brother of yours that makes you such a stickler for the rules."

"How about that brother of yours who breaks all the rules?"

My gasp and her *"damn"* sounded simultaneously.

"Hannah, Gracie, I'm sorry. I didn't mean that. I mean, at least not as bad as it sounded."

Harry assured me years ago that Karen would never side with me against her brother. In a cruel twist of fate, I had lost Harry, and through the next year I thought I could find happiness with Ric. At the point when our relationship was poised for the next step, word came that Harry was alive.

Karen helped Ric put his life together. I'd often wondered how deep her resentment ran. I'd caught a glimpse today.

I waved off further comments and followed Hannah down the stairs. I didn't want to see the area, but I didn't want to deal with Karen. Our relationship of late had tottered between best friends always and cautious spectators as she struggled with her future with Hannah and I dealt with Harry's son and the boy's mom, Harry's ex-lover.

"Here's where they were pulling up the floorboards," said Hannah. "It's in the corner above the cupboards."

We stopped at the bottom of the stairs. More boards had been pulled up and two ladders poked through the gaping holes. I assumed the police had ripped up all the planking to get to the remains. I wondered why they'd limited their scope of search to the small area.

I jumped when the answer came from above us.

"This is a crime scene with an ongoing investigation. No one is allowed beyond the tape—that's why it's there." Ric Kramer glared at us from the top of the stairs. His dark eyes held no amusement at the sight of six women ranging in age from early thirties to eighties clumped like goose down at one end of a quilt. No one mistook his ire.

He lifted the tape and motioned us under with a sweeping wave as though seating us at a corner table at Chez Paul.

"How lucky that I forgot my jacket."

Josephine moved quickly considering her age and the steep stairs. She took Ric's offered hand and peered into his face. "Yessir, you are most agreeable." She continued to hold his hand. "Did I mention earlier that my niece, who I'm sure is rollin' her eyeballs, is a good woman, with a good government job, and is single?"

"Aunt Jo, that's enough!" Juliana crowded around her aunt and ducked under the tape while avoiding Ric who tried to hide the hint of a smile.

"Ouch!" Josephine yelped. "Child, I don't believe you pinched your Auntie Jo." She appealed to Ric. "Isn't there some law against elder abuse? Maybe you should take her in and speak with her about taking advantage of her elders."

"Miss Josephine, I doubt anyone has ever had the ability or courage to take advantage of you," Rick said smoothly.

I swear Josephine batted her eyes as she allowed him to nudge her under the tape. The rest of us scampered past him avoiding his stare. He closed the door and re-attached the tape.

"This," he said, pointing to the tape, "stays put."

"Auntie, I will be in the car which will be leaving in five minutes." Juliana nodded her head toward us. "I enjoyed meeting you. Thank you for your hospitality and," she said as she stared at Josephine, "your tolerance."

Hannah walked to the front door with her. I saw her press something into Juliana's hand. No time to wonder about her shenanigans. I hoped Ric's return had nothing to do with me. I escaped to the kitchen and busied myself cleaning up. Had I the presence of mind to pick up my purse in my exodus, I could have sneaked out the back door and been halfway to the Eisenhower before anyone noticed. I patted my pockets to check for keys. No luck.

"Thinking of lamming out the back?"

I hated when Ric seemed to know my thoughts.

"I came back to see you."

"I was just leaving."

"Gracie, wait. What's wrong with you? You take off every time I try talking with you. It's like I'm some kind of pariah."

"To me you are, you have to be. I'm trying to build a family with Harry and Will. I can't be distracted or de-railed by your agenda." I'd said more than I wanted to and felt the rush of heat fill my cheeks.

"A distraction, eh? I'll take that as a good thing."

"Don't take it as anything. Please, Ric. This transition to shared custody is tough and I'm trying hard to make it work."

"How hard is Harry trying? Seems he never thinks of what's best for you, only what serves him best."

"How dare you talk about my brother that way," Hannah said angrily. "You have no right to comment, chasing Grace like a lovesick puppy."

"No right?" Ric's eyes glittered dangerously. "Your dear brother left his wife to chase across Europe when she needed his protection and support."

"Chase across Europe indeed! He was meeting his son for the first time. You, on the other hand…"

Karen cut off her. "Hannah, you need to stop. You don't know everything."

"I know enough," Hannah insisted. "I know what Harry's told me."

"Yes, and he's always been forthcoming with the truth," Ric said sarcastically. "Your family didn't even know what he did for a living. By all means, believe him."

I'd heard these arguments before and had led the defense on behalf of Harry. Sensing Hannah's fury, I felt I should be jumping in now. Instead, my senses turned inward and their voices faded while the room chilled. I stood still understanding that this feeling might bring a sense of discovery about what lay below me in the basement. Did I want this? Could I stop it? I turned my eyes to the window in the back door, careful to make no other motion.

He stared at me through the smudged pane. Older than I'd thought from the glimpse I'd had. Sadder than I could bear to see another person. He touched his hand to his throat, to the pendant around his neck.

"Gracie?" Jan Pauli spoke from the doorway, her voice louder than the rest. "Gracie!"

My eyes turned outward and my first sense was that the cacophony of name-calling had stopped.

"I came in when I heard the shouting. What's wrong, honey?"

My dad's lady friend, my ex-cleaning lady, asked with

concern. I knew the others would mirror her sentiment, and I felt overwhelmed. "Is she having one of them spells? 'Cause I felt it too."

Josephine pushed past everyone to reach for my hand. A calm I didn't expect flowed from the contact.

"I felt a heavy weight, a sadness no one should bear alone. It was coming from in here. I felt it, child. Did you see him?"

"See who?" Ric checked the back door. He stepped out a few paces and returned. "No one's been out there. The earth is soft; no footprints."

I shook my head. "I didn't see anyone. Just tired. Tired of the arguing. I'm going home." No one moved.

"Grace, wait. We were out of line," Ric called.

"Gracie, I'm sorry," said Hannah. "That was stupid of me. Harry can fight his own battles."

"Please, Grace, don't leave this way," pleaded Karen.

Josephine led me out of the kitchen. "This girl needs to breathe and think her own thoughts. She be fine, this girl." She patted my hand, then released it.

She stayed in the doorway while I retrieved my purse and left. I wondered if she would have prevented anyone from following me.

Juliana waited at the curb. She rolled down the window. "Is she even thinking about leaving?" She tried for a stern tone, but the affection she held for her aunt softened it.

"Your aunt is one remarkable woman. She'll be out soon. I think she accomplished what she came for."

Juliana glanced at the house then me. I continued walking to my car. She called out, "I don't understand."

"That's a good thing."

FOURTEEN

THE DRIVE HOME gave me time to sort out what happened. When I pushed too hard at a solution it eluded me, but if I let my mind go blank the synapses usually flowed and sorted the extraneous data from the germane. A cup of Cinnamon Nut Swirl and some quiet while I studied the photos would help the process.

Not to be. My father's car was at the curb. Normally, I'm pleased to see my dad anytime of the day or night. Should I leave the photos in the car? No use drawing attention to them and I didn't want to bend them to fit them in my purse. I tucked them in the visor.

"There she is."

I heard my dad's voice lift with fondness. He stood next to Harry at the island. It was apparent he'd just arrived or Harry would have pressed a drink of some sort in his hand by now.

"Hi, Dad." I hugged him and planted a kiss on his cheek.

Jan walked quickly through the doorway. "Whew, thanks for the use of the powder room."

I stared at her and I'm sure my mouth sagged in disbelief. "I just left you…"

Jan's laughter caught me off guard. "No, that wasn't my twin. Although that would be handy. Your father pulled up practically on your heels—or wheels—and we came straight here."

"But I left first! I would have seen his car."

"Gracie, you always stay on I-88 to Rt. 53. If you'd get

on I-355 and exit at Maple, you'd shave seven or eight minutes off your commute."

Harry nodded his head. "I've told her, Mike."

It was a guy thing. Seven or eight minutes in the scheme of things didn't seem that crucial. I'd rather have the extra time to noodle.

I hadn't expected Harry to be home either.

"Gertrude called Walter to tell him you'd just left. He dropped me off here. Guess Gertrude is staying with Karen and Hannah tonight."

"How's Will?"

Harry shrugged. "Eleven and confused."

I thought Harry seemed blasé about his son's current behavior. My dad interrupted my thoughts.

"Yeah, well, they're still confused at thirty-two."

Oh, oh, that meant me. Now to the reason he scurried here.

"Jan told me what happened in that house. I want to hear it from you. She said you seemed lost in thought, almost ill, then you took off with barely a goodbye."

I hated seeing the concern on his face.

"Dad, I'm fine. I felt odd at the house. Everyone was shouting at each other and I sort of 'zoned out' for a moment to get away from the fray."

"Gracie, I saw your face. You were staring out the back-door window. There was no doubt you saw something."

Here it comes. The "Gracie, you've got to fight this. You don't want to suffer like your mother did" plea.

Do they think I enjoy seeing and feeling what I don't understand?

He wouldn't bring up Mom in front of Jan. He wouldn't.

He didn't. "Honey, when Jan told me about how your face went pale, I got worried. We were coming out to Naperville anyway. I thought we'd swing over."

"Mike, Jan, sit down, please. Let me get you something to drink." Harry's host mode kicked in and gave me a moment to settle down.

"Coffee, tea, or soft drink? We've some takeaway from Joyful's Café, lemon and custard tarts and raspberry bars."

As many years as my husband had been in this country he still popped up with an English term every now and then. "Takeaway" did make more grammatical sense than "takeout", but I didn't think it would catch on.

Jan caught it immediately and gushed about how "darling" that sounded. My dad rolled his eyes. This is how it was with my English husband; women loved his accent and colloquialisms.

Minutes passed choosing refreshments and passing plates, glasses, and cups. I took the time to wash up in the powder room, carefully wiping streaked mascara from under my eyes and vigorously brushing my hair into a fresh style.

Everyone was comfortably occupied munching and sipping when I returned. I slipped into the space next to Harry. When we've company, he insists they get the bench facing the yard. With the light in his eyes, I hoped any further scrutiny from my dad would be difficult.

In an attempt to further distract my father, I launched into an account of the day. I drew Jan into the story by asking for confirmation of facts or her opinion on a statement.

Of course I made the foray into the basement sound like fun until Ric came along. "Can you believe how Josephine flirted with him trying to get Ric to hook up with her niece?"

"Poor girl, she was embarrassed and went out and waited for her aunt in the car." Jan shook her head. "I can't imagine her aunt isn't always like this. She needs to get a thicker skin."

"Perhaps she agreed with her aunt's assessment of the fine Inspector." Harry smiled. "He has been known to turn a few heads."

I didn't want to talk about Ric in any way that might include my head in that number. A tiny pause drifted over us until my dad lumbered into the conversation.

"But what made you turn pale?"

So much for diverting his one track mind. I should have known better.

I knew my eyes darkened in preparation for the lie I spoke. He'd know, but what could he do, ground me? He'd be disappointed; it was his ultimate weapon over me.

"I thought I saw a face at the window. I'd been blocking out the arguing, letting my mind go blank, humming *Frere Jacques* in my head. I glanced at the window and saw an old, black man. A moment later a branch brushed against the pane and no one was there."

"So you glanced at the window, thought you saw a dark face, then realized it was the arborvitae outside the back door?"

When Harry asked that way it sounded plausible enough for me to believe it. I nodded.

"Must have been, but in that moment I guess I felt weird." I glanced at Jan, then at my dad, and pretended a shiver while grinning. "Guess it did give me a start."

I was a moderately good actress as long as I didn't have to look anyone in the eye during the commission of a "whopper", the term my brothers used when we were kids for my less-than-honest accountings.

"Refills?" I slid out and carried my mug to the counter. I fiddled with the coffeepot, giving my eyes a chance to lighten before turning back to offer more coffee or tea.

Harry shook his head and slid out from the bench. "No

thanks, darling. I have an appointment in a bit and need to change."

I thought he looked great dressed as he was—snug jeans filled out in all the right places and a sky-blue polo, the fit accentuating his broad chest and shoulders and the color a near match to his eyes. On reevaluation, maybe he should change. I smiled at my assessment.

"Amused, are we?" said Harry.

I caught Jan's eye and saw my catalog of Harry's attributes mirrored in her eyes. We each blushed and grinned. In that moment we drew closer, another lace in our relationship pulling tighter.

Harry and my dad exchanged glances.

"Mike, I think there's something afoot here. I for one am happy to have the occasion to leave." Harry's eyes twinkled.

"Are you doing anything fun? Maybe I'll go with you." Jan poked him in the ribs.

"Only a boring meeting." He glanced at his watch. "Good to see you." He shook hands with my dad and leaned past him to kiss Jan's cheek.

"We should be getting on the road, too. Still have to find this store Jan's heard about."

Dad slid out and motioned for a hug. I stepped into a Morelli bear hug and relished the childhood comfort that it brought.

"Behave, young lady. No foolish snooping into, you know, those kinds of things. You're too sensitive, just like your mom." He whispered the last part, *just like your mom.*

He didn't used to whisper. Didn't he want Jan to know? My aunts always whispered about my mother, but he never did. Not until now.

I kissed him goodbye and pulled out of his grasp.

Mental illness wasn't a crime to be hushed and hidden.

He never treated my mother's manic depression that way before. Before Jan, that is.

He wants to enjoy someone who isn't suffering. He enjoys avoiding the frustration that he can't help someone he loves. He wants to spend his "golden years" loving again.

Okay, okay. I get it. It still upsets me, but I get it.

Jan bussed my cheek and I caught the scent of her *Happy* perfume. Everything about Jan screamed fun loving, even her cologne. I couldn't be angry with her because she wasn't tormented.

"Let's hit the road before that store closes," Dad said. "Jan's got an idea that my kitchen cabinets need sprucing up so we're going to some fancy smancy store, Restoration Hardware, for new drawer pulls. I could trust a store called Lou's Hardware or Joe's Hardware."

"You'd like the prices better, too," Harry said with a grin. "They command, we obey." He bowed and flourished his arm to include Jan and me.

Dad grimaced. "Ain't that the truth."

Jan took my dad's arm. "Let's go before it gets any thicker in here."

The way she smiled when she took his arm made me happy for him. Still, I was sad that my mom wasn't the one with him. She'd been dead for over five years, but my heart wished her with us every day.

When my dad started dating my ex-cleaning lady, I had to come to terms with the fact that he had moved on. My brothers had moved there, too. I, the apparent hold out, moved more slowly. *She was my mom.*

I swallowed hard and pasted some kind of grin on my face. Dad and Jan had already gone out the garage door that Harry held open. Only he saw my teary eyes. He leaned toward me and lifted my chin. His lips brushed the tip of my nose.

"I shan't be long. Wouldn't go at all if I didn't need to."

He left quickly and I stood alone in the garage watching the door roll down, closing me in darkness. The dark never bothered me; the shadows scared me. I moved to retrieve the photos from my car's visor.

I spread them on the island counter and took a moment to pour a fresh cup of coffee. A knock at the nook window startled me and coffee sloshed across the oak surface. I mopped at the puddle with a napkin and searched for the source of my distraction. My neighbor, Barb Atwater, stood at my nook window. She wrinkled her nose and tilted her head in apology.

I waved her toward the back door and rushed to let her in. Barb's short light brown hair curved around her ears and lay perfectly coifed. I gave a quick thought to the mare's nest that must be my hair by this time in the day. I have a tendency to tug, twist, and generally mess up any hairstyle. I forced myself not to lift a hand to my head to pat or smooth it.

"Sorry, Grace. I knocked, but you must not have heard me."

Barb wore sneakers, jeans, a sweatshirt and a light windbreaker, her basic walking outfit.

"Did I miss the memo," I joked. "We walk in the mornings."

Barb fixed me with an arched eyebrow. "You forgot." Not a question. A statement. "The coach house? The Lisle Woman's Club flower sale?"

The promise I'd made moved to the forefront of my mind. I'd agreed to let the club stage their flower pick up in the coach house. Barb was committee chair and they always used her garage. Unfortunately, it had sustained damage when a tree snapped during a windstorm and crashed through the roof.

The small structure would be perfect to take delivery and house the flowers until everyone could pick up their orders.

"Oh, gosh. I had forgotten. Are they delivering today?"

"No, tomorrow. I'm here as planned to rearrange or clear out the space. You don't need to be out there, but I need the key."

"I'd love to help. I'm not sure what's in there. It's been awhile. I've been meaning to clean it up and offer it to Will as a playhouse. If eleven-year-old boys do that."

"Call it a clubhouse and you'll be a hero." Barb's son Devin was my idea of a great kid. Of course, so were my nephews Joseph and Jeffrey and Tracy's boys, Matthew and Benjamin. Would I someday add my stepson to that list?

"I just poured a coffee. Let me put it in a travel mug. Want one, too? It's Cinnamon Nut."

"Hmm. Sounds good."

I lifted the key from the plaque on the wall. One of my nephews had made it in woodshop. Across the top read, *Right where they belong.*

"Here's the key. You can scout it out while I get the goodies."

I play-tossed the keys to Barb and she snagged my less-than-stellar throw. She grinned and turned on her heel heading for the coach house. Her quick, light step belied her early fifty-something age. I continually hoped I'd be as trim and energetic in twenty years. I did the "pinch" on my waist and realized I could use her athletic build now.

I pulled out two travel mugs, one labeled with Harry's company name *Knights' Publishers* and the second reading *Regina Rebels*, compliments of my alma mater's women's soccer team. I lingered at the cake plate, tempted to bring out a few pastries. Barb didn't have a sweet tooth and I was fast developing a sweet depository around my waist. I scooped up the photos instead and hurried to the coach house. I'd offer an intellectual tidbit rather than a caloric one.

The interior wasn't nearly as cluttered as I remembered. After a nutcase from Harry's past life with British Intelligence had launched a mortar shell into our living room, the restoration crew had moved the salvageable furniture into the coach house during the renovation. I thought more pieces, that on closer inspection were too damaged, had been left in the coach house. My family had handled the entire renovation project while Harry and I recovered from the trauma by spending almost three months in England with his parents.

I handed Barb the Knights Publishers mug. She adored anything English, especially Harry. I saw her eyebrows lift when she accepted the mug.

"Thanks. Smells delicious." She sipped and nodded. "Hmmm. Perfect."

"This isn't as bad as I thought."

"Not at all. If we move that small table and those chairs and that loveseat all to one side, and the boxes and that trunk to the other, I'll have plenty of space in the middle for the plants. By the way, I don't have your order yet, do I?"

I grinned and shook my head. "No, and you don't have my dad's either."

"Ah, but there you are mistaken. I talked to Jan and have their order in the books." Her smile faded a tad and I realized my face must have caused the drop in grin wattage. I always ordered the flowers from the club for my dad. He and I would sit down over coffee and decide how many hanging baskets of wave petunias, how many flats of impatiens for under the bushes that lined the yard, how many geraniums for the front walkway. I hadn't been able to slip a smile on my face in time and my hurt or surprise must have shown.

Barb turned away and moved toward the square oak table scorched up one leg and across a quarter of the top. I'd hoped sanding would remove the mark, but the restorer had said it was too deep. I'd thought to sand it, use filler, seal it, cut down the legs and paint it for a table for the twins.

"Let's push this against the wall and put the three chairs around it."

The fourth chair to the set had been destroyed. Curtains that had been singed or smoke damaged lay in a heap across the loveseat, which was part of the living room set Harry and I had picked out at Marshall Field's, our second purchase after our bedroom suite.

Barb cleared her throat. "Or we could line up the boxes and the trunk on that side." She walked across the room and easily lifted a small sealed box. I could see the square black writing on the side, *books*. A lawyers' bookcase, the type with the glass panels that lifted over each shelf, had shattered in the explosion. Eight manageable cardboard boxes held the books that had survived the blast.

The trunk had been in the coach house almost two years ago since I'd found it in the basement of Gertrude's boardinghouse. Had it been less than two years that I'd made the painful discovery about my long-missing aunt's fate? My mother had died before she knew the secret of her older sister's disappearance from Regina College years earlier.

Today, I'd spent time in Gertrude's basement uncovering another secret. I felt as though I'd come full circle.

I pointed to the trunk. "It's empty. Let's move it to that corner and load the boxes inside." With a point at which to begin, we made fast work of clearing the center of the room. We folded the drapes and dropped them into a large plastic bag. Barb offered to cut them short to fit the windows in the coach house.

The table fit well against the wall with the chairs tucked in at the three open sides. I'd left the photos lying on it and Barb saw them now. "What are those?"

"We worked enough. Have a seat while I fill you in."

I pulled out a chair and motioned for Barb to sit also. The breeze kept the interior from becoming stuffy and in short order I had her up to speed. My neighbor's eyes widened and widened until I thought her contacts would dry up and pop out. She blinked several times and shivered.

"Grace, how do you get involved in all these, these…"

"Bizarre cases?"

"Yes, bizarre. Perfect word for what keeps happening to you."

I shrugged. "I don't know. I find myself drawn to the sites, almost pulled." I rolled my shoulders and took a deep breath. "Anyway, these are the items that were found with the, um, remains." I pointed to the photo of the shoe clip. "Hannah is positive this is shoe jewelry from the 1920s or 1930s made by Chanel. I thought they only made perfume."

Barb nodded. "Me too. What's this?" She held up the photo of the odd metal square.

"Not sure. I have to get to the library—"

"I know what it is." Barb's voice rose in excitement. "It's a slave tag, Grace."

"A what?"

"I've seen them on display at Graue Mill. It's a tag, I think made of lead, which the slaves wore around their necks to identify what kind of work they did, like house slave or overseer or field slave. Devin worked on a merit badge at the mill. They had one of those reenactment events and the program explained how slaves escaped North to freedom. The woman who presented it is Glennette Tilley Turner. She wrote *The Underground Railroad in Illinois.* It was fascinating, so I bought the book. Pierce Downer used his home as a station on the Underground Railroad.

"You think the skeleton they found could be the remains of a runaway slave? That would be bizarre."

"Yep. *Bizarre.* Right up your alley. You can borrow the book if you want. I think I put the pamphlets from the event in the book." Barb stood up. "Oh, I'm late. I have a dinner tonight."

She wrinkled her nose. "Doctor stuff. Yuck!"

"Hey, that doctor stuff keeps you in bonbons." I joked.

"Yeah, there is that." She grinned. "Thanks for the coffee. I'll be by in the morning to sweep out before they arrive."

"Barb, wouldn't it make more sense to come by after the plants are gone and sweep out?"

"Good point. I'll just drop off the book."

I gave her thumbs up and she scooted through the break in the rose hedge.

The coach house had been a frivolous last-minute addition with roughed-in plumbing for a small bath and kitchenette. I don't know what we were thinking, except when Harry revealed his plans for a greenhouse I blurted, "And a coach house, too." Harry thought it a "capital" idea and here I sat.

A plan replete with carpenter's measurements grew in my mind. This could be a great guest cottage. The contractor hired by Hannah could work here too. In my mind's eye I imagined the wood floor and wainscoting, the Franklin stove centered on one wall, the day bed resplendent in Laura Ashley linens, the gleaming copper-bottom Revere Wear hanging from hooks, and the large floral-themed rugs.

"Wow, this is cool."

Will's voice startled me. I jumped up as though caught doing something naughty. My skin flushed with embarrassment.

"Hullo, what's all the fuss?" Harry's eyes searched my face.

I don't know why I felt "busted", as my nephews would say. I grinned. "I didn't expect you so soon. Actually," I said, "I didn't know when you'd be home." I stopped before I yammered something to Will like *"and I didn't expect you at all"*.

Harry rushed to explain. "We needed to clear the air about some things, and his mother forgot—"

"Lily. Her name is Lily," Will interjected.

Oh, brother. They'd cleared the air all right. Who was Harry kidding.

Harry's face clouded and he continued without an adjustment "—that although tomorrow was a free day from school, she had already made appointments."

So Will bounces back to us on a day he is supposed to be with his mother.

I knew Harry's feelings about Lily's and his custodial agreement. He was working through the courts to establish his rights as the biological father. In the interim he had to tread carefully around Lily's largesse lest she decide to dangle less *Will time* in Harry's face.

In an attempt to change the subject, I explained about the flower delivery tomorrow. "Barb left a few minutes ago and I was just thinking about what a great—"

"Clubhouse. This would make a great clubhouse." Will rushed in to explore the entire space. "We could get one of those little refrigerators and keep pop in it. And we could get one of those long tables and build models out here."

Will's voice droned on while Harry's face beamed brighter with each proclamation. There goes the guest cottage. I gathered my photos and the travel mugs and headed for the house. I'd drop these off, then visit the barn for some solace. I had some general cleaning and straightening to do. I should ask Will to help, but I didn't want a confrontation.

I thought of what my dad would say. "Tell that kid that if he lives under your roof, he follows your rules and he helps out." In other words, get your eleven-year-old butt out to the barn and help me muck stalls. Maybe another time.

I heard April's soft *snicker* and wondered at her acute hearing, then realized someone was in there with her. I heard Will's question. "We have to shovel all of this?" His incredulous tone made me snicker.

"When you keep animals you take on their care. Can you imagine April here grasping the shovel with her teeth and pushing the straw about?"

Will giggled in response.

"And what about Cash Cow? Shall we have him rear up and push the wheelbarrow with his front hooves?" Harry's exaggerated scenario and accent had Will in belly laughs. "Opposable thumbs," he continued. "It sets us apart, gives us great possibilities, but also keen responsibilities for those who can't do for themselves because we choose to keep them for our pleasure."

When he put it that way, it sounded dreadful to keep any animals in confinement. I shook off the idea that April and Cash would be better off running free on some distant open range and walked into the barn.

"How nice to have the help. Thanks, Will."

Harry smiled and swung his arm around Will's shoulders. "Labor Men to the ready." Will rolled his eyes. "Gracie, lead April out and we'll tackle her stall first."

I lifted the lead off the peg outside her stall and offered it to Will while holding out my other hand for the shovel. "I'll hold that while you lead her out. Clip her to that ring over there."

He hesitated for a second. "Really?" His tentative smile widened when I nodded.

"Sure. You have to learn how to get her out before you clean the stall." I slipped him a couple of baby carrots. "Always have treats on you when you come to the barn. April will snuffle your hand even without a treat. She's such a flirt, but something tasty is always appreciated."

Will held out the offering and was rewarded with a gently slurp of his palm.

"Scratch her muzzle, then slide your hand under the halter strap and snap on the lead. If she didn't have her halter on you'd have to slip that on first. Now lift the latch and let the door swing all the way open before you lead her out."

He led April (she knew the routine better than I) to the opposite wall and secured the clip. April would stand there anyway because she knew after her stall was cleaned and she was brushed there would be an excellent chance for an outing.

"Can I do Cash?"

"Not until we clean out April's stall. We don't want them out at the same time. Too crowded."

"How about I take it from here?" Harry wanted to have Will to himself, perhaps to talk out their previous problem or maybe just to have guy time. I wanted to stay and be part of the bonding. I liked Will best when he was around horses; he seemed to tolerate me, even like me then.

Harry and Will's faces held the same expectant expression. I shrugged and slapped an empty grin on my face. "Sure, I'll check around later, white-glove inspection."

"Huh?" Will's head swiveled from Harry to me.

"It's an expression that means we'd best be good at our mucking." Harry ruffled Will's hair and pulled him against him for a quick hug before he pointed him toward the stall.

"I believe you can leave that," he said, reaching for the shovel I held. His whispered, *"thank you"* was heartfelt. I nodded, then reached up to kiss his cheek.

I walked back to the house expecting to feel disappointed, but the thought that I had a couple of hours to settle in with the new ideas Barb had given me drove the melancholy away.

I hadn't realized I'd carried one of the short ropes from the barn with me. The two-foot length begged to be twisted and formed into knots. My fingers rubbed the rough twining, the sensation relieving some pent-up jitters. Tying a few knots would be a great way to clear my head.

Bowlines? Yes. Five? No, twenty. Too many. You asked. Ten? Oh, all right.

FIFTEEN

I KNEW THE barn chores would be done and the two of them would claim their reward and take April and Cash for a ride though the meadow. A part of me would like to be included. More of me understood they needed to spend time together to catch up on all the things parents and children intrinsically know about each other from years of common contact.

I rinsed out the travel mugs and filled my angel mug with fresh coffee before turning my thoughts to the photos. I spread them across the nook table, pleased to see they were sharp in detail. I stared at the square medallion wondering about the person who had worn this around their neck. If this was a slave tag, then logically one of the skeletons had to have been a slave. How had they died in the basement of an Oak Park home? Could this house have been a stop on the Underground Railroad?

The doorbell interrupted my thoughts. I wasn't expecting anyone and was surprised to see Karen and Clare standing on my front porch.

Actually, Karen stood there, expertly holding her daughter on one canted hip. Wonderful perches those hips. Even the thinnest moms manage to have them or get them when needed.

I swung open the door and reached for my niece. "Hi, sweetie pie, I'm happy to see you." Clare rewarded my sing-song tone with a grin and outstretched pudgy arms. I swept her to my chest and hugged her. "Mmm, you smell yummy."

I proceeded to chatter all the way to the kitchen. Karen placed her tote bag on the bench. It appeared to be filled with books. She pulled her shoulder bag off and rolled her neck and shoulders.

"That's a sure way to end up with a bad neck," I said. "What's in the bag?"

"Library books. I called Debby and asked her to suggest some books on the Underground Railroad in Illinois." Karen grinned and emptied seven books onto the table. "*Voila,* instant reference."

Debby was a friend we'd known since college and the librarian at the Oak Park Library. She and I had attended grad school together at Regina. I stayed on to work in the college library while she landed a peach of a job in Oak Park.

I cuddled Clare and smooched her cheeks until she shrieked in delight. "Pour yourself a coffee and we can start reading. Harry and Will are in the barn. They're cleaning stalls before going riding. We'll have plenty of uninterrupted time."

Karen grinned. "Not while she's in the picture."

A moment of pain swept over me. I'd wanted to know those things first hand. Harry and I had planned to adopt a child at the same time with Hannah and Karen. They were applying for a girl and we for a boy. Through a quirk of fate, they adopted twins. A month before our paperwork was to be submitted Harry discovered he had a ten-year-old son. He'd thought it best for us to put the adoption on hold and get to know William Harry Marsden.

Clare's pink fingers tugged at my lips and thoughts of what could have been retreated under her touch.

"Mmmm, more smooches, baby girl?" I sat on the bench and settled Clare on my lap. In addition to books, Karen had several toys in her tote. She placed Clare's own chubby storybook and Missy Mew, a plush tiger cat, in front of her. Clare squealed with joy and pulled Missy Mew to her mouth.

"Let's see how far we get." Karen pushed two books across the table to me and took two for herself. The others she stacked neatly at the end of the table. She removed two small pads of paper and two pencils from the tote and passed one set to me. "In case you need to jot down something."

I smiled. "Is there a better combination than a teacher and a librarian?" Although I hadn't worked as a librarian for five years, in my heart that was my calling.

"None better," Karen answered and lifted her mug in a toast. We clinked ceramic and grinned like kids.

"Barb was over earlier and she identified this photo. It's a slave tag worn to identify what type of work the slave did. You know, like a field worker or house slave. She says there's a great display of information about the Underground Railroad at Graue Mill."

"Sounds like a road trip."

"And lunch at York Pub."

"Yes, Gracie, we'll stop for food."

Anyone who knew me knew I hated to miss meals. From childhood I always knew when it was lunchtime and would leave play to go home for food. The joke was, if I ever ran away from home, it would only be until dinner. As an adult it became easier to plan around meals, slipping breakfast, brunch, lunch, or dinner into the outing plans.

We began reading and soon became engrossed in the tales of bravery and sacrifice jumping out at us page after page. I especially admired the story of the Crofts, a young couple who pulled off an incredible disguise in their successful bid for freedom. Mrs. Croft, a light-skinned woman who'd worked in her owner's home and therefore spoke in a more genteel manner, disguised herself as a man and, in the company of her "slave" husband, made her way north. The daring journey required her to wear green tinted glasses to hide her eyes and a toothache sling to disguise her beardless face. Because slaves weren't allowed to learn to read or write, she wore an arm sling to prevent the necessity of signing her name. Through their courage, some help from unusual sources, and the grace of God, they'd made it to safety.

"Listen to this," Karen said. "Mainly young men were successful in their flights to freedom. Older slaves felt they didn't have the reserves of strength necessary to make the arduous journey and therefore stayed behind to help others find their way. Many older slaves, if they were owned by 'nicer' families and had a useful skill like blacksmith or furniture maker, were not as confined and watched. These slaves risked their lives to aid runaways making their way through the area. They would bring food and clothing to the hiding places that were known to the slaves but not to the plantation owners or the slave catchers.

"The most trusted of these slaves would act as 'Waysayer', a person who would meet with the runaway slaves and tell the route that they knew to be safest. All slaves were told to 'follow the North star', but more direction was needed to find the safe stops along the way. Young slaves who had made it to the North returned to get word to others on where to stop and who they could trust. They would make the dangerous trip back to the plantations to help others. Usually they would arrange to bring a group back with them.

"The Waysayer, could never seek freedom for himself or herself. Their most necessary job was to learn the safe routes and repeat them to runaways. Even if they could write, it wouldn't be safe to have the routes written down for fear the slave-catchers found them. It would mean certain capture and return to their owners for the runaways; to most, a fate they considered worse than death."

"If we use that accounting, the skeleton must be a young man or woman," I said.

"Why not both skeletons?"

"The shoe clip. The other skeleton can't be from the same era. I would think the newer skeleton is a woman."

"Maybe the other one, too. There wasn't much room in there. I don't think a full grown man could have fit."

I thought about the man I'd see at the side of the house. He hadn't been tall or brawny.

"Maybe a boy?" Karen continued.

I shrugged. "I guess we'll have to wait until the police get their results."

Clare stretched out her arms and Karen lifted her to her lap. The baby reached for her mom's nose. Karen 'meowed' and Clare giggled and touched Karen's nose again and again to elicit the meow.

"You are so silly, my silly girl." Karen kissed Clare's fingers, handed her a baby biscuit to distract her, then leaned toward me. Her eyes gleamed with gossip. I knew that expression and anticipated a good story.

"Can you believe my brother is seriously contemplating having her move in with him?"

My brain froze. I felt my eyes widen and I'm sure my jaw slacked.

"Geez, Grace. Oh my God, I thought he told you. He told me he was going to tell you. God, Gracie, I'm sorry."

This is what you've wanted. For him to find someone to love; for him to leave you alone. Now you've got what you wanted. This is what you want.

Of course it's what I want. Don't be absurd. I'm only surprised. I never imagined he'd want to marry another cop.

Who said marry? He's moving in with her. There's a big difference.

Absolutely there is. Maybe he's not too sure of his feelings.

Is that wishful thinking on your part, Gracie girl?

"Grace? I am sorry. He told me two weeks ago that he was telling you. He wanted you to be the first to know, but I overheard him talking to Marisol—"

"Marisol Nunez? Why was he telling her?"

Karen stared at me in most unsettling manner.

"Grace, he wasn't telling her, he was finalizing the moving arrangement for next weekend."

"Why would he finalize those with her? Does she know Nancy Royal?"

"Nancy Royal? Grace, that was over months ago. Don't you remember, I told you Marisol had taken a leave from the FBI and moved back to Aurora where she grew up?"

"Yeah, kind of, but what's that got to do with it?"

Suddenly, the picture came into focus. I'd heard comments about Ric and his police lady friend, but I'd assumed they meant Nancy Royal, a Lisle police officer.

He was asking Marisol, the beautiful FBI profiler who had physic abilities and great curves.

"Oh, I see. Marisol. Guess I got behind in Ric's affairs." I tried to sound flip and unimpressed, but I heard the catch in my voice. Clearing my throat didn't fool Karen. "That *is* news, and a first. He's never wanted to share his castle." I smiled and patted Karen's hand. "How about a refill before we do more research?"

I fiddled with the coffee maker and searched the cabinets for packages of cookies. The traitorous tears slipped easily down my cheeks. I resisted swiping at my face with my sleeve; I felt Karen's eyes on me before I heard her soft voice.

"You know you were the first person he really loved. Gracie, this is his chance to move past you and find some happiness." I heard her rise and walk to my side. "I love you, Grace, but I love him too. You have your happiness. Please let him have his."

Did I have my happiness? Would Harry stay with me or eventually choose the path of least resistance and reconnect with Lily? That choice would thrill Will. Was I subconsciously holding Ric in the wings? I'd hate to think I was that insecure and self-absorbed.

"Grace, when you left him you didn't see, never knew, the half of what he went through. You were busy nursing Harry back to health. No one understood how devastated Ric was over your dismissal of him."

"Dismissal? Geez, Karen, you make it sound like it was an easy choice for me, like I didn't love him, miss him." My voice lowered to whisper. "Want him."

Dismissal indeed. Like I hadn't cried myself to sleep anguishing over the choice I'd made. Harry's parents must have thought the sobs they heard were for their son as he lay recovering from horrible injuries suffered on his last mission for their government.

Karen shifted Clare to her other hip and put her arm around my shoulders. "I'm sorry, Grace. I didn't know. You were in England with Harry. You made that choice. Please don't hold onto Ric now."

"Is that what you think, that I'm holding him as 'backup' in case things don't work out with Harry?" I'd never before said it out loud. My best friend's silence answered for her.

"Is Uncle Ric your boyfriend?"

SIXTEEN

I NEVER HEARD Will enter the room. He stood in the doorway, his eyes gleaming with possibilities. The resemblance to his father at that moment took my breath away.

Karen answered smoothly, "My brother dated your stepmom a long time ago. But now, he is going to share his life with a special lady who he loves very much."

"Like my dad did with my mom before I was born? Like Grandpa Mike and Jan? Like you and Aunt Hannah?"

The list about covered all the relationships in the family. I wondered how Karen would handle this. Before she could answer, Will said, "Is anybody getting married?"

Harry stepped up behind Will. "Who is getting married?"

Will twisted his neck to peek up at his dad. "Uncle Ric. He's sharing his life with a special lady who he loves very much," Will parroted.

Harry stared at me over his son's blond head. "I'd pay a pretty penny to see that," he said.

"Oh, you have to pay way more than that, Dad. You have to give them an envelope with money, lots of money."

Harry smiled. "It would be my pleasure. How do you know about wedding protocol?"

"Adam, one of the kids in the troop, his older sister is getting married. He hears all kinds of stuff about weddings. Like his parents hope people will at least 'cover their plate'. We're not sure with what. He didn't hear that part. Probably a napkin."

We burst into laughter. Harry ruffled Will's hair and pulled him into a hug. Will looked bewildered but pleased to be the center of attention. Clare shrieked with delight at all the laughter and her response made us laugh harder.

Harry stared at me, watching for a "tell" that the news of Ric's engagement bothered me. I struggled to keep a neutral expression on my face. With my eyes wide open and a smile lifting my lips I thought the word *ocean* over and over in my head hoping for the calm that came with associative therapy. I felt a lessening of the tension in my neck and shoulders and smiled genuinely, I thought, at my family.

"Wonderful news, let me know when they hold the chap's bachelor bash. I'm keen on attending."

Karen grinned at Harry. "I'll bet." She scooped up Claire. "It's getting close to her bedtime. Keep the books, I have them for two weeks."

Several kisses and hugs later and we three Marsdens stood alone in the kitchen. I liked the thought of that, *we three Marsdens*.

"Where have you scampered off to up there?" Harry touched my temple with his forefinger.

I crossed one arm over my chest and rested my elbow on my hand while I tapped my head with my finger. "Hmm, thinking about where I put those white gloves."

"Dad, is she serious? Really going to inspect our cleaning with white gloves?"

Will's squeaky voice caused more laughter. I smiled and he got the joke.

"You'll become accustomed to her sense of humor, son." Harry assured him.

"Yeah, maybe, but I'll never get used to your big words. Can't you just say 'get used to'?"

The expression of chagrin on Harry's face was priceless.

I put my hand up to "high five" Will. "I've been asking him that for years. Don't worry, you'll get used to it."

Will and I burst into laughter. Harry pretended to be cross, but the laughter percolating in his heart escaped in shorts bursts between his comment of, "Would *My Fair Lady* have stood a chance of gaining an award if they sang, 'I've gotten used to her face'?"

"What was wrong with her face?" Will asked.

More hoots of laughter until Harry sat down shaking his head, muttering, "colonists". He noticed the books.

"Who is back in school? You've enough here for a term paper. He picked up a slim volume. "*The Underground Railroad in Illinois*." He picked up another. "*Ride to Freedom*." He read a few more titles, then stacked the books neatly at one corner.

"Sorry to say, the British started all this." He motioned toward the stack. "By the time the British Empire came to its senses and outlawed slavery they had been instrumental in spreading it halfway around the world. The irony was that for an American slave to be safely free, he had to move far beyond the borders into Canada or sail for England."

"Do you think the people they found in Aunt Karen and Aunt Hannah's basement were trying to go to Canada? Would they go to Midland like you did?"

Will referred to my erstwhile attempt to enjoy a brief respite with my childhood friend, Joan, in her cottage on Georgian Bay. It hadn't been a respite at all, rather a tragedy of lost lives over greed and superstition.

"I never heard mention of a settlement of slaves," I said. "Of course, we never thought they'd find what they did in the boarding house. When your dad and I were down in that basement two years ago, there were only a bunch of trunks crammed in there. We never suspected a false floor."

"Really? Not even you, Dad?" Will's voice pleaded for a glimmer of super-hero powers.

Harry smiled the smile of a boring dad with a regular job, like when a bespectacled Clark Kent would avoid danger. Will might never know how his father had risked his life for the British government taking on missions that required his special skill. Harry was out of that business now and that suited us. But oh, what exciting stories he could tell. Maybe someday he'd share that part of his life with his son.

"Would Uncle Ric have known?"

Harry's blue eyes clouded and I spotted the flicker of frustration forming on his face.

"Nope, he was down there too and never suspected a thing." I answered.

"Oh." Will's voiced sounded flat. No heroes today.

I brushed my hands together and cleared my throat. "Dinner will be ready in an hour. You two have time for another quick ride. Any takers?"

That moved us off the subject. Will dashed for the mudroom with Harry in hot pursuit. I heard them laughing and banging their way out the back door. With the two of them gone, I had time enough to drive out and pick up a bucket of chicken and all the sides. Harry could preach about the nutritional value of Brussels sprouts when he planned dinner.

I glanced at the stacked books. Something was wrong. They were stacked all odds and ends, not by size.

Won't take but a minute. You know you have to.

I know, I know. Okay, one time through.

I handled the books into size order with the largest on the bottom stacking up to the smallest on top.

How about turning every other one at right angles. You know, straight, sideways, straight, sideways.

I said, one time through.

My fingers rearranged the books even as my mind attempted not to. One of the slimmer volumes slipped from my fingers. I grabbed at it and trapped it, pages pressed open, against the table leg with my thigh. *Nice save*, I thought and plucked it from its snare. The open page showed a picture of Graue Mill and the mill owner's home and another home adjacent to it. I'd been to the mill through the years and never recalled seeing this other home. I sat down and read the paragraph under the photo.

The Coe family operated a station from their home situated less than 300 hundred feet from another station in the Graue home. A tunnel connected the two homes and enabled them to transfer "passengers" at a moment's notice when slave catchers were searching the area. The Coe home provided excellent subterfuge as Joseph and Aida Coe often entertained well-known performers from the Chicago stage."

Interesting, music and song in the salon while you're smuggling slaves through the tunnels. I turned to the index to find more about the Coe family whose house no longer stood. Nothing there. The next three books also had nothing. But the fourth one, *Riding North to Freedom*, showed a sepia photograph of Aida and Joseph Coe in fancy dress. My heart beat faster as I scrutinized the photo, zeroing in on the pendant around Aida's neck. The photo was old, but I knew what I saw. I grabbed the glossy photographs from the counter; the pendant matched the piece found with the skeleton in the cupboard.

How was that possible? The shoe clip was made in the 1930's by Chanel. And it's a shoe clip, not a pendant. The clip was copied from the pendant. Is the skeleton a Coe descendant who had the pendant, then commissioned the clips? I slipped the photo in the book to mark the page and set it to the side.

I searched the other books for other old photographs and found one immediately. The metal pendant used to designate slave status was easy to find and it matched the crime-scene photograph. That photo became a page marker and I set that book aside.

Now my index search would be for any mention of a station or conductor in the Forest Park or Oak Park area. Obviously, the owner before Gertrude's family, or maybe the one before him, had been an Underground Railroad conductor. I skimmed the indices of each book with no success.

Think, Gracie, think. You used to do this for a living.

My internal admonishment worked. Public records, tax records, census records, all records, beautiful records. It would be there—names, sales of property, etc.

I stood and whirled round to grab the phone. I knew the perfect person for the job. She should be home by now.

Karen answered on the third ring. I explained my discovery and theory. She jumped onto the same page with me and knew who we had to ask.

"Sure, I'll call Debby tomorrow. She'd love to follow this thread back to the spool. I'll call you after I talk to her."

"Okay, take care. Kiss those bambinos for me. Good night."

Our friend Debby Preiser would be perfect to handle this task. She'd always been the most intuitive of my circle of librarian friends, always a sixth sense of where to search next.

Part of me wondered why I didn't take it on. Part of me knew I didn't want to delve too deeply and be drawn somewhere my spirit shouldn't go. Even now, miles away from his Oak Park grave and over a hundred years removed from his death, I felt a sense of presence so strong a chill crept across my shoulders.

SEVENTEEN

THE DOOR BANGED against the mudroom wall and Harry shouted for help. He carried Will through the door and rushed into the living room to place him on the couch.

"I told him not to go through the woods. April knew better, she tried to turn back." Harry's eyes stared at the goose-egg-size lump on his son's forehead. "My God, Grace, he hit a branch and tumbled off her back."

Will's pale face served to accentuate the harsh red mark above his brows. He stirred and opened his eyes straining to focus. "What happened?" His voice wavered with fear.

"Honey, lie still. I'm going to get some ice for that bump." I hurried to the kitchen and pulled out a small package of frozen peas. I grabbed the kitchen towel with the orange poppies and wrapped the package.

Harry reached for the bundle. His hand shook while he gently applied the cold pack to Will's forehead.

Will flinched and Harry anguished. "Sorry, son. Stings a little, but it will help bring it down. You rode into a branch and popped off April's back."

Will closed his eyes and seemed to relax. Harry panicked. "We need to take him to Emergency."

"I'll drive; you sit in back with Will." I wasn't sure if his injury warranted emergency services, but I wasn't willing to take that chance. My brothers all had had their share of bumps but no one had been conked out to my recollection. "Let me call Devin and ask him to round up April and Cash."

Harry lifted Will and I preceded him through the kitchen into the garage to open doors. While Harry settled Will in the back seat I called Barb and quickly explained. She said she'd get Devin right on it.

I grabbed my purse from the counter and slid into the front seat. The ride to Good Samaritan took less time than I thought it would, although Harry squirmed with impatience.

The emergency room entrance glided open for us. The triage nurse rushed to Harry when she saw him carrying the still figure. Another nurse pushing a gurney appeared. She helped Harry lower Will to the surface. They took Will and Harry behind the curtained area while I remained outside.

I fiddled with a length of yarn tied to the metal ring on my purse. My fingers produced a taut line knot, then undid and retied it. I appeared nonchalant; only I knew I had ten to tie and untie before I could go in search of a coffee. My mind drifted to the puzzle of the remains found in the basement. According to Josephine two young women of excellent means visited the boardinghouse. Why would Gertrude's mother know rich people from as far west as Hinsdale? How did an expensive piece of jewelry from a wealthy family end up in the final resting place of whom? One of those women, Trixie or Dolly? Were they part of the Coe family?

Easy enough to find out if Karen had been able to enlist Debby's help. I knew any emergency room exam would take a bit of time, time I could use to make a few calls. I fed all my quarters into the black box to insure an uninterrupted conversation.

Karen's hushed voice answered on the first ring, which made me think the babies might be napping.

"Sorry, hope I didn't wake the kids."

"No, they're at the park with Gertrude. I'm watching this PBS documentary on, of all things, the Underground Railroad in Illinois. What do they call that when you've never heard of something, then everywhere you turn you see a reference to it?"

"Bizarre?"

"No, there's a term for it. Never mind. This segment is on the area near you, Graue Mill. It used to be Fullersburg; not the mill, the area. The lead in for the next segment mentioned Maywood. I wonder if there were any stations further east. Maybe the boardinghouse? Would that give it landmark status? Man, that could mess up my plans."

I noticed two things immediately. First of all, Karen was holding a conversation with herself. Secondly, she had referred only to herself when mentioning the renovation plans. I waited for her to take a long enough breath to interrupt her.

"Did you reach Debby with our plan?"

"Left her a message on her answering machine," was her quick reply. She probably resented being cut off in mid soliloquy.

I quickly explained what I'd seen in the photo and asked her to add the name Coe to Debby's list.

"Do you recall if Josephine mentioned the last name of the two debs, Trixie and Dolly? And were those their real names or what Josephine and Clarisse called them? Somehow they don't seem like debutante names to me. Do they to you?"

Karen had grown up in Oak Park society tagging along to events with her mother and aunt. She'd attended debutante balls, had her own debut. I deferred to her on all matters *hoity toity*.

"They could be family nicknames, but I'll bet Josephine and Clarisse addressed them 'Miss something' to

their faces and made up the names for their private use.
I'll let you know. Right now, I want to finish watching
this program. Absolutely fascinating. If we have landmark
status…"

I gently replaced the receiver and waited for any change
the instrument might regurgitate. A lone quarter dropped
into the return.

"There you are." No accusatory tone, only fact. "The
nurse pointed me in this direction."

Harry looked much relieved. Exhausted, but relieved.

"They're admitting him for observation, and since I am
not his legal guardian, or anything legal, I cannot sign the
papers. I'll have to reach Lily and have her okay it somehow."

The edge in his voice grew sharper with each sentence.
I knew it killed him that legally he was nobody in Will's
life. Tracy had suggested he get a signed document from
Lily stating that he had the authority to make emergency
medical arrangements in her absence. Lily wouldn't consider it. She'd merely cautioned Harry not to put Will in
harm's way.

"So once again I'm trying to track down his globe trot-
ting mother. I left a message on her machine."

A nurse approached from behind Harry. I nodded at her
and he turned around.

"Mr. Marsden, Mrs. Marsden called and approved the
paperwork. We're taking Will upstairs to his room."

"She identified herself as Mrs. Marsden?" I blurted.
My stomach tightened.

The nurse nodded and checked at her clipboard. "Yes,
Lily Marsden," she read from her notes. "Do you want to
go up with him now?"

Harry sprang to her side. "Yes, of course." He turned to
me and held out his hand. "Come up with us."

I froze to the spot feeling hurt and horror that his ex-lover flagrantly adopted the use of his name—no, my name—Mrs. Marsden. Harry didn't seem surprised. Did he not hear, or did he not care. Did he maybe wish she'd been his first Mrs. Marsden?

"Gracie, are you coming?"

Harry and the nurse waited.

I shook my head and mumbled, "I'll catch up. Have to use the ladies room."

"He'll be in 2120." The efficient nurse turned and Harry followed, glancing back once to smile.

Was that an, *I'll explain everything about the name thing later* smile? If he knew she'd been using his name, he'd have lots of explaining to do.

I did use the ladies room, did find the coffee machine, did call and check on the horses, and finally did make my way to room 2120. The door to the room was open and the view unobstructed. Harry and Lily sat on the hospital bed on either side of Will who appeared remarkably chipper. Harry held a travel mug, a match to the one in Lily's hand. Two blond heads bobbed in acknowledgment while Will spoke about his ride through the woods.

I took my dark head and plain Lipton away from the doorway and retraced my steps to the lobby. Eventually Harry'd come down. I'd spotted a small bag on the floor near the foot of the bed. Lily would most likely spend the night. I know I would if I had a child who'd been injured. If I had a child…

Suddenly, I didn't want to wait, didn't want to hear another explanation about, *she's his mother, what can I do?* He could take her car, or call Walter, or walk. I knew my anger was unreasonable, but it's all I had to hold onto right now.

The ride to my dad's house in Berkeley gave me enough

time to calm down, a little, and compose my thoughts before I arrived. I saw my brother Marty's car in the driveway. He'd moved back in with my dad when his wife, Eve had asked for a trial separation. It had been almost six months. They were talking, but he was still living in his old bedroom. His moving back must have cramped my dad's new romance. I dumped that thought out of my brain before it could take hold. *Parents aren't supposed to have romance.*

Another car pulled up to house as I turned into the driveway.

EIGHTEEN

JOSEPHINE HOSSACK AND Juliana Dodd walked up the drive toward me.

"Good evening, Mrs. Marsden." Juliana extended her hand.

"Please call me Grace." I smiled at her and her aunt. The older woman stepped closer and patted my shoulder.

"I am happy you are joining us for dinner with your father and Jan."

That explained why they were here, but why would my dad invite them to dinner? I didn't think he'd even met them. Jan had, and I guess her relationship with my dad extended to inviting her friends to dinner. Why not her condo in Naperville?

My mind was churning, but my manners kicked in automatically and I made small talk while we walked up the driveway. Marty answered the door and registered surprise when he saw me.

"Hi, Sis. Coming to dinner or just passing through?" The two women stared. I hadn't lied, just hadn't confirmed their question.

Geez, I used to live here. I'm not the interloper.

"I came to see you and found out dinner was a possibility. Serendipitous, I'd say."

"Martin, don't leave folks on the porch for pity's sake. Bring them in," called my father.

We trouped in and were made instantly and thoroughly welcomed. Mike Morelli loved entertaining. He'd had little opportunity beyond family when my mom shared his life. In the short time he'd known Jan I'd hear of a few impromptu and a few planned dinner parties. I couldn't begrudge him his new joy; only wished it could have been with my mom.

Changes in the décor reflected a woman's influence. Things matched. The television wasn't the focal point. In fact, wasn't even in the living room.

Jan hung the ladies' jackets on a new wrought iron coat tree. Each 'branch' ended with a glass doorknob to hold the article of clothing. Clever and retro. Maybe from Jan's condo. Maybe from Restoration Hardware.

"Hi, honey. What a nice surprise." My dad leaned forward to hug me and I loved the feel of his strong arms around me. We rocked side to side and did our big squeeze and *hmmm* grunt before we released each other. We always hugged, only sometimes, in public, more quietly. "You're staying for dinner aren't you? Is Harry out there?" Dad asked peering behind me.

"No, he's with Will and Lily." I explained the riding mishap quickly, not wanting to spoil dinner. "I came by to see Marty for a few minutes."

"You're staying for dinner. Jan's already set out a spot." I checked the table and it was set for six. I didn't doubt that if I had barged in with Harry and Will, Karen and Hannah and the twins, the table would have expanded to accommodate.

I nodded and slipped out of my jacket searching for an unoccupied knob.

My dad slipped his arm around my shoulders. "Crazy looking thing. We got it at the fancy hardware store. Nonna Santa's house, where I grew up, had those kinds of glass doorknobs. It's growing on me. Maybe I like old things more as I get older." He grinned at his assessment.

"Let's hope that statement doesn't include me," Jan said from across the room. Her soft voice, laced with a smile, left no doubt that she was confident about his attraction to her.

My dad spoke in a stage whisper, "Am I in trouble?"

"Depends how you answer." I laughed too hard to add more.

"Easy, Dad," Marty called as a warning. "It's a mine-field out there."

Jan held up her hand. "Enough. Mr. Mike and I will discuss this at a later time." She grinned and crooked her finger at my dad. "May I see you in the kitchen."

"Oww. Mr. Mike." Marty fanned his neck with his open hand pretending to cool off. "All the kids on the block call my dad Mr. Mike. Watch out, Mr. Mike," Marty said, mimicking a young voice.

We laughed as my dad sauntered past the table. He turned and smiled. "Nonna Santa's pasta primavera coming up."

JAN HAD DISCOVERED something about Josephine and Juliana that intrigued her. They were reenactors of Revolutionary War times. I'd seen Civil War re-enactors several times, mostly as a kid tagging along with my dad's scout troop when they had family camp trips. I'd never seen anything about our fight for independence.

"Next weekend Civil War people will be at Graue Mill. They're interesting, but I prefer the first war. I'm fascinated by that era." Jan's eyes sparkled with interest. I noticed my dad watching her and in his eyes I saw the excitement he felt at being with someone so happy to be alive.

The teeniest part of me wished for the millionth time that he'd seen that with my mom. I let it go and rejoined the chatter.

"Will's troop is going to be there." My dad spoke with authority. "I'm sort of helping out. Mr. Riggs needed another adult to ride roughshod on those palookas."

I smiled at his description. Once a scouter, always a scouter. I wondered how long it would take for "gramps" to get involved.

"They're planning a campout near Starved Rock. I've already talked Don Craig into helping out on that one. It's practically in his backyard."

Marty snorted water through his nose and immediately grabbed his napkin and dabbed at his face.

"Sorry. I just got a picture of 'Grumpy Old Men' in Boy Scout shorts."

Everyone shook with laughter and even my dad struggled to keep a stern face. Jan rescued her beau and asked their guests, "Are you behind-the-scenes organizers, or dressed-up characters?"

Josephine did a kind of snort of her own, more a chastising sniff. "People of color have limited roles."

Juliana lowered her gaze to her plate and her fingers fiddled with the spoon at her setting. Jan's expression never changed. I wondered if Josephine was about to embark on a familiar rant.

"Not many parts for black folks ceptin' for the ones of slaves." She shrugged. "Can't rewrite history. Leave that to the politicians." Her hand patted her already-perfect curls. "I work on the costumes, got a real talent for sewing. Juliana, she reads up on the history and makes sure it's right."

The older woman's voice was warm with pride and her eyes gleamed with affection for her niece.

"You research the periods?" Research was always my favorite part of library work and writing.

Juliana nodded. "We were attending our first re-enactment, actually stumbled upon it after exhausting the craft show booths at the fair. We were fascinated by the living history. I heard someone standing nearby comment that the uniforms worn by some of the soldiers represented a different 'campaign' and that earlier they'd noticed the flint piece someone used hadn't been invented yet.

"I went home and checked the library and found out that voice in the crowd had been half right. The flint could have been in use, but the uniforms were definitely wrong. I contacted the organizer and offered to check out battles and encampment sites for their troupe. That's how it started and we've been involved ever since, seven years now."

Jan loved reenactments. She'd participated in a couple of events on the Riverwalk in Naperville. I knew she wanted to get more involved and pull my dad into the fray. I tried to picture my dad as a Colonist or a Red Coat. I could imagine him only as a publican perhaps with Jan as a serving wench. I felt the heat rise to my cheeks and prayed no one noticed.

"Let's all go watch them next week," Jan said. "It'll be fun. We can have lunch at the York Tavern afterwards."

Nods crisscrossed the table and I guess we all had a date. The ex-librarian in me wondered about Juliana's research techniques. I'd have to introduce her to Debby at the Oak Park Library.

Dinner conversation moved from weather to books to movies and back to re-enactors. Josephine repeated a funny story about how seriously some of these re-enactors took their craft.

"So this fool gets the idea he should recreate some of the mistakes the soldiers at Jamestown made that first winter. He, but he don't tell nobody, boils up a pot of leaves from the Jimson Weed and passes them off as "greens" that the soldiers watched the Indians eat. He was hopin' that those that ate them would get a buzz, nothing compared to the crazies those soldiers came down with in Jamestown. Not many of the 'troops' are ready to eat so he stuffs his face with most of them greens and washes 'em down with root beer ale. 'Bout thirty minutes later this fool has got his boots off, his tunic off, and he's swinging his sword all round hisself like he was fightin' devils."

Josephine stopped to drink some water, but I suspected it was to build suspense. She told a story well.

"What happened? Did anyone get hurt?" Marty rushed to ask.

Josephine grinned. "That swinging sword was worrisome and no one wanted to step in close. We had two brothers, firefighters, who'd had some training at subduing frantic people. They managed to each grab an arm, and once that sword stopped swinging, a couple of other guys jumped in to help."

"What happened to him?" Jan's eyes were fixed on the storyteller.

"No one suspected what he'd cooked up, but fact was, the pot was mostly empty, and eatin' was what he'd been doing before he'd went crazy. They sent him and the pot to the emergency room. Nurses pumped his stomach. He recovered and explained his stupid idea. 'Course he never went back to that there troupe."

She shook her head slowly. "It's hard enough to get folks to eat their greens without some fool poisoning hisself."

"Enjoy these greens; no Jimson, a little escarole, a few dandelion leaves, and a bit of arugula steamed lightly and seasoned with olive oil, salt, and pepper." My father uncovered the bowl he'd carried to the table.

The phone rang and Marty popped up to answer.

My dad had two phones, one on the wall in the kitchen and one in a bedroom/office. Marty came back from the kitchen and nodded toward me. "It's Harry."

"Great. Tell him he's in time for dessert," my dad offered.

Marty handed me the "Autumn Harvest" colored receiver and dragged his forefinger across his throat. Guess I was in trouble.

"Hi, Harry," I said.

"What in heaven's name are you doing? Why would you leave and not even say goodbye to Will. He asked where you were. He wanted to know if April was okay. What's the matter with you?"

Indeed, what was my problem? I loved Harry, wanted to love Will. Everyone had adjusted to Will in our lives, everyone but me.

"Grace, I'm spending the night here. I wanted you to know."

My heart lurched and I felt breathless. Too much time passed.

"Good night, Grace."

NINETEEN

I STARED AT the phone as though the fault lay in the plastic instrument and slowly replaced it on the hook. I returned to my chair and slid easily onto the seat, smoothing my napkin across my lap. Juliana was explaining a bit of history on Civil War era cooking accoutrement. I wondered if she'd researched anything on the Underground Railroad. I know they didn't re-enact slavery, or did they? I waited for a break in her narrative.

"Does any of your Civil War research touch on the Underground Railroad?"

Josephine's shoulders straightened. "Not hers, honey, but mine sure does." Her wide smile touched each of us.

"Excuse me, Gracie, but is Harry joining us for dessert?"

I'd hoped this question would be sidetracked.

"No, he and Lily are spending the night at the hospital."

The sewn edges of my napkin rolled between my thumbs and forefingers. As a toddler I'd practically rubbed through the satin edging of my baby blanket. The motion comforted me.

No one commented, and bless her soul, Josephine wise-cracked, "more for us then" and continued her explanation.

"My research is done at the churches and town halls. If you think about it, in those days where did folks go when they needed to have a talk 'bout something happening? Who kept track of marriages and deaths and births?" She paused and nodded at her niece who stood up and excused herself. "I have something that I thought you might like seeing. A woman in Ottawa, Illinois, give it to me after I talked with her about the farmhouse that she lived in as a child. She was ninety-five in the summer of '82 when I met her. None of her grandkids or great-grandkids cared a spit about that part of our history. When she saw how keen I was on telling that story, she gave it to me."

Juliana returned with a sturdy dress box, the kind you'd get from a high-end department store. She suggested we step into the living room away from the food. She placed the box on the coffee table and lifted the cover. Inside laid a quilt protected in a zippered plastic bag. Juliana unzipped the side and slid out the one time vibrantly hued quilt. The colors had faded with time and exposure, but nevertheless, were remarkably distinct. Josephine explained the process of dying the cloth, a process the African slaves had brought with them, and how this knowledge sometimes earned a slave a position in the plantation owners' homes rather than in the fields.

"It has different designs on each side. Unusual, wouldn't you say?"

She was right. Most quilts would be showy on one side and plain on the side that would rest against the sheets.

"That's 'cause this here quilt was a road map and signal." She smiled and warmed to her topic. "Stops on the Underground had to have a way to signal the slaves coming through as to where it was safe to stop. And if the slaves weren't in no need of spending the night, but jest wanted to keep moving, they had to know they was going right."

Josephine stepped closer to the quilt that Juliana held up. The quilt was about four feet wide by four feet long. When Juliana held it up completely open, I noticed there were two different designs on the same side.

Marty offered to hold up the quilt since at his height it was easier to do. Juliana gratefully relinquished the job.

"You noticed something different?" Josephine asked.

Jan spoke first. "There are two different designs on the same side."

Josephine smiled her approval like Jan was a star pupil. I felt a jab of jealousy. I saw it too.

I shook my head to stop the thoughts.

"You don't think so, Grace?" Josephine spotted my head movement.

"No. I mean, yes. I was thinking of something else."

Her eyes focused hard on my face. I didn't feel flush, but would in a moment if she didn't stop staring at me.

"Why did they quilt that way?" Jan asked. Josephine broke eye contact and grinned.

"They had messages to send and they had to do it right under them slave catchers' noses." Her pride in her ancestors' clever and brave acts rang in her voice. "They always kept a few elements the same, making it look to be a pattern with slight changes on each panel. What they always kept was the sign of the drinking gourd."

Marty, who'd decided it was easier to hold the quilt in front of his body rather than to the side, popped his head around the material. "That was because of the drinking gourd song, right?"

Josephine smiled. "You are absolutely right. No one dared to write down nothing for fear the slave catchers would find it, and most slaves, ninety-nine percent, weren't allowed to learn to write and read. Each panel has the drinking gourd, which is the Big Dipper. This tells the runaways to follow the Big Dipper and go toward the North Star."

Josephine pointed to a panel of alternating light and dark stripes with a yellow center. "This here piece is called the Log Cabin. The yellow center means it's a safe house, but one with a black center is a station. In the same piece they put the sign of a road with a steeple and a moon. That meant the church was safe, but only at night. When they flipped the side it showed the gourd again, but it showed caves and hills to tell them where they could hide during the daylight hours. And these triangles all pointing the same way, north, is called Flying Geese."

"Man, that's amazing." Marty shook his head. "How did you learn all that?"

"Most times it was struggling through books and papers. Sometimes, though, I got to meet someone who'd heard the oral history of their family."

The doorbell rang and my dad hurried to answer it.

"About time you two got here. There's still some dessert, but just barely." My dad stepped aside.

Walter and Gertrude entered the room and minutes were spent with kisses, hugs, and handshakes.

The quilt was admired by Gertrude, then rewrapped and boxed. Juliana leaned it against the wall by the front door. The conversation shifted back to the re-enactment with Jan convincing Mike and Marty that they should join her at Graue Mill. She would be in costume at the Civil War site.

Walter and Gertrude said they'd come and watch. Who was I to say no.

"I'll ask Harry and Will when Lily brings them home tomorrow."

Walter's startled expression caught me by surprise.

"Why you *tinking* Missus Lily *ist* taking them up to bring home?"

Sometimes Walter's syntax made following his thought process difficult. I glanced around the table and all eyes seemed to be asking the same question.

"I thought since she was staying overnight, she'd bring them home."

"Missus Lily not spending night." Walter sounded confused.

"She's not?" I heard the delight in my voice.

"Nein, she come and leave *tings* for Will." He checked his watch. "She *ist* on airplane for Brazil. Miss Hannah, too."

"What? Lily and Hannah went to Brazil? Why?"

Gertrude sighs and shrugs her bony shoulders. Her high-pitched voice seems higher when she answers. "I am not sure. It is business with camera for Missus Lily, and Miss Hannah she is going to help find best places." Gertrude tucked a wisp of hair back under a rubber-tipped bobby pin, then folded her hands in her lap.

I thought the bag belonged to Lily. I walked out on Harry and Will because I was too hurt, no, too proud, to walk in and find out.

"Walter, I'm assuming Harry asked you for a ride home tomorrow?"

He nodded.

"I'll call in the morning and find out when Will's being released."

Walter nodded more vigorously.

I suddenly felt exhausted. Too much stress between Harry and me. I wanted to go home and curl up with Elmo and my new Judge Knott mystery. I stood to start the lengthy process of saying goodbye the Morelli way.

"Thanks for dinner, scrumptious as usual. I'm going to hit the road before I get too tired."

I hurried through hugs and kisses. My handshake with Josephine was turned into a hug when she pulled me into her ample bosom. Juliana accepted my hand and smiled as though next time there might be a hug.

I bumped the box at the doorway and felt goose bumps creep along my arms. *What in heaven's name was that?* Instinctively I knew to be glad I hadn't touched the quilt.

TWENTY

ELMO GREETED ME in the kitchen with loud mewls intended to raise my guilt level for leaving him home alone. I petted and pampered him, lifting him into my arms for serious ear scratching.

I wanted to check on April and Cash. I knew Devin would have groomed them and turned them into their stalls, but I had to say good-night and explain. With Elmo tucked securely under my arm, I grabbed some treats and made my way to the barn.

April's soft whinny comforted me. Before I opened the door I heard Cash's gruffer snortle.

"Hello, my friends. What a strange turn of events, eh?" I smiled at my speech. I'd grown accustomed to hearing 'eh' when I visited my girlfriend in Canada and had adopted the quirky style of language. I knew it would wear off eventually and I'd be back to confirming affirmatives with my inherited, 'yes?'

"Quite a day." I shifted the treats to the fingers holding Elmo's collar and let him nibble at one while I palmed a baby carrot for April. I offered her the treat. "Will is okay. The hospital is keeping him for observation. His dad is with him; it's okay."

She gently snuffled the treat off my open palm. Cash craned his neck toward us.

"Wait a second, you big baby. I have treats for you, too." He greedily snared the treat from my palm. You had to be vigilant with him when you put your hand out.

"All right, my pals, time to turn in." I hadn't let Elmo onto the floor. I wasn't in the mood for him to squirrel behind the tack to play hide-and-seek. I scratched his ears and kissed the top of his head. "Let's go in Elmo, time for bed."

My nighttime regimen allowed me time to unwind and let my brain wander through the day. While I washed and moisturized my face, briskly brushed my hair and diligently brushed my teeth, my thoughts scurried to gather the essence of my encounters and exchanges, to deposit all in the vault where my brain would catalog, reclassify, and register the bunch.

During this down time I tried not to have additional thoughts. Tonight new ones popped in at an alarming rate.

Why hadn't I walked into the hospital room?

Why had I reacted to the quilt in that manner?

Could that quilt have once lain over the rail at Gertrude's house?

Could the man I saw at the house have studied that quilt for guidance over 100 years ago?

I slipped into bed intending to read myself to thoughtlessness and sleep. I picked up one of the books Karen had brought and searched the index for any mention of quilts. It gave only one reference about the purpose of the quilts and the cleverness of the quilters.

Imagine running for your life, living by your wits, and hoping the directions on a quilt are still valid. Was that why the *Waysayer's* job was critical? To let runaways know a certain road was no longer safe, a safe house had been compromised, a previously trusted person had sold out to the owners. I closed the book and turned off the light, sliding down under the covers and pulling my pillow with me. I had set my alarm for 5:30 to be up in time to walk

with Barb before helping her set up the coach house for
the Lisle Woman's Club plant sale.

AFTER TOSSING AND turning for over an hour, I left my
sleepless bed to make tea. Harry insisted a *cuppa*' cham-
omile tca would promote sleep better than warm milk.
We'd find out.

I heard a soft tap against the windowpane. It was, un-
mistakably, the rap of knuckles against the windowpane
in the back door of the mudroom. The hair on my neck
stirred with the primeval urge to run.

Had the lights attracted an equally restless neighbor's attention? It could only be Barb. Would she venture
through the dark at three o'clock in the morning to check
up on me? She wouldn't know Harry wasn't home. Might
she assume something was terribly wrong with Will and
sleep was not an option?

The tapping sounded again, a little louder and more urgent. I couldn't cower in my kitchen, but I didn't have to
unlock the door. I moved purposely to the mudroom flip-
ping the switch to flood the immediate area with high-
wattage light. The switch had been installed to trigger
the outside lights on the barn and coach house. We joked
that we should alert O'Hare airport when we flipped the
switch to avoid diverting incoming air traffic.

From the darkness of the mudroom my eyes search the
yard for a person, any movement. Was this some teenage
prank? Were Devin's friends going to the wrong house? I
started to relax believing that the kids had realized their
error or just scattered when the yard went to high noon. A
smile came with a sigh of relief. I lifted my hand to douse
the lights and I saw it. Near the barn, on the top rail of the
corral, hung the quilt.

TWENTY-ONE

IMPOSSIBLE, I THOUGHT. My eyes weren't seeing clearly. It was probably a horse pad or blanket that Devin had laid there and forgotten.

You didn't see it when you went out earlier. You'd never miss that. You would have seen it wasn't where it belonged. A place for everything and everything in its place.

Stop! I could have missed it. I was focused on April and Cash, giving them treats, saying good-night.

A place for everything and everything in its place.

Slowly and with a sick feeling in my stomach, I knew the quilt hadn't been there when Elmo and I went to the barn.

Well, it's there now, Gracie girl. What do you suppose it wants from you?

It doesn't "want" anything. It's inanimate. Stop confusing me.

Inanimate. Interesting word. From the Latin for lack of life or spirit. It wants you to bring it in. It has something to tell you.

I had learned a long time ago that when I lost ground with myself I couldn't be sure of anything. I'd lost a significant amount of ground with that last exchange.

I wasn't going outside. I turned and ran up the back-stairs to my bedroom, diving under covers, neglecting to kick off my slippers, cowering and willing my body to stop shaking.

In a few moments I sensed rather than heard movement

in the air above me. I peeked around a crease. My body stiffened with fright. The quilt hovered above me. It was as if an occult hand held the patterned cloth as it slowly descended on my shoulders and head, its unaccountable weight smashing the air pockets of my comforter and cutting off my breath.

My legs and arms felt heavy as though they'd turned to wood. In the split second before self-preservation kicked in, I wondered if my body had become the railing on which the quilt would hang to welcome or warn slaves.

I pushed up with my arms, lifting it inches from my face. I could breathe again. "No!" burst from my lips. I pulled up my knees and used them to hold the cloth from settling on me again. My arms were tiring.

"Our Father, who art in Heaven, hallowed be thy name." I choked out the words. "Thy Kingdom come, Thy will be done," *this couldn't be His will*, "on earth as it is in Heaven."

My arms strengthened or the quilt weakened. I didn't care. "Give us this day our daily bread and forgive us our trespasses," *I have much to be forgiven,* "as we forgive those who trespass against us."

My arms were straight up, elbows locked, making it easier to hold the quilt off me. "And lead us not into temptation, but deliver us from evil."

The quilt floated away from me. "Amen," I whispered, secure that my prayer had protected me.

The colorful cloth slowly dropped over the blanket stand at the end of the bed. It settled down, smoothing out the wrinkles and lying still. Until when? Until I'm asleep?

I sat up abruptly and the contact with the headboard woke me.

I gulped ragged breaths of air to fill my lungs. I felt a rage to scream. My eyes quickly scanned the room for the quilt until, wide-awake now, realization flooded my body with relief. *A dream! A freaking, scary dream.* My fingers reached for the carafe on the nightstand. The tepid water soothed my dry throat.

I stared at the blanket stand. The Battenburg lace topper lay across the wooden stand just as I'd left it.

Okay, it was a bad dream.

I tried to remember my last *awake* thought. The tapping? Was that real? Had I been downstairs making tea?

Only one way to know. I flipped back the covers and had my answer.

TWENTY-TWO

BARE FEET! Thank God. A dream, that's all it was. No tapping on the window, no quilt on the corral, and best of all, no quilt in my room. I swung my legs out of bed and dashed for the shower.

I turned the spigot to hot and waited for the blessed stream of water to wash away the sweat and fear. I lathered, rinsed, and repeated three times, then realized I had to stop. The sensation to continue scrubbing my skin was reaching a danger point for someone like me. I slammed the dial closed and stepped out quickly soaking the bath mat before I grabbed my towel. Even toweling could be excessive and I carefully patted my body dry before wrapping the towel around my dripping hair.

My skin glowed pink, like with a mild sunburn. I'd dodged the obsessive washing bullet, but just barely. As a child, my parents had to monitor my hand washing and later my showering. I stared at my image in the mirror.

Why are you so weird?

No answer. Never got one.

I gently applied moisturizer to my face and neck. I needed to get dressed and get some fresh air. An early morning ride would clear the cobwebs. I looked at the twisted bed linens and marveled at the night I'd spent fighting off a cotton monster. I tried to laugh but felt the sound stick in my throat. I'd wash the sheets later.

It was pre-dawn when I walked into the mudroom. The lights were on outside. An icy prick of fear touched my spine. When had I turned them on? Had I been down here after all investigating the tapping? My throat tightened. The corral's empty rails assured me of some sanity. I must have been down here. I must have—

The rap on the window inches from my face sounded like a shot in the small room. I screamed and jumped back from the door.

More rapping.

"Grace, are you all right? Grace."

Barb Atwater's strong voice was filled with concern.

"Grace, answer me. I'm calling the police."

My hand grasped the doorknob and slowly opened the door to my frantic neighbor. She rushed in, waving a hammer and checking nervously for signs of an intruder. She lowered the hammer.

"What's wrong? I heard you scream."

I bent over from the waist, leaned my hands on my knees and took a few deep breaths. "I'm fine. Sorry for the scare," I said staring at my shoe tops. I wanted to give Barb time to compose her expression. I straightened and looked her in the eyes.

"I didn't sleep well and was sort of daydreaming when you tapped on the door. It startled me, that's all."

"Oh, were you going to ride? Don't let me stop you. I'm putting some signs out front to direct the plant truck and the ladies from the club." She motioned with the hammer to a few placards leaning against the outside wall next to the door. "Thanks for turning on the lights. I wasn't sure if you remembered that I asked. I figured if you were up you'd hear my knock."

"You asked me to turn on the lights?"

"Sure did, when I was here cleaning the coach house. Don't let me interrupt your ride. I need to get these in the ground. The truck rescheduled for a 6:30 delivery."

Barb left, grabbing her signs and swinging the hammer as she walked.

I must have automatically turned on the lights last night for Barb. I felt immensely better and my spirits lifted considerably. I stepped out the back door and shouted to Barb before she turned the corner. "I'll have coffee ready when you're finished."

She turned and smiled. "Deal."

I skipped to the kitchen lighthearted with the knowledge it had all been a frightful dream. The aroma of Cinnamon Nut Swirl filled the room within minutes and I watched as the final drip left the funnel. I filled two mugs and hurried out to enjoy some conversation with Barb.

"Perfect timing," she said. Her long-legged gait brought her to my side before I'd covered half the distance to her. When we walked in the mornings she adjusted her stride to mine.

I handed her the steaming cup. "Let's sit in the coach house." I'd brought the key and opened the door.

The card table and chairs Barb had set up earlier was a perfect perch while we waited.

"How many plants are you expecting?"

She consulted some papers she'd brought with her. "Twenty-three flats of petunias, seventeen flats of wave petunias, forty-one flats of impatiens, fifteen flats of salvia, and thirty-seven geraniums. I'm not sure about the herbs and tomatoes."

"Man, that's a lot of flower power," I joked. Barb was in her forties and a child of the sixties.

She deadpanned, "Peace, love," and flashed the peace symbol.

The truck rumbled into the driveway. Barb directed the unloading and staging of the colorful cargo. I pulled my order form from her neatly stacked pile and perused the selection. Within moments I had filled my order and placed the flowers in the shade at my back door. I'd plant them later or tomorrow.

I continued selecting and grouping flowers by the order forms until some volunteers from the club arrived to help Barb. She introduced me to Joanne, Wendy, and Bea.

"Grace, thanks for your help and your carriage house. They'll take it from here." Barb sat down and lolled against the chair back. She shooed the trio towards the flowers with a languid wave of her fingers. "Ladies, wake me when it's over."

Crossing her arms over her chest, she pretended to snooze. I lifted an old garden hat from a peg and laid it on her head to complete the picture. Barb grinned, but kept her eyes tight shut. Then two cars pulled up the drive and she snapped to attention.

I left her to her customers and headed back to the house. It was too early to call the hospital. I poured cereal in a bowl, left it dry, and refilled my cup. Elmo curled around my legs when I sat down at the nook. I picked out an oat morsel and tossed it across the floor. He shot out from under the table and pounced on the defenseless tidbit. I tossed another that he crunched quickly. I flipped a third piece, then a fourth until, in a moment of surprised frustration, I flung an entire handful of cereal at the surprised cat.

He stared at me, canting his head to one side. We'd never played this game before. He hesitated, then eagerly sucked up each tiny ort.

What is wrong with you?

Everything, okay.

I realized I was in plain view of the Lisle ladies and wondered if anyone had seen me pelt Elmo with dry cereal. I smiled. It was funny on one level, a desperate cry for help on another.

An eating pattern evolved forcing me to eat two at a time by positioning one on each side of my mouth and crunching on the count of two after which I could take two sips of coffee. I munched the remaining cereal and sipped my coffee for over an hour. *Two* felt good, felt necessary.

At eight o'clock I called the hospital and Harry answered the phone in Will's room.

"Hi. I'm sorry I left last night. I thought Lily was staying. I didn't want to…" *Didn't want to what? Intrude? Be a third wheel?*

I heard Harry sigh. "It's all right, Grace. I suppose someday you'll believe how I feel about you."

My heart ached to hear his flat voice.

"Does this call mean you'll be here rather than Walter?"

I wanted to say something clever, full of love and warmth. I stammered, "Uh, yes. Yes, I'll be there. What time?"

"They're making him eat breakfast. I'd say by ten we should be signed out."

Gracie, say something loving and special.

My brain refused to create beyond the basics.

"I'll be there."

"Yes, well, see you then."

The phone connection broke and I leaned against the wall. Our conversation could have been two strangers setting up an appointment to meet for the first time.

Is that what we'd become? I climbed the stairs to get ready. Elmo followed me weaving in and out of my legs. I had time to throw in a load of whites and straighten out the bedroom.

I loaded the washer and folded a few towels. After the night I'd spent under the covers I wanted to change the sheets and air out the comforter. Elmo leaped effortlessly onto the bed. He sidestepped my hands when I grasped the lilac and green patterned material and whipped it off the bed.

My gasp startled my furry companion, my only witness. He bolted from the room as I stared at the slippers tangled at the foot of the bed.

TWENTY-THREE

IN SLOW MOTION fear I turned my head toward the blanket stand. A rush of heat overtook me and my legs buckled against the side of the bed. Gone was Nonna Santa's embroidered coverlet. Instead the crude outline of the drinking gourd lay over the heavy wooden holder. The stand swayed under my lurching weight and toppled with me to the floor.

"Grace, are you up here?"

Barbara's voice sounded from the hallway.

"Oh my gosh! Are you all right?"

She rushed into the room and around the side of the bed to where I crouched on the floor. She lifted the holder to its upright position. "How in heaven's name did this happen?"

The cool Battenberg cotton brushed my cheek and I knew there would be no gourd to point out. I slowly moved to a sitting position and leaned against the bed. Barbara knelt next to me.

"You didn't hit your head, did you?"

I shook it to reassure her. "I tripped over Elmo while he waltzed between my legs," I lied. I thought to embellish but remembered my younger brother Marty's advice to keep lies simple. He was the best liar I knew.

She stood and offered her hand. I scrambled up using the bed. "No use repeating history," I joked when I didn't take her hand.

Barb laughed. "We'd make a silly sight all tangled in

the linens. I assume you were headed to the laundry. I'll give you a hand."

The last thing I wanted was to explain the pair of green flip-flops in the bed.

"Not necessary. What's up?" I walked toward the doorway and she followed me down the stairs and into the kitchen.

"I came in to let you know that only seven orders are left and they belong to various Morellis and/or friends of Morellis. We set them on the side between the coach house and the hedge."

"Do you want a check for everything and I'll collect from them?"

"That would be fine. Pay now or pay me later when they pick up their orders."

"I'll pay now. They can owe me." I grinned. "Who knows? Maybe I'll charge storage fees and collect the price of my own order." Barb smiled at my proposed chicanery.

"I had another reason for barging into your home."

"You wanted more coffee?"

"Well, that would be nice, too. But no. I came in to tell you that one of the club ladies used to live in Forest Park and her neighbor's house was a stop on the Underground Railroad."

A chill crept across my shoulders and I rolled my neck to shake it.

"Are you sore from falling? Maybe you should put some ice on your neck."

"Just a kink. It feels better already." I eyed Barb suspiciously. "This news popped up in casual conversation?"

My friend flushed, then straightened to her full height. "Of course not. I told everyone about the skeletons in Gertrude's—hmm, I guess its Hannah's and Karen's—basement. Anyway, here is the woman's name and number.

She'd love a phone call. Apparently, Maywood and Forest Park each claim to have official stops in their communities. She thinks Oak Park is too far from the river to have been logistically feasible." Barb shrugged. "Have at it, Nancy Drew. But if it gets interesting, don't forget your old chum."

Is that how my friends see me?

What did you expect? You've been exposed, involved, whatever with five old murders.

I didn't go looking, you know.

Looking, smooking. It comes to you. You get that, don't you?

Yeah, I get it. Don't like it, but I get it. I'd hoped it had stopped at five.

Is five your lucky number?

No, seven is.

I groaned at my thought that there might be two more instances of old deaths and restless souls.

I realized I over-poured Barb's cup a split half second before she did. I hoped she attached the groan to my spill.

"Whoa, there. I'll need a straw to get that started."

"Sorry. I lost track."

"Seems so," Barb said as she leaned in to slurp the coffee from the brim. "I'll call you later with the total amount. Take a break and rest. I think you may have rattled yourself when you collided with that stand."

I flashed her a quick smile. "Thanks. I'll catch you later."

She lifted her cup and slipped a paper towel under the bottom. "Later."

THE MORNING BEGAN with my having all the time in the world to do some housework, even run an errand or two, before I needed to be at Good Samaritan to pick up Harry and Will.

I assessed my accomplishments while I parked in the hospital lot. One load of clothes and I couldn't remember if I'd actually put in the soap; no errands and running ten minutes late. I rushed through the lobby to the north elevators and up to the second floor. I reached the room in time to hear them conversing.

"Mom's always late, too. Why are girls always late?"

Harry's chuckle made me smile.

"God made men and women different in many ways. He gave men precision timing—think of a finely made Swiss watch—and he gave women a sundial."

Hoots of laughter stopped abruptly when I stepped through the doorway. Will actually had the good grace to sputter and pretend to cough. His dad renewed his laughter partially at his son's reaction.

"Enough girl bashing or you'll be walking."

Harry tapped his watch and pretended a consult with Will. "Not bad."

"For a girl."

They grinned and crossed their arms over their chests at the same moment.

"Oh, brother. Are you two ready to leave, or is there more to this routine?"

Harry moved first and slipped his arm around Will's shoulders. "We are ready." He propelled his son toward me while lifting Will's duffle bag from the chair.

"How are you feeling?" I asked.

"Good, nothing hurts. My headache went away."

"That's good. April says 'hi'. Well, more like '*heihei-hei*'", I said, mimicking horse talk.

Will rolled his eyes at my lame attempt at humor. I followed him out the door, aware of the look of approval on Harry's face.

I could do this with Will. I have two younger brothers

that I said dumb things to all the time when we were kids. I always made them laugh.

He's not your kid brother, Gracie. He's your husband's son with another woman.

You know, that's your problem. Always bringing up the "son" thing. He's just a kid. If you treat him like you treated Marty, he'll be fine. Marty turned out...okay, bad example.

"Grace?" Harry waited for an answer to a question I'd missed.

I smiled and shrugged.

"Where are you parked?"

We were in the lobby approaching the doors. I'd missed the entire trip.

"The main lot, east end," I murmured, upset that I could zone out so easily. I had to get that under control.

I wanted to tell Harry about the quilt and the terror. Now was not the time. Would there be a time to share this with him or anyone else? How much weirdness could I ask him to accept before he decided to pack it in and hook up with a normal person?

I drove and kept my thoughts to myself. I tuned in and out of their conversation from the backseat. My father's car was parked at the curb when we approached our house. Dad stepped out of it carrying a large shopping bag. Jan had only her tote with her. They followed me as I pulled into the driveway and pressed the garage button.

"Hi, Gramps!" The words burst from Will as he scrambled from the backseat. "Hi, Grandma Jan."

"Hi, sport." Dad hugged Will and gently tapped the top of his head. "One tough melon."

Harry followed more slowly and shook hands with my dad. "Hello, Mike." Harry nodded at Will. "Tough heads the whole lot of us."

Everyone followed me inside where it was easier to hug. My dad engulfed me in the usual Morelli maul—like a bear hug and side to side shuffle.

He looked around at us. "Everybody good?"

Three heads nodded.

"What's in the bag, Gramps?" Will had called my dad "Gramps" from day one. Harry's parents were Grandma and Granddad. All the adults were titled except for me. Even Jan was 'Grandma Jan'. He hadn't yet found a spot for me.

"Two things. One from me," he said, pulling out a football. It wasn't a new one, rather an old, used one. "This football belonged to one of best little running backs I ever raised." He nodded at me, "*Gracie Quick*."

Father and son together squeaked, "Really?"

No one had used that nickname since junior high. We burst into laughter and a slight flush crept up my neck.

"Really," my dad assured them.

"Awesome!"

"Amazing!"

The generational gap showed in their responses.

Jan grinned. "That would make her Amazing Grace."

I groaned and rolled my eyes. "I hated that adjective. You can't imagine how people, even teachers, overused it."

"Sorry, couldn't resist."

Harry put his arm around my shoulders and announced in a serious tone, "She saved this wretch." He stared into my eyes telling me more, willing me to hear his thoughts.

"Thanks, Gramps. You said there were two things?"

Leave it to a kid to put life in perspective.

"This one is from Grandma Jan." He lifted a riding helmet from the bag. This item was obviously new and undoubtedly purchased at The Riding Store on Hobson Road. I'd been a long-time customer.

Harry and I glanced at each other in embarrassment. We insisted Will wear his helmet when he rode his bike, but never transferred the thought to riding a horse.

I watched Will heft the helmet. Would he balk at another restriction?

"Awesome. This is like what you wore in that picture Mom has of you." He glanced up at Harry. "You know, you're wearing those puffy pants and boots."

Harry smiled with a memory he'd corralled. More to himself, he said, "Can't believe she still has that." Then to us he said, "It's a photo taken ages ago in England when I played a summer of polo."

"I thought you played soccer."

"Soccer was my sport, Will. But one summer Matthew Collings got up a group of us and we fooled around with it at his parents' estate. Matthew was the resident rich kid. We, most of us, rode well and we wanted to see what the ruckus was about playing the game. Actually, we wanted the photos atop a polo pony to impress the girls."

He had the good grace to blush at this point in his narrative.

"We discovered it's a beastly difficult sport and happily returned to our true avocations." He grinned. "I can't believe your Mum kept that."

My heart tightened. I would display that photo if I had it; strikingly handsome Harry wearing jodhpurs, a polo shirt, and his helmet while sitting astride a magnificent animal. I stopped the envy train from moving too far along the tracks by countering with what I had in the way of photos. I had the side-by-side shots of both boys on horse back as children. Harry, thirty-five years ago; Will, five years ago.

Will nodded. "Yeah, next to the one of you when you

were a little kid sitting on the pony. Grandma gave it to her when we visited."

So much for one upsmanship.

"Hey, maybe if I get a pair of those puffy pants and wear my helmet, I can get a picture like you, Dad."

Even I joined in the laughter.

"Did the doctor say there was anything you couldn't do?" Dad asked Will.

Will accorded my father with the same respect as shared by the kids on the teams Dad coached. Dad talked to them and expected them to know their minds. He could have asked Harry that question, but instead he let Will know he had a say-so in his relationship with his Gramps.

"He said not to fall off horses any more."

I laughed so hard my eyes teared. I saw Jan wiping at her cheeks, too.

Dad engulfed Will in a hug. "Why don't you and your dad go have a game of catch. Go easy on him. Remember, he thinks football is played with a round ball you kick."

Harry pretended chagrin. "*Foot* ball, get it? You colonists have yet to learn the primo sport in the world."

"I thought that was shopping," said Jan.

The men in the room rolled their eyes and groaned. I high-fived her.

"Okay, manly men. When you go out to play, take him with you." I jerked my thumb towards my father.

"Yeah, come on, Gramps. You and me against Dad."

"Oh, no. If you're bringing in him, I say we get the ringers in, too. Grace and Jan, you're drafted."

Jan and I took the challenge and followed them out to the yard. Will, in a stroke of genius, determined the teams.

"Dad, you don't know how to play, you go with the girls." He stage whispered, "Sorry," to Jan and me.

"Gramps and me will receive." Will flipped the ball to

me. "Don't let Dad kick it. That's probably the one thing he does pretty good. You know: *foot* ball."

The kid was hilarious. It felt like a Morelli bash and banter. Lily didn't have this. In that moment, I felt ashamed. Everyone should have this kind of love in their life. I promised myself to be more tolerant of her.

Jan punted the ball and the game was afoot. Of course we played Morelli rules. When Dad caught the ball he threw it to Will, who by this time was standing behind us. He caught the ball and scored while his dad sputtered, "I don't think that's allowed, Mike."

I'd seen the play a million times, but hadn't wanted to spoil the fun.

Will jumped up and down in the "end-zone" shouting, "It worked. It worked."

Walter walked around the side of the house. Will spotted him first and yelled, "He's on our team!"

The expression on Walter's face told us he wasn't here to play. His words shocked us. "I'm sorry to be stopping." He lowered his voice to exclude Will. "Another body they find."

I knew Walter; there was more.

"Gertrude *ist tinking* it is body of her brother Kurt."

TWENTY-FOUR

"Her brother? She never mentioned a brother."

Will approached the somber group. Jan put her arms around his shoulders and led him off a ways to explain the news. It wouldn't mean much to Will, but it would keep him from piping in with questions.

Walter continued. "Ya, he was young man for war. They was not citizens yet, her family, and the German government write him that he must serve Deutschland."

I knew this must be difficult for Walter. His own allegiance during that war was not on our side of the pond. He'd flown one mission against England before his plane was shot down and he crashed into the English countryside and into the Marsden family's life.

"He not want to go to Deutschland, but he not want to fight against his people. Americans look funny at young men not fighting. Gertrude's *vater* he changes name from *Kloopsweringern* to *Klops* to make a fit in better. The *vater* is wanting to be much American and he tells Kurt he must fight for Americans. Kurt he is much angry that he says he will go to Canada to not fight anybody. He argue *mit* his *vater* long time at night and in the morning Kurt is no home, is nowhere. He is gone with no goodbye to his sisters and *mutter*. *Ist* great sorrow for them. They wait for letter, but nothing comes. After war, no Kurt comes home."

"Oh my gosh, Gertrude must be devastated." I felt my stomach churn at the thought of losing one of my brothers, never knowing what happened.

My mother had lived that life, always wondering what had happened to her older sister who went missing years before my mom came to this country. I knew secondhand about the anguish of not knowing.

"At least she knows," I blurted. No one reacted. I guess we'd all been thinking the same thing.

"*Ja,* she knows but now she is knowing too much."

Jan had rejoined the group. "Where is she, Walter?"

"She is with the mamas and the babies."

We smiled at his reference to the Kramer-Marsden household.

"Are the police at the house now? Do they know where Gertrude is?" Harry asked.

Walter nodded. "*Ja,* there *ist* more peoples and more yellow tape. But Karen come fast and take her away."

Harry took Walter's elbow. "Come inside. You need a drink." My excellent hearing picked up the sotto voce, "And we need a plan."

A plan for what? Or whom? Did Harry think the police would go after Gertrude again? Surely they wouldn't think she had anything to do with her brother's death. Someone did—obviously her father. Would they accuse her of being an accessory? Could she have known and stayed silent? Impossible!

I heard my dad's voice call me. He asked a question.

"Sorry, Dad. Say again."

"I asked if these flowers are my order." He added under his breath, "For the second time."

Will giggled, and the sense of a younger brother enjoying a chastisement from Dad overtook me. Maybe I could be a big sister to him. After all, he didn't have one of those. Not that I knew of.

"I have yours, Hannah's, Gertrude's, and Mr. Riggs'."

Will puffed out proudly. "I gave him the order form.

He said we might use this as a fundraiser for the troop. We could use the money for new tents. We have a bunch with busted zippers."

"Broken," Jan and I corrected.

"Sheesh, like stereo."

We laughed at his use of one of my Dad's favorite expressions. What eleven-year-old says, "sheesh"?

"Anyway," Will said, waving his hand to dismiss the grammar police, "all we need is a 'ways and means' chairperson." He fixed those Marsden eyes on me. "Mr. Riggs says it would only take one hour a week.

We roared with laughter, each of us having been involved in scouting. Will grinned, not sure why it was funny, but enjoying the spotlight.

Dad clapped an arm around his shoulders. "C'mon, help me load up my order." Jan slipped her arm around my waist as we watched them work. This was a first, but it felt natural. I let myself relax and reciprocate.

"You might want to consider being 'ways and means'," said Jan. "It's a great way to get involved with Will's troop, meet other parents. After all, it's only one hour a week." She squeezed my waist, then walked over to supervise the loading of the plants.

I should get more involved, I thought. Dad was offering his help, Harry was going for outdoor training, and I was already a merit-badge counselor for Horsemanship.

Will came bounding over to where I stood. "Gramps and Grandma Jan said I could go home with them and practice with the baseball team if it's okay with you. Can I? Please?"

I knew Harry had wanted to spend time with Will, but I also knew he'd been sequestered with Walter for a bit. I hoped I was making the right decision.

"Absolutely. Your Dad and I will pick you up at…" I looked to my father for a timeline.

"We'll be finished by four."

"Four o'clock it is."

"Thanks." Will turned to race to the car when Dad's raised eyebrows and head nod stopped him cold.

"Oh, yeah." He swerved and barreled toward me for a good-bye hug. His thin arms wrapped around my waist in a satisfactory way. "Thanks."

An instant later he was back on course for the Impala. I hugged my dad. "Thanks," I whispered. "Reminds me of Marty."

"Yeah, he does. More and more."

I walked him to the car.

"See you later."

"Tell Dad bye, okay?" Will shouted out the window.

"Okay."

I watched them pull away and wished for an instant I'd gone along. The conversation taking place inside my home would not be lighthearted.

ENTERING THE HOUSE, I overheard the tail end of Walter's tale. The story Walter had been told was that after her son's disappearance, Gertrude's mother took ill and died within the year. I could imagine that knowing your husband killed your son would take that kind of toll.

I stopped in the living room on my way to the kitchen to tell Harry about Will.

"Thanks, darling. We're about finished here. I've called David to recommend an attorney. In the meantime, we're meeting him at the Oak Park Police department. The Inspector's sister, the interference queen, will bring Gertrude there."

"If it's not backtracking too much, when did they find

his remains? I thought they were finished examining those little cupboards."

"The remains weren't in a cupboard. The body had been buried. The technicians were back yesterday. When they were checking out the remaining cupboards one of the men noticed that a preponderance of the family's goods was piled in that corner. They took some photographs of the pile, then began to move it away. They discovered a tunnel that over the years had partially collapsed. They surmised it must have been an escape route."

"That makes it sound like the boardinghouse really was a stop on the Underground Railroad."

Harry nodded and continued. "The technician assumed everything had been jumbled at that end of the cellar to hide the tunnel. Didn't seem logical to block an escape route, something that might be needed at a moment's notice. He then wondered if the pile had been created to cover something. He decided to dig where the stuff had been and within a few shovelfuls found the remains. The shallow grave had needed the extra protection of extraneous items."

The picture of a father digging a grave for the son he'd killed bought bile to my throat. I swallowed hard and kept quiet.

Harry saw my discomfort. He stood and stretched his arms over his head. "Darling, would you brew up some of your wonderful chocolate-flavored coffee to go?"

I knew he was giving me an out from the suffocating atmosphere.

Suffocating indeed. But why? It wasn't that hot outside and the windows were open. A stiff breeze had cooled the house earlier. I heard Harry speaking from a distance. How odd. He was asking me something, but I couldn't make it out. The room was stifling and the air was thick with a foul smell, a cloying, oppressive odor.

Was I hallucinating? If I think I am, then I'm not? Is that how it goes? I wanted to sit, but my legs seem rooted to the spot. What on earth...then I spotted it. The quilt had found me. I saw it on the sofa next to Walter. Didn't they see it? I lifted my arm to point, but it stayed leaden at my side. My mouth opened and shut with no sound. The quilt quivered slightly preparing for flight. The edges curled under, ready to push off in a mighty thrust that would end when it smothered me.

TWENTY-FIVE

"GRACIE," HARRY SHOUTED. He was at my side in time to steady my swaying body. I pushed fabric away from my face until he caught my flaying arms and I realized that there was nothing there but air. Cool air.

He guided me to the chair. "What on earth happened to you?" His blue eyes darkened with concern. I saw the confusion reflected in his thoughts. Were they thoughts that he'd married a "Looney Tune"?

Harry shook my shoulders. "Gracie? What is it?"

I was fine now, but how could I tell them I thought the quilt was trying to kill me? *My God, I must be nuts.* I rolled my neck and took a few deep breaths.

"I felt lightheaded and hot all of a sudden. I'm fine now. Really, I am." I kept my voice steady and asked, "Where did that come from?"

"It was in cellar with all *dose tings* they find. I don't know who it is they find; I'm thinking is maybe another slave. Me and Gertrude break law and go to see. The family *tings* are spread closer to stairs and she remembers this quilt from when she was little. She and sisters use it for covering the dolls in cradle. We keep looking and she is excited to remember happy times. Then she sees belt buckle on floor near grave. She scream and cover her face in quilt. She scream more and more and I must carry her up stairs to couch. She know then ist her Kurt that they took away.

"Miss Karen comes to take her home with her and Gertrude is holding this and gives it to me when she gets in car. I don't go back inside."

"How horrible for Gertrude," I said with a shiver. "Harry, do the police know the identity?"

"No, that's why we are meeting up at the station. One, Gertrude and Walter shouldn't have been down there. Two, they should have called the police immediately. Three, he has to return the damn quilt which could be evidence, although I doubt it." Harry spoke with more assurance than I felt.

The quilt lying next to Walter had the same design as the quilt I'd seen on the corral and on my blanket stand.

I stood and felt no residual weakness. "I was on my way to make coffee. Mocha Madness was the request, I believe."

I slapped a smile on my face and headed for the coffee maker. I wanted to think. I wanted to talk to someone who might have some answers.

Within ten minutes I'd brewed coffee, poured two travel mugs and kissed and hugged them out the door. I felt a sense of relief when the quilt left with them, although it was obvious to me it could return at will.

I dialed the number for Josephine and she answered promptly.

"Hello, Grace. I had a feeling you'd be callin'. What is it I can do for you?"

I knew I'd been right to call. "I'd like to come out and see you this afternoon. Would that be okay?"

"That'd be fine."

She gave me directions to her niece's home in Eola. I called my dad to fill him in on what was happening and asked if he could keep Will a little longer. I knew there'd be no problem.

JULIANA'S HOME HAD one feature that set it apart. Some homes had banners and flags of flowers, sports teams, animals, etc. Her house had a quilt laid over her porch railing. No doubt her aunt's influence.

She met me on the porch and invited me to sit down on the wicker chair. She'd already set a pitcher of lemonade and two glasses on a tray on the table between the chairs.

"I wondered if we'd talk again."

Her opening remark made me wonder about the sensibility of this meeting. I peered into her dark eyes and jumped into their depths. "What do you know about the quilt that came to visit me?"

I wanted to slam her with my feelings before she could sense anything about me and use her mumbo jumbo talk about the spirit world. I watched her eyes flicker with doubt, then relief. Not the reaction I expected.

She reached her hand across the table and patted mine. "Praise Lord, you are connected."

"Don't bring the Lord into these shenanigans. I want to know what you know about this 'wandering' quilt."

I don't know if I expected her to confess that she'd somehow planted the quilt. Why would she? For her book, to add a sensational chapter? I stared hard at her, wanting a logical answer.

My resolve to stand firm crumbled when I saw the sadness in the tired lines of her face. I felt remorse at my verbal attack. I had been brought up to respect and cherish the elderly.

"I'm sorry. Please, forget what I said."

"No, child. You had a right to push, but I never meant no disrespect to the Lord. I gave praise because I believe angels bring us messages from them that can't rest in peace.

"I've been thinkin' on this man found in that cellar. He'd be most likely too old to think he'd outrun them slave catchers. In my talks with people who was children in them times, or wit them that heard the stories from their kin, I'm thinkin' this man was a *Waysayer*."

She poured more lemonade into my glass. I hadn't realized I'd drunk at all.

"I've heard the term. The purpose of the *Waysayer* was to send the slaves in the right direction with as much information about safe hiding places as possible. If the *Waysayer* left, there'd be no one to help the slaves. They'd run a higher risk of being recaptured."

"I've been ponderin' that same notion. I heard tell some stories about slaves that were offered safe passage if they would send back word that would guide the slaves to a trap. The bounties paid to slave catchers kept those devils in whiskey and women."

Her voice strengthened with her anger. I patted her hand and she acknowledged the gesture. I saw her shoulders relax.

She continued in a calm voice. "Ifin' the *Waysayer* had found out that his information was guiding his people wrong, he might of come north to warn those he sent, maybe even find the house posing as safe."

The premise seemed sound. "What if Gertrude's house was the poser and he was killed when he confronted the owner? We need to find out who owned it during that time."

She grinned. "That's easy. My Juliana knows about all them records 'cause she is a government employee. Juliana already looked up that man in the city records and the church records. Those days the church oft did more record keepin'. She thought it'd be good background for my book."

I wondered at her niece's industrious investigation. Why would she be so quick to search out those records? Karen and I were doing the same, but we had a vested interest in

Gertrude. Maybe it was like Josephine said, some 'color' for the book that sounded dry with only photos and snippets of misremembered stories.

"The owner of the house in 1853 was jailed. They said he was helping slaves get to the river. In them days you could lose your house if they fined you heavy. It says John Alfred Coe spent three days in jail and sold his best horse to pay his fine. Juliana found out he died the same day he was freed."

I gasped. "They killed him?"

"No, no. The newspaper story says he was killed by his horse. He was rushin' and hurryin' and he pulled and jangled that animal till it reared up, threw him, and caught him full in the chest with a hoof."

I shivered, understanding the power of a panicked horse. "What happened to the house? I mean, did they sell that too?"

She shook her head. "Mr. Coe had a daughter who married well. They had no use for the house. He had a brother who had no need for the house either and let it stand empty." Josephine's eyes sparkled with something beyond this story. "Know who she married?"

I shook my head.

"Wilhelm Graue." A grin filled her face.

"That's amazing. There must be a connection between the two. We know for a fact that Graue Mill and some of the surrounding homes were safe houses."

Josephine's grin receded to a wistful smile. I had little time to wonder at the change.

"Honey, we need to talk about your connection, not theirs."

There it was—freak time.

I pushed the chair away from the table and started to

stand. She reached up and grabbed my hand, urging me to sit.

"It's no shame to be chosen to have this gift."

"It's not a gift. I don't have anything beyond odd feelings and sensations that make me feel, make me think…" I couldn't finish the thought.

"Child, you are by no means going crazy, if that's what you'd be thinkin'. I know crazy when I sees it, and you ain't got it."

She shook her head with vigor, and unbelievably, I felt assured. Most of my family mumbled things like, *"don't think thoughts like that,"* or *"don't let your mind wander."* How refreshing to hear someone state unequivocally that I wasn't nuts! Okay, I'm not nuts, I'm gifted. It sounded better than crazy.

Josephine interrupted my thoughts. "What did you see. Will you tell me?"

I took a deep breath and rushed through the entire event starting with seeing the quilt on the corral and finishing with watching it twitch to life on my sofa. I watched her eyes, in fact held on to the contact to help get the story out. She never wavered in her encouraging gaze. I didn't see doubt or fear when I described the sense of being suffocated; I saw instead compassion for my ordeal.

When I finished I took a deep breath and leaned back in my chair. Only then did I realize I'd been holding her hands across the small table. I blushed and pulled my hands off hers.

"You say the quilt Walter had with him had the same designs?"

I nodded and shivered in spite of the mild day.

Josephine stared into the distance, not seeing anyone or anything from this era. Her dreamy gaze seemed to bridge time. I sat quietly nurturing the thought of being "gifted", not "crazy".

I can do gifted. I like gifted.

After all these years, who is going to call you gifted out loud when they've been snickering crazy under their breaths and behind closed doors?

Score one for the alter ego.

Josephine's fingers tapped the tabletop. The staccato pattern soothed rather than jarred my thoughts. She snapped her fingers together. "We need that quilt. I want to study the pattern. Who has the quilt?"

"They were taking it to the police."

Josephine's demeanor changed on a dime. She stood abruptly and seemed to tower over me. "We cannot allow that. It's crucial I examine that particular quilt."

I stared at her openmouthed. She took my hands and pulled me out of the chair.

"I gets so excited when I hears about a new quilt I ain't seen. Didn't mean to put a scare in you."

I let her lead me to the stairs. "Let me get my handbag and you can take me to the quilt. We gotta' move on this. It's important." She turned to go inside.

"You mean 'crucial'." I couldn't see her face, but I saw her step falter before she went inside. What in heavens name just happened? It was like someone else channeled through Josephine for a few moments.

What? Now you think she's possessed?

Of course I don't. Do I? I mean what do I know about her? Do I want to be alone with her?

Shhh. Here she comes.

She can't hear us. Can she?

I shut down my internal argument and led the way to my car. "I don't know where Harry and Walter went first and I have no way to reach them. I'll take you to Karen and Hannah's house."

Josephine prattled on about never having ridden in a Jeep before and how practical it would be for when she went quilt and story hunting. Her monologue took up most of the drive to Oak Park. Josephine changed topics several times, something I do when I'm nervous. I glanced at her when she finally stopped talking. Her fingers plucked at the tassel on the clasp of her handbag. The thin threads rolling between her fingers seemed to comfort her. Had I found a kindred spirit, another afflicted with OCD? The question was on my lips when we pulled up to the curb outside the brownstone.

New questions formed when I saw the police on the stairs.

TWENTY-SIX

"UH-OH. POLICE ON the porch can't be good." She studied the two uniformed officers, but turned quickly when one of them casually glanced in our direction.

If I hadn't been stressed I would have burst out laughing at her deadpan understatement. As it was, she made no move to get out. She turned in her seat.

"Maybe it's best not to intrude at this here time."

I stared at her. She didn't want an encounter with the police.

"Let's go find out what's happening. Maybe they still have the quilt and we could get it before they do."

I had no intention of snatching the quilt out from under police noses. I only wanted to see her reaction.

Her eyes widened. She shook her head once slowly, then two quick shakes. "If you want to go inside, you go. But I'll be waiting here." She crossed her arms over her ample chest and melded to the leather seat.

The two officers had entered the brownstone by the time I decided on my course of action. My nature wouldn't let me drive off not knowing what was unfolding inside. I looked for Walter's car on the street. Maybe they'd parked in the alley. I turned to my passenger. "Suit yourself. I'm going in." I matched my actions to my words and left her staring straight ahead.

She had her reasons. Maybe she didn't trust the police, or maybe she'd had a run-in with them, though I can't imagine for what. I rang the bell and waited.

Ric Kramer opened the door. His tentative smile strengthened when he realized I was alone. "To what do I owe this pleasure?"

"It's your sister's door you've answered, not yours. Anyway, I came with…" I turned to point at Josephine, only the passenger side was empty. Either she'd slipped out or slumped down. Either way, I didn't care. I was growing tired of all the games, including Ric's. I waved my hand toward the inside and continued, "Ah, I came with an idea about the people in the cellar."

Ric stretched out his arm and waved me along like a maître d' offering the best table. "They're in the living room."

Conversation stopped to acknowledge my appearance. "Gracie, hi. What a surprise," said Karen. "Are Harry and Walter with you? Gertrude's waiting for them." I turned when a soft voice from behind me said, "I'd hope to see you again."

Marisol Nunez walked toward me holding a tray loaded with cups, saucers, spoons and napkins. Gertrude deftly relieved her of the burden while murmuring a thank you.

This was awkward. Marisol was the FBI agent whose life I'd saved last year. We'd become friends, even kept in touch for a few months afterwards.

"Hello, Marisol. It's good to see you, too." It was incumbent on me to acknowledge her engagement. My mouth dried up and my tongue swelled to fit the cavern.

Not now, not now. Please let me say something intelligent or even normal. Normal is good.

I'd been fingering the large grommet on my purse strap, sliding my baby finger in and out. I'd almost finished the last set of five when Karen, trying to be helpful and smooth out the moment, reached for my purse.

"Here, let me have your bag. Sit down." In one quick

movement she pulled the strap from my shoulder, twisting the grommet and bending my pinkie the wrong way.

"Ouch!" I grabbed for the bag. "Wait, my finger. Ouch."

She let the strap drop and I worked my swollen digit out of the ornamental grommet, then let my bag drop to floor.

"I'll get some ice," Gertrude offered.

"Sorry, Grace." Karen stared at my finger. It had mushroomed to the size of a breakfast sausage.

I felt stupid being the center of attention for such a stupid reason. This was Marisol's moment and I spoiled it.

Would they think I did it on purpose?

Oh yeah, I'm sure. Anyone would break their finger to avoid saying 'best wishes' to their ex-lover's intended.

When you put it that way...

"Here is ice." Gertrude handed me a small package of frozen peas and a hand towel. "Sit now and you feel *gut* in little while."

I winced when I laid my hand on the cold pack. I glanced at Marisol. "Best wishes on your engagement." I smiled and a weight lifted from my body. "To both of you." I turned my head to include Ric. His smile hesitated, his eyes questioning. "You're lucky she said yes."

A chorus of agreement arose until we were all laughing at Ric's expense. Marisol and Ric smiled into each other's eyes, their faces mirror images reflecting their feelings.

In that moment, I wished Harry were here to see Ric look at Marisol. A few months earlier that expression had been reserved for me.

Are you okay with that?

Yeah, I am. I really am.

Rather than sensing a void, I felt a surge of happiness lift my spirits. My thoughts shifted to why I'd come here.

"Wow, that was amazing," Marisol said looking at me.

"She went from the cat that ate the canary smile to a weight of the world frown in two seconds."

"She never did have a poker face, but that was a quick change. What's wrong?"

I blushed at their comments and took a deep breath to steady my thoughts and hopefully my eye color. "I came because I thought Harry and Walter were coming here to be with Gertrude if she had to go to the police station. I don't know why they haven't arrived yet."

Ric interrupted me. "They called about five minutes before you arrived. They had car trouble, but they're in route." His neck reddened when Gertrude and Karen stared at him. "Sorry, the phone rang, the doorbell rang. It happened so fast I forgot to…" He shrugged and slapped a crooked grin on his face while mumbling something about walking and chewing gum at the same time.

I waved off his explanation. "I hope they get here soon. I didn't expect the police would come to get her."

Ric, Marisol and the two cops burst into laughter. Karen and Gertrude smiled. I felt the heat rising around my neck and felt entirely stupid.

Marisol noticed my discomfort and stopped laughing. "Okay, fellows, enough. Her take on this makes sense if she doesn't know who you are."

She turned to me and explained. "Grace, these are two of my colleagues, Joe Bennett and George Shaw. They're in town from Maryland and I wanted them to meet Ric. Guys, this is Grace Marsden, the woman who saved my life last year."

I shook hands with them. "I thought FBI people didn't wear uniforms." On closer inspection the shirts were different from the local ones I'd seen.

"Usually true," said Bennett. "But today we participated in a ceremony at the Daley Center."

"That ought to take the edge off Josephine." I realized I'd mumbled that out loud.

"Josephine? Ms. Hossack?" Karen asked.

"Yes, the one and only. She wouldn't come in when she saw the two officers. She acted like she was on their most-wanted list." I chuckled, but they weren't getting the joke.

"Yes, the one and only describes her, Mrs. Marsden. We know Josephine Hossack." The two men exchanged a look.

"I'll keep an eye on the Jeep. You fill her in," George said.

"Have a seat, Mrs. Marsden. I'm sure this will interest you."

TWENTY-SEVEN

I yanked the door open and glared into the car. Josephine had the decency to look upset. She squirmed back up into a sitting position. Her expression was a blend of contrition and humor.

"Did you have a good visit with your friends?"

"I did." I extended my hand to help her out. "Two of your friends would like to say hello, *Professor* Hossack."

She looked at me with those big brown eyes, then smoothed her curls and grinned. Reaching out to accept my help, she bounced out of the vehicle.

"Grace, I never intended to trick or ridicule you or your friends. It's just my way when I'm working."

Her speech pattern, cadence, even accent had changed. I sputtered, stopped, then tried again. "What, when, why…" So much for controlled sputter.

She smiled generously and patted my hand. "I suspect I have some *'splainin'* to do. Let's go inside." Her purposeful lapse made me smile at how we were all taken in by her speech. How different our assumptions and maybe our reactions would have been if we'd met her as a professor of African American Archaeology.

I heard a car pull up and turned to see Harry and Walter hurrying towards us. Harry slowed his steps. He looked surprised to see me, even more surprised to see Josephine.

"Now I know why you didn't answer the phone at home. One mystery solved." He smiled at Josephine. "Nice to see you again, Ms. Hossack."

She beamed and, I swear, batted her eyes at him.

"That would be Professor Hossack," I said, stressing the title.

Harry's eyebrow arched in question.

"Yep, the chair of African American Archaeology at the University of Missouri."

Harry's smile broadened and he extended his hand. "Well done Ms...Professor Hossack."

She definitely batted her eyelashes. "Please, call me Josephine."

Walter, who had stood by silently during the reintroduction, shifted his weight from one foot to the other, drawing Josephine's attention to the bag he carried.

"Is that the quilt found in the cellar?"

Neither Harry nor Walter showed surprise that she knew about the quilt. Walter nodded. "I am bringing back so police not be angry with Gertrude when she move it."

"Ric and Marisol and two of her FBI friends are inside. They have nothing to do with the investigation; they're in town for a few days and wanted to meet Marisol's guy."

Why didn't I say fiancée?

I watched Harry's face while he processed the Ric and Marisol parts. His poker face gave up little. I thought a saw a glimmer of something in his eyes. Was it relief or suspicion?

"May I see the quilt before you return it?" Josephine's voice sounded eager and excited. "Please?"

Walter shrugged and handed her the bag.

Josephine started forward, then stopped. "Would you mind if we did this more quietly at the boardinghouse? I'd like to have a sense of the entire picture."

At that moment I didn't want Harry and Ric to interact. I didn't want to hear the words they'd exchange. I too preferred the quiet of the empty house.

I turned and faced Walter. "Harry and I can drive Josephine to the house while you bring Gertrude. If anyone asks, just say that you and Harry are taking her to the police station to give her statement."

Walter's broad smile transformed his worried expression. "*Hölzerner splitter.*" He turned and walked up the steps.

"What did he call me? What does that mean?"

"I'll tell you later; we'd best be on our way." He hurried us to the Jeep. He was right. If Karen found out where we were going, they'd all want to come along. Ric would probably try to stop us, and Marisol and her pals would show up, too.

The drive to the boardinghouse didn't take long. Josephine sat in the back cradling the bag to her chest. Harry stared straight ahead.

"So, what did he say?" I asked.

Harry chuckled. "It's a saying. Difficult to translate. He complemented you, in a way."

A sideways glance showed him I wasn't satisfied.

"It's like when Americans say a 'chip off the block'. Literally it means a wooden splinter or a splinter made of wood. He referred to the devious plan you devised."

"Would that mean, Mr. Marsden, that Grace has been influenced to some degree by your devious ways?"

Josephine's voice held humor when she spoke.

"Please, call me Harry. I'd be careful whose ways you called devious, Professor Mizzou."

Josephine's hearty laughter filled the space around our heads. "Point made. No pots and kettles in this car."

We parked in front of the boardinghouse and slipped quietly into the house from the side entrance. The sense of being watched overwhelmed me as we crossed the threshold. This was the door where I'd seen something, someone. I glanced at the slender bush at the corner. *Could I have seen the bush swaying as others thought? It was the height of a person. Was this the door the slave had used to gain entrance to sanctuary?*

"Some sanctuary." I jumped when I heard the words spoken out loud.

"Come again?" Harry asked.

Josephine answered slowly. "I was just thinking that the slave who died here most likely thought he had found sanctuary."

"Why would you say *sanctuary*?" my voice squeaked. I couldn't help myself. "Why not say, 'safe haven' or 'shelter'? Why 'sanctuary'?" I flung my arms out in frustration.

Harry stepped closer. "What is it, Grace?"

I shook my head and turned away, embarrassed at my outburst. A shadow fell across the window in the door.

"There!" I shouted.

TWENTY-EIGHT

HARRY AND JOSEPHINE followed my outstretched hand and turned to face the door.

"Relax, Grace. It's Walter and Gertrude."

I felt the pinch of tears and clenched my teeth to keep quiet.

Harry looked at me with concern, and Josephine, well, she stared a hole through me. She stepped past Harry and greeted the newcomers.

Gertrude bustled into the room and immediately asked if we wanted something to drink. Harry had already poured a glass of water for me and motioned for me to sit down at the table. He sat next to me and watched me sip my drink.

He leaned his head close to mine. "What was that about?"

I shook my head, still not confident I wouldn't cry.

Josephine removed the quilt from the bag. Harry noticed and spoke up. "Take that in the living room, won't you? Spread it out in there."

Josephine fixed me with a puzzled expression and carried her parcel into the living room. Gertrude followed with drinks. Walter leaned against the doorjamb with his back to us. I smiled at Harry. "Thanks," was all I could manage.

He covered my hand with his. I liked the warmth and the calmness emanating from him.

"Gracie, we'll get through this, I promise. I don't know

why you tune into the past, people's pain and sorrow. But each time it's happened, you've been in danger. I'm not taking any chances with your safety. I've made some inquiries about the people connected with this house. Some of what has come back is interesting but not criminal."

I slipped my hand out from under his and stood up. "I feel better knowing you're on the job." I quipped. "Will your ethics allow you to share the 'interesting' part with me?"

Harry pulled me down on his lap, engulfing me in a hug. He whispered, "I've all sorts of interesting parts I'm willing to share with you."

We heard Walter clear his throat. "I see if they are being ready," he said to someone in the other room.

I whispered, "Are we being ready?"

Harry sighed and released me. "Definitely beyond ready; more like randy."

I moved off his lap and ran my hands over my hair guiding the sides behind my ears. Harry stood and straightened his shirt. I felt like a teenager caught necking.

Walter stepped back to let us pass. Harry led the way into the living room. He smiled at the ladies. "Forgive the delay."

They nodded and would have forgiven him most anything.

I sat on the sofa to be as far from the quilt as possible. Harry sat next to me. Josephine looked at me, at the quilt, then back at me. In a clear voice devoid of any bad grammar she asked me point blank, "Is this the quilt you saw in your…" She hesitated and I felt myself begin to blush. "…dream?"

My mouth felt dry and I wished for the water I'd left in the kitchen. I nodded. "At first, I thought it was like the one you showed us at my Dad's house. It was on the corral fence and I saw it for only a moment before I…"

I wondered if I should tell them I dove under the covers fully clothed and shod. The memory of that scary event evoked in my brain an image of me as a horse, my unruly dark mane caught up in show braids.

"Before you…" prompted Josephine.

I focused on her face where I saw no incredulity, no accusatory moue. She would not be shocked. Maybe she'd heard stranger things than what I was about to reveal.

"I was frightened by the sight and rushed up to bed. It was late and I was tired." I felt the blush creep up my neck and I knew my eyes darkened with the anxiety of the telling.

Harry offered me the lemonade he'd accepted from Gertrude. I sipped at it gratefully while gathering my thoughts and my voice.

"I woke up with the sensation of the quilt smothering me. I struggled and pushed the fabric off my face. It retreated to the blanket stand and seemed to wait."

There, I'd shared my bizarre story. I waited for the stares, then the "plausible explanations" people always tried to conjure to avoid using the "C" word. Only problem with their explanations was that they sounded crazier than my experience.

Josephine reflected on my answer. "Could you have seen two different designs?"

I replayed my first encounter with the quilt from the safe distance of memory. In my mind's eye I could see the outline of stars. It had been different from the quilt in my room.

"The one I saw outside was more like the one you showed us. The one in my room was exactly like this one." I surprised myself with my own certainty.

Josephine's eyes gleamed with excitement.

"What about my experience makes you happy?" I challenged.

She quickly crossed the room to stand over me. "I am not pleased by the trauma you suffered. If my actions led you to believe that is the case, then I apologize and ask your forgiveness. Enthusiasm for one's cause should never eclipse one's obligation to other people."

Her eloquence touched each of us; no one spoke or even moved.

Harry's voice broke the silence. "What is your cause, Professor? Grace is on target in noticing your interest in this quilt. An interest that goes beyond a new find, I presume?"

The question hung in the air and settled squarely on her shoulders. Sometimes the auditory signals I receive create vibrant pictures for my mind to grasp and store. I assumed most people reacted to auditory cues the same way. I learned to stop describing what I heard/saw when other kids stared at me in shock. My breath slowed, I froze to the spot and watched—I hoped in only my mind's eye— as the quilt lifted from the table, circled behind Josephine and settled gently around her shoulders. I forced my eyes away from her face, using only my peripheral vision to watch her reaction. I'm certain my eyes were pansy purple and a dead giveaway, if anyone noticed.

She straightened like she felt the weight. Her eyes widened. She rolled her neck, and slowly raised her hand to her shoulder. Josephine looked at her hand, then down to the quilt she saw lying on the table. Her nostrils flared and she breathed faster.

The others recognized her distress, but not the cause. Josephine's raisin eyes, tiny islands surrounded by white, stared at the quilt. Slowly she reached her other hand up to her shoulder and crossed her hands pulling the invisible quilt closer. Her breathing calmed and her eyes relaxed.

Then the quilt gently loosened from her grip as she opened her fingers. Her posture seemed to record the sensation of the material slipping off her shoulders. I saw in her eyes an unspoken question. I answered in silence.

"Professor, you are looking strange. Coming here to sit." Gertrude pointed to a nearby chair. "I am bringing more lemonade." She waited until her guest sat before bustling off to the kitchen.

Harry stood in front of Josephine who now leaned back in her chair. His body blocked my view of her face.

"Something occurred in this room that I'm certain my wife and you experienced. Whatever it was seemed directed at you, not Grace. For that I am grateful. Until I know your cause, I can't be sure that Grace won't be attacked or approached or whatever bloody hell just happened here. Her well-being is my cause."

Gertrude placed a glass on the table within Josephine's reach, then hurriedly stepped to Walter's side. He placed a comforting arm around her shoulder.

Josephine sipped at her drink, lowered the glass to her lap, and looked up at Harry. "Your wife is not in danger; no one here is. I have encountered something I have never experienced in my thirty years of research. Please, sit down and I'll explain as much as I know."

Harry sat down next to me and lifted my hand into his. I felt a surge of calm and leaned closer to his arm.

"During the course of my research I began hearing a similar story from people I interviewed. These people were either young children during the time of slavery remembering snatches of conversations or the grandchildren of slaves recounting an often-told and possibly altered family story. I could never be sure of the veracity of the Judas Quilt."

Each of us stirred at her words and inadvertently stared at the quilt on the table. I waited, half expecting it to twitch in protest.

"The oral tradition is a powerful one. Usually one family member is entrusted with the telling of the stories for that family. The stories are passed from generation to generation supposedly intact and unembellished. In early cultures the stories were memorized and repeated verbatim as part of tribal ceremony.

"The story of the Judas Quilt changes little from one telling to the next. Slave catchers captured one of the slaves who made it north. He was shackled and tied to a rope in preparation to be dragged along the road behind the horses as an example to other runaways who might be in the area. The slave broke down and bartered for his freedom. The slave catchers hatched a scheme to enable them to easily catch many runaways and earn top bounty. They promised the slave freedom for himself and his wife, whom he'd left behind, if he would go back under the guise of telling his people a safe route to the North. They wanted his wife to make a quilt that would direct slaves waiting for a signal to the caves near the river. The slave catchers would get this quilt anonymously to a known sympathizer who would display it on his railing. The runaway slave pretended to be heroic in his return and plan. He convinced his wife to try for freedom with him, assuring her that he knew the safe route."

Josephine sighed. Her body reflected a heaviness of spirit as though the retelling brought the tragedy alive to her.

"At this point the story splits. I have heard accounts that the husband and wife were killed once they delivered the quilt. Another version is that the wife found out and was killed trying to destroy the quilt. Yet another says she

slipped away in the night and made it back to the plantation to warn her people." She shrugged, as if not sure how
to close this tale. "There are as many endings for the story
of the Judas Quilt as there are storytellers."

Gertrude stared at the door to the basement. I could
only imagine how her mind must keep coming back to
the thought that she'd lived her life worrying and wondering about a brother who'd left her, only to discover a
tragedy of her own. I watched as she dragged her eyes
back to Josephine.

"You *tink* black man in cellar *ist* man come to take the
quilt away?"

"I believe he was a *Waysayer*. When he found out the
route was not safe, he either came north to warn people
who'd just left, or he wanted to find the safe route. Maybe
he knew about the quilt. We can't be sure."

"Why did there have to be something erroneous stitched
on the quilt?" I asked. "I thought if the quilt was placed
outside, that meant it was safe to approach. Why didn't
the slave catchers just watch the house for when the quilt
was out?"

"Good question, but I don't know all the patterns and
what they meant. I do know that where this house is lo-
cated made it tricky on both sides of the slavery issue. Even
in the 1850s, it wasn't isolated. That made it difficult for
slaves to approach without being noticed. I never would
have suspected this location for a station on the Underground Railroad. Apparently Mr. Coe felt strongly about
abolition and took risks."

"That would make it easier for slave catchers, wouldn't
it?"

Josephine smiled at me. "Depends on the sentiments of
Mr. Coe's neighbors. Oak Park has always been a forward-
thinking, tolerant community. Even though the Fugitive

Act of 1850 put the law squarely on the side of the slave catchers, many communities protected runaways and even fought off their pursuers.

"After the Jim Grey case, when John Hossack and his friends rescued Jim Grey as the Marshal escorted him from the courtroom, abolitionists became more assertive. Grey made it to Canada. Hossack was indicted and stood trial. He was fined and served ten days in jail. Because of his actions and others' refusals to follow the law in the case of captured slaves, slave catchers preferred to capture slaves away from the prying eyes of do-gooders. If runaways could be directed to an isolated location, the slave catchers would be assured of easier captures resulting in more bounties."

A knock at the back door interrupted Josephine's story. Harry answered it and returned with Karen and three bulging brown bags.

"Gene and Jude's, everybody. I thought there might be some hungry people here."

I looked beyond her. Harry shook his head slightly. Josephine must have wondered the same as I. "Did those two young men come with you?" she asked Karen.

"No, they took Ric and Marisol to dinner. I called the girl who occasionally sits for the twins and she came right over."

"How did you know we'd be here?" I asked.

"Um, a little bird told me?" She grinned. We turned to Gertrude who suddenly appeared quite flustered. Blushing, she ducked her head and tugged at several wisps of hair that had escaped from their nest. She weaved the thin strands back through the sturdy bobby pins without ever meeting our eyes.

"*Liebchien*, I *vas* telling you don't tell no one." Walter's admonishment was hardly stern. I think he wanted to go on record with Harry that he had tried to keep a lid on our plans.

"Oh, Walter, don't be upset. I forced it out of her," Karen lied easily. "C'mon, we have Gene and Jude's hot dogs and Italian sausage. Let's eat before it gets cold."

No one argued, and during dinner, no one mentioned the graves in the basement.

"Mmm, Gene and Jude's. I haven't had one of their hot dogs in years." Josephine spoke from behind a mustard-stained napkin. "They're just as good as I remembered."

"Josephine, why didn't you tell us who you were when we met?"

She smiled. "I figured that question might come up." She wiped her lips. "I have found through the years that I'm more easily accepted into black family's homes, especially the elderly, when I present myself as a woman with a similar background."

"Don't you feel you're insulting the people you meet by pretending to be this homey, minimally educated person?" Karen's question resonated with me. I nodded my head.

"I am the sum of my parts and I like to think that the Josephine you first met is just as viable and true as the one you see wolfing down hot dogs." She reached for another wrapped dog. "I love the thin strips of pickle."

It was difficult to be upset with her for any length of time. Maybe she was right; we all had different phases, personas that lived compatibly within us.

"Okay, I'll give you that," Karen said, "But how and when did you go from working for the family next door to being a professor?"

"The way everyone does it. I went to college and graduate school." Her eyes gleamed with amusement. "Just because my mother and I worked for a family, we weren't poor. I attended the Oak Park and River Forest Township

High School. I'd always had a great interest in history. My teachers encouraged me to apply for a scholarship to Missouri in an emerging field. I was accepted and my aunt and I left for Missouri."

"Your aunt went with you?"

"Yes, ma'am. She'd been watching out for me since my mama passed. She wasn't about to let her sister's daughter move to another state and go about her business like she had no people. She found work cleaning for a family near the university. The plan was for us to stay there until I graduated, then we'd move back home. My father and brothers couldn't leave the business. We'd see them on the holidays when we'd come home. During the last two years of school they'd come and visit us.

"My dad and brothers loved to fish. They found great areas to fish in Missouri, and they started hatching plans to move there. Housing was cheaper and my dad had been tinkering with the idea of opening a hardware store while still offering his smithy work to the area farmers. Hossack Hardware opened on Main Street and my family successfully immigrated to Missouri."

"You began tracking any leads about slaves and safe houses with the hope of verifying or debunking the emerging legend of the Judas Quilt."

Josephine stared at Harry. "You like to cut right through it, don't you?"

Harry smiled. "Cut to the chase, I believe you Americans say."

She set down her glass and wiped her moist fingers on her slacks before carefully picking up the quilt. "I believe I have found the Judas Quilt and it will rock my world as one of the important finds of the 20th century. It's incredibly important to be able to accurately piece together a nation's history. I also believe that the remains of the slave in the cellar belonged to a *Waysayer* who risked his life to secure safe passage for his people.

"In my research on this house I have already seen a drop in the number of times the house was mentioned in any accountings of the period. I thought it was due to the death of the owner, but there is another explanation."

She shifted in her chair and held the quilt on her lap. I thought I saw a twitch of movement and I glanced at her face to look for a response. She continued in the voice I didn't connect with the Josephine I'd originally met.

"The *Waysayer* would have told those he left behind that if he didn't return by a certain date, they should consider this route unsafe and let no one use it. He never made it back, and no one ever used the route again."

You could have heard a pin drop when she paused. In fact, a pin would have been pleasant. The low moan emanating from below gripped my heart. I heard the gasps over my own.

Harry and Walter rushed to the head of the stairs and cautiously began their descent. Josephine took a position at the top of the stairs. Her curiosity more motivating than mine, I chose to sit still. Karen moved next to me and I suspected would be grabbing my hand any minute. I watched the quilt. I hadn't meant to.

A shiver, a twitch, and the Judas Quilt lifted from where Josephine had placed it when she rushed away. The floating fabric ignored the opening to the graves from whence it had come but rather moved directly to the front window.

Karen had picked up the real quilt from the arm of the chair and refolded it, placing it on the table atop the bag. Her interference distracted me, but not my vision of the quilt invisible to her eyes passing easily through the glass and settling on the railing of the porch, claiming a position it had taken long ago.

The moan grew louder and my instant concern was for Harry and Walter. They'd been down there for what seemed too long. Gertrude walked past me in no hurry at all. In fact, she seemed to move in slow motion. And Karen's speech sounded slow and slurred across the room. The room suddenly turned icy cold.

TWENTY-NINE

HIS DARK FACE glared through the window. I watched him search the room until he found Josephine. I saw her shoulders twitch. As kids we'd say someone stepped on your grave when we got that spontaneous twitch for no reason.

She had reason to twitch. Her shoulders spasmed again. She turned toward the window, but I knew she didn't see him. He knew, too, and turned his eyes to me not in anger, but in confusion.

The clouds slid over the late afternoon sun filling the room with unexpected light. I squinted at the window. He was gone. Was he ever there?

Harry and Walter appeared at the top of the stairs helping a young man up the steps. Shock and confusion flowed in the form of exclamations and questions.

Harry's clothes and hands were smeared with dirt. The boy between them was covered in dirt and dust. He looked scared and exhausted. They helped him to a chair. Karen had a glass of water ready for him. He accepted the glass with murmured thanks.

"Does he need medical attention?" Josephine asked.

"Maybe an ice pack for his head. He's taken a nasty bump, but his thick hair absorbed a lot of the shock."

"I have *sometink* to help." Gertrude rushed to the kitchen and returned with an honest-to-goodness red rubber ice pack that she'd filled with ice. So much for my frozen pea packet.

She handed it to the young man. "*Dis vil* help."

He'd never seen one of those; he was probably used to sports wraps and packs. He placed it against the lump just beyond the hairline. Harry spoke true; if this kid had hit his forehead instead of the top of his curly head of hair, he might still be out cold.

"Let's hear your explanation for trespassing before we call the police."

The young man gulped the water and returned the glass to Karen. He held the pack to his head and his gaze swung from one of us to the other. I wondered what he thought— were we a bunch of old people to him? What could he tell us that would turn the tide in his favor?

He coughed and cleared his throat. He fixed his stare on Josephine, the only black person. "I've never been in any trouble, honest. My father would kill me if I had to call him from the police station. It's because of him that I'm here."

"Your father sent you to trespass?" Harry asked in a neutral tone.

"No, no. I mean it's because of the stories he told and because my great-aunt saw this article in the paper and my mother drove by and remembered—"

"Hold on," Harry interrupted. "First of all who are you and how old are you?"

Josephine stared at the young man, her expression cautiously curious.

"My name is Jack Johnson, Jr. My friends call me 3J. I'm nineteen and I'm not a criminal. I'm sorry I came into your home." He hesitated, not sure whom he should be addressing. "I really only wanted to see what my—"

"Oh, dear Lord! You're Clarisse's nephew's son. Your father is Jackson, isn't he?" Josephine stepped closer to the young man. "Yes, indeed. I do see the resemblance."

Jack looked as shocked as we did. He shook his head slowly. "You know my great-aunt?"

"I certainly do. Oh, my goodness, what a coincidence." Josephine grinned with delight.

"No more coincidence than what brought you here, Professor. Your niece saw the article and passed on the information. You hopped the first plane to ostensibly visit Ms. Dodd." Harry's tone sounded pleasant, not accusatory. "No surprise if someone else saw that article and mentioned it to a person once connected to this house. How can we be certain that your father didn't send you, perhaps to remove something incriminating to him?"

Jack began to stand, then noticed Walter's close proximity and sat back down. "That's crazy. My dad's got nothing to do with this. He used to play here as a kid and told me wild stories about a tunnel in the cellar and pirate's treasure. I didn't even think the house was real. Then my great-aunt read about this place and said she used to work here. She kind of validated what my dad had been saying. I thought it would be cool to come here and see...well, look around and..." His voice stopped.

He probably realized how lame his story sounded. I believed him. It was just the sort of thing my youngest brother, Marty, would have done. I'm sure of it.

Josephine believed him, too. She put her arm around his shoulders and faced Harry. "I don't think we need call the police." Jack visibly relaxed under her arm.

"I had no intention of doing so," Harry assured her. "I only wanted some straight answers. Tell us, son, how did you get stuck in the tunnel?"

Jack asked for another glass of water and if he could use the bathroom. Karen offered to heat up one of the hot dogs for him while he washed up. What teenager wasn't always hungry?

I watched Walter and Gertrude approach Harry. I couldn't hear the conversation. Gertrude came and hugged me good-bye and left with Walter. I'd forgotten they needed to check in with the police. Harry saw the concern on my face. He motioned for me to join him at the window. I slipped my arm around his waist and leaned my head against his shoulder.

"She'll be fine. David is already there and he has everything set up." He kissed the side of my head. "How are you doing with all this?"

His question snapped my head up and caused me to look out the window. The railing was empty.

"What's wrong?"

I turned to glance at the quilt. It wasn't on the table. Walter and Gertrude must have taken it to turn into the police. It couldn't mean anything to them, but it had been found at a crime scene. I leaned back against Harry.

"Nothing, I thought they forgot the quilt. I have to talk to you. Not now; tonight though, okay?"

"Before or after we pick up Will?"

Oh, gosh. I forgot about Will. I'm some stepmom. Leave the kid with my dad all day and night. My dad! I think he said he and Jan had plans.

I twisted around to face Harry. "I have to call my dad. I think he has plans, but I don't know what time. I forgot about…" I caught my breath before I said "Will". "…his plans." I rushed to the kitchen and found Karen using the phone.

"Thanks, Natalie. I'll be home soon. I really appreciate it."

Karen hung up and saw me. "The sitter gave the kids their baths, but she has to study. I'm going to have to leave before the 'rest of the story'. Fill me in, okay?"

"Absolutely. Karen, when is Hannah getting back? I mean, is she with Lily the entire time?"

"I have no clue. She told me she couldn't pass up this

opportunity to do the site finding for Lily's shoot. It's something she's always wanted to do." Karen took a deep breath and swallowed. "I don't know what's going on anymore."

I regretted asking and not being able to spend time to cheer her or let her talk more. We each had other places to be. It happened that way more and more.

I hugged her hard. "We'll get together for a long talk soon."

She hugged back. "Say good-bye in there for me, will you?"

"Sure. Go on."

She turned for the door, then turned back to me just as quickly. "Wait, I forgot to give you these." She pulled several pages from her tote bag. They were covered with her precise handwriting. "Research I did at the library on Lydia and Lucy Coe. Sad story. Gotta' go."

I had no time to wonder what she meant. I dialed my dad's number.

"Hello."

"Hi, Marty, it's me. Can I talk to dad?"

"Nope. He and Jan left for dinner."

"Oh, what about Will?"

"They told him if he started walking, he should reach Pine Marsh by midnight. Jan made dad loan him a bike." Marty waited a beat. "What do you think—he's here with me and we're watching movies."

"Thanks, Marty. Harry and I are in Oak Park and something came up, but we'll be there later. I'm not sure when, but we will."

"Gracie, relax, breathe. Take your time. We have two more 'G' rated movies, then my stuff plays. *Ciao.*"

He broke the connection. I grinned and hung up the phone. Will was in excellent hands. We'd make a Morelli out of him yet. I froze, thinking of the motive behind that thought. I would have liked to erase Lily's gene pool and input and make Will a combination of Marsden-Morelli. I would have loved to create a Marsden-Morelli of our own. That would never be.

"Did you get through?" Harry asked.

I couldn't let him see my thoughts. Instead, I nodded and fiddled with the cord. "Marty's in charge. They're watching movies."

"Movies?"

I felt in control of my expression. I smiled up at Harry as I walked past him. "Don't ask."

JACK SAT ON the same chair as before, but his face and hands were spotless, his clothes had been brushed off (I made a mental note to check the bathroom), and his hair was groomed. All in all, he appeared a more confident individual than the one Harry helped up the stairs.

"Professor Hossack says I shouldn't say anything without my parents being here." He lifted his chin slightly. Josephine shifted in her chair, preferring to keep her eyes on Jack.

"She does, does she?" Harry's calm voice held no malice. "You are of a legal age to speak without your mom and dad present."

I thought that particular phrasing might send a challenge to a teenager who felt, as they all do, that they're adults and should be treated accordingly. Harry was offering to talk to him as an adult. What nineteen-year old could resist? Not this one.

"I don't think they have to be here; she does."

"Jack, you really should wait." Josephine admonished the boy in a teacher tone of voice.

I saw Jack stiffen a little. Harry saw it too and drove home his point.

"Maybe you should listen to Ms. Hossack, Jack. She's an old friend of the family, sort of a surrogate parent as it were."

That did it. Jack's body language screamed his intent even if his voice was level. He turned away from Josephine and faced Harry.

"Like I said, I only wanted to see the place my dad had been talking about ever since I was a kid. I think he really believed there might be something of value down there. I'd read about these urban explorers that go into condemned and closed buildings to search for artifacts. I thought it would be cool to explore this house, kind of looking for whatever my dad thought was important all those years ago.

"When I got down there I realized it was a pile of junk. I saw the yellow tape around the hole. Just about the time I figured out something more had happened than what had been reported, I heard people on the stairs. I panicked. The only place I could hide without being seen was in the tunnel. I turned off my flashlight, ducked in a few feet, and hunkered down real quiet to watch."

"Jack, you weren't quiet at all. Walter and I didn't use those stairs until we heard you moan," said Harry.

Josephine and I nodded, but the boy ignored us, his gaze intent on Harry.

"I wasn't watching you guys. I was watching the woman and the man with the gun."

THIRTY

"WHAT ARE YOU talking about?" Josephine asked.

"I'm telling you why I backed so far into the tunnel. When I saw the gun I rushed farther into the tunnel. I could see a little ways in front of me because they'd turned on the light in the basement. They had a flashlight, too. It cast a strong beam when they came down the stairs. But the farther I went in the tunnel, the darker it got. I looked down to cup my hand around my flashlight before turning it on. That's when I ran into something. Whatever it was, it knocked me out."

Josephine was on her feet and at his side. "Thank God they didn't come after you. They must have heard you fall." Her concern was genuine. She'd bonded with her best friend's great nephew whether he wanted it or not.

Jack shrugged. "Maybe they saw the tape and decided they shouldn't be there. Or maybe they were too old to crawl around all the stuff down there. The man was thin, but he had a bad limp. I think what they were after wasn't near the hole or the tunnel."

"What makes you say that?" Harry's tone was tense as he focused on Jack's face.

"Almost as soon as she cleared the last step, the woman said, kind of excited, 'Over there, there' and pointed at the opposite wall. Then I saw the gun and ducked for cover."

Harry's expression darkened. "Jack, I'm sorry to do this to you, but we have to involve the police." He held up his hands to stop any further comment. "I'm not ringing them because of what you did, Jack. Three bodies have been found in that cellar. We don't know the cause of death of any of them. Anyone who shows up after decades, seemingly points to one of the graves, and brings along a man with a gun, is police business. You may have been feet away from whoever was responsible for killing one or more of those people."

Jack's head bent forward. "I just don't want any trouble. I'm a sophomore at DePaul. I can't afford to miss school and have this on my record."

Harry smiled and clapped the young man on the shoulders. "Jack, you're not in trouble. You are going to be a witness. Just tell them the truth about why you were here. You'll be a hero with your friends."

Harry's cheery spin didn't appeal to Josephine.

"And he'll be a target for someone who still worries enough to have a bodyguard. I don't like it." She crossed her arms over her chest. "I think he should go home and keep quiet."

Harry stared at the older woman. He saw the concern on her face, heard the tremor in her voice. I think he understood her fear even though he hadn't lived in this country during the sixties when civil rights were hard fought for and won.

"It won't be that way, Josephine, I promise."

She held his gaze for a long moment before making her decision. "See that you do."

She sat down, leaning back heavily against the chair's ample back, showing every bit of her seventy-something age.

Harry made the call and we waited for the police to arrive. I called Marty and explained why we'd be detained even longer than. 'No problem', he'd said. 'In fact, let him spend the night and we can pitch tents in the back yard. It's time for a burn anyway.'

My brother referred to the fire pit the boys had dug out and lined with leftover bricks they scavenged from building sites. Every few weeks we'd gather the garden brush and cut branches and have a burn.

At this moment, I'd have rather been there than here. The doorbell announced the arrival of the police. Harry led a detective into the living room and made the introductions.

Howard Barber looked like an older version of Denzel Washington. Josephine, still his senior by at least twenty years, perked up. I know she appreciated an attractive man, but his assignment to this call made her comfortable about Jack's treatment.

He shook hands with each of us and remained standing. "Is the owner of the home here?"

"You missed her by a quarter hour. She has eight-month-old twins she'd have to bring along. Shall I ring her?"

Detective Barber shook his head quickly. "No one is living here, correct?"

We all nodded.

"I have a tech coming out to padlock the doors once we leave. Someone will call the owner of record and let them know."

He faced Jack. "Son, let's you and me go below and you tell me everything you did, saw, and heard. Don't leave out anything even if you don't think it matters."

Jack popped out of his chair, then swayed like a buoy in high winds. Harry and Barber grabbed for him and slowly lowered him to the chair. Harry guided the boy's head forward to his knees.

"Keep your head down until the room stops spinning."

Harry lifted his hand from Jack's curly hair. "Dammit." He held his hand palm forward for us to see. A brown smear across his fingers explained his exclamation. "Jack, keep your head down." Harry parted the boy's thick hair and probed the area.

Jack's shoulders twitched and Harry knew he'd found the spot. "Sorry, son. You have a small gash right behind the lump. It's not bleeding. It doesn't appear to need stitching, but it's your head not mine."

Jack slowly raised his head. His clear eyes focused on the detective. "I stood up too fast. I'm fine. Let's do this." He rose from the chair and took steady steps to the basement door.

We followed. Detective Barber turned at the top of the stairs. "I've got it from here, folks. Wait for us in the living room."

The doorbell rang. Detective Barber grinned. "That would be my tech. Someone please let him in."

He followed Jack down the stairs and we had no choice but to return to the living room. The tech, Peter Dwyer, went to work on the back door.

Josephine paced the living room, circling the coffee table with each passing. Her pattern tripped the wire in my head. I counted the steps she took and allowed my mind to drift. Her feet slowed and blurred.

Odd, the count is off. The quilt was off. Nothing is as it appears.

The sound of heavy steps broke my erratic train of thought. Detective Barber's jacket bore the results of his spelunking efforts. He carried a small notebook with writing on at least two pages. I couldn't help wondering what he'd recorded, couldn't help thinking I'd almost caught a thread of all this.

He brushed off his sleeve where he must have leaned

against the side of the tunnel. "Anyone know where that tunnel leads?"

"Detective, up until I heard this young man moaning, I'd never seen the tunnel."

"What about the owner? Would she know?"

I shook my head and chimed in. "No, I'm sure she didn't. She's been the owner for only six months. Maybe Gertrude would know."

"What *ist* she knowing?"

Walter strode into the room followed more meekly by Gertrude.

"How did you get in here? He's not supposed to let anyone…" Detective Barber waved it off. "Please sit down." He turned to Gertrude. "I wanted to know about the tunnel. They told me you would know where it leads."

Gertrude sat next to me. Walter remained standing with his hand protectively placed on her shoulder. We quickly filled them in on the latest twist in the cellar. Gertrude ducked her head a few quick bobs and cleared her throat.

"As little children, my brother…" Her voice caught. She cleared her throat. "My brother, he *vas* brave and follow tunnel. It *vas verboten* by our parents, but he did not listen. One time he is gone for too long and we, my sister and me, are fearing for him. We tell our *vater* and he goes to find him, but he don't go through the tunnel in the cellar. He walked outside and back behind the house.

"Later, my brother is home *mit* our *vater* who is angry with Kurt who is angry *mit* us. He don't talk to us for two days, but then he tell us the tunnel goes into a small room in the bottom of the barn near Chicago Avenue."

Gertrude paused.

Detective Barber turned toward the front window before looking toward the kitchen. "The tunnel leads off behind the house that way," he said, pointing at the kitchen. "I never realized how close this block is to Forest Park; it's only one block over. It's possible." He encouraged Gertrude to go on.

"*Ist* noting more. After, our *vater* put old furniture in front of tunnel and he tell us no more we go there. Even Kurt, he listens."

Josephine interrupted. "Do you know where the barn was, if it's still standing?" The excitement in her voice intrigued me. She faced Barber. "We need to contact the African American Archeology Network and get a team out here to search the tunnel and find that barn or what's there now."

Josephine paced between the window and the couch. "Sometimes groups of abolitionists would map a grid of stations. If the slaves came off the Des Plaines River in Maywood, they might transport them a short distance to a barn or home, then leapfrog them to a station closer to the railroad line. Those places would be closer to the commercial part of town. In like manner, if slaves came in on the train, but had to get off before a major city where slave catchers were watching the terminal, they could stay at a place like this until dark. Come nightfall, they'd use the tunnel to leapfrog to the barn, then to the station near the river, and continue on the water."

"Ma'am," Barber's deep voice interrupted. "This is a crime scene. No matter how interesting your premise, no one gets anywhere until I say so. Like the lady said, 'go there no more'." He folded his arms across his chest as a visual aid.

"We'll see about that," Josephine muttered.

Harry stepped into the breech left by their disagreement. "Detective, if you've finished questioning this young man, I think we'd best get him home. Lad's all done in."

At Harry's words, everyone focused on Jack. He smiled weakly. "I am a little tired, and my head hurts."

Talk about understatement.

"I've got his contact information. Leave a number where I can reach you," Barber said, pointing at Josephine. "And you," he added with a nod toward Harry.

Harry slipped a card and pen from his pocket and passed it to Josephine who scribbled Juliana's home phone number next to Harry's printed one.

"We're padlocking the house. Please inform the current owner. If she wants information on when we can release it, have her call me." Barber handed his card to Harry. "Call me if any of you think of anything else, especially you, son," he said, turning to Jack. He handed out more cards. "Go out the front. I'm sure my tech has the back door locked."

"I'll get my things from the kitchen. Hand me your glass, Jack. Might as well clear up." Josephine took Jack's glass and her own and followed me into the kitchen. I sensed she wanted to talk to me. I crumbled up the fast food sacks and tossed them into the garbage. Josephine set the glasses in the sink.

"Grace, when we were waiting for Harry and Walter to come upstairs, I got the distinct feeling of being watched. Not by you, not by anyone inside." She looked me straight in the eyes. "Was there someone else?"

I knew my eyes flashed purple as I lowered them to the task I'd set for myself. I ran a wet dishrag over the table. How much could I tell her? Suddenly the temperature in the room dropped. The dark face stared in at us. He shifted his gaze to Josephine. I raised my hand and pointed to the window in the back door. "Him. He was watching you, is watching you now."

I lowered my arm and rubbed my hands together. I didn't expect her to see anything. I was wrong.

THIRTY-ONE

HER SCREAM BROUGHT everyone running. Harry burst into the room with Barber a close second. Josephine held one hand clapped to her mouth and pointed to the door with the other.

I turned to Harry who had rushed to my side. "I saw that man again. She saw him too." My heart lifted with this realization. No one else had ever seen the people I'd seen. Now, someone had. He must be real.

Barber couldn't yank open the door because of the padlock. He quickly radioed the cop outside. "While he's checking, tell me what you saw."

Josephine squared her shoulders. "He was a black man, thin, shaved head, young, maybe early twenties."

Shaved head, young? What was she saying? Why was she lying?

I stared at her, about ready to ask her, when Barber's radio crackled. He moved toward the living room. "Good job, bring him in."

We trailed in behind him. Walter opened the front door to the police officer and a young black man. My mouth sagged. He fit Josephine's description to a tee, except anyone could see he wasn't in his early twenties.

If she saw him, why did I see the other?

Because you're still the only one who sees them.

I crossed my arms over my chest, the fleeting joy I'd felt disappearing and leaving me sad.

"Jeffrey, I told you to stay in the car." Jack said. "You promised you'd stay in the car."

Jeffrey shrugged and took and interest in the toes of his sneakers.

"Is he your brother?" Everyone looked at me. "Younger brother?" They behaved like Benny and Matt.

Jack nodded and moved next to Jeffrey. "He didn't do anything. He wasn't supposed to get out of the car."

Josephine looked at the two of them. "His shaved head makes him seem older, but now that I see him up close I see my mistake. How old are you, son?"

Jeffrey's voice shook when he answered, "Sixteen."

Jack put his arm around his brother's shoulders. "It's okay. You didn't do anything."

Josephine stared at the boy. I couldn't read her expression. It seemed out of place for the circumstances.

Barber cleared his throat. "It would seem we're back to vacating the building and padlocking the door. Again, please take your belongings with you." He moved to the door and extended his arm like an usher waiting for us to follow.

I had grabbed my shoulder bag when we left the kitchen. I felt in the side pocket for the papers Karen had given me. I had no need or desire to return to that room. Gertrude was making a sweep of the kitchen; she'd handle the dish-rag, wherever I'd left it.

Josephine leaned down next to the chair she'd occupied and lifted her bag to her shoulder. It bulged where I hadn't remembered a bulge, but then I hadn't scrutinized her beach-bag size tote.

Harry nudged me toward the door. "We'll drive the pro-fessor"—Harry lingered on the title—"home. Walter can see to the Gertrude. The Johnson boys are free to go. The police will be in touch with their father, a fate neither son is eager to experience. From what I overhead, their dad is a no-nonsense fellow. Probably won't approve of what his eldest has been up to."

Josephine had exchanged phone numbers with Jack. I figured she had every intention of meeting with her old friend. I briefly wondered if Karen and I would still be in touch in forty years. Sheesh! Forty years would put us in our seventies. I considered Josephine with a new appreciation. *Tough old broad* is what my Uncle Jimmy would say. He sure knew how to turn a phrase. I pursed my lips, blocking a grin from forming.

The ride to Eola was long and quiet. Josephine broke the silence. "I want to apologize for not being forthcoming when we first met. The persona of Juliana's old eccentric aunt from Missouri serves me well. People have a tendency to talk around me and over me. It's necessary in my work that people feel unfettered in my presence."

I thought "unfettered" an odd word to use.

"What exactly is your 'work', Professor?"

"Please call me Josephine, Harry. Each time you use the title it sounds accusatory, all things considered."

I saw Harry's lips curve. "All right, Josephine." His smooth as silk voice worked its charm.

Josephine leaned forward as much as her seatbelt allowed. "My work takes me to all areas of the country tracking down oral traditions about slavery, but most specifically stories about the Underground Railroad. When I can verify that a home, barn, church, or any structure was a station, I try to find and secure artifacts from that area. I have a grant to create a catalog of African American artifacts from that time period. I don't have the Native American Graves and Repatriation Act to help me protect what I find. On the one hand, if no one is alive to claim it, I don't have any problems keeping what I find.

On the other hand, if no one can accurately identify the article, I have no provenance. We've uncovered journals, diaries, ticket stubs, newspapers of the times with articles on slave catchers—"

"You took the quilt. That's the bulge." I turned in my seat and pointed at the bag on the seat.

"Is that true?" Harry asked. "You stole the quilt from Gertrude?"

"It wasn't hers."

"It was more hers than yours," I challenged.

Josephine sighed and leaned back. "Like I said, I don't have the NAGRA to help me protect what I find. Gertrude doesn't own it and certainly couldn't account for its origins." She folded her arms across her chest.

I sat back in my seat and stared out the window. Thoughts clamored for my attention. Should I challenge Josephine in front of her niece? Would that make a difference on whether she kept the quilt? Did I really care if she kept it? Her passion for finding the truth about the quilt impressed me even if her methods didn't.

We pulled up to the house. I'd made my decision. I didn't know Harry's feelings. He opened the doors at once and let Josephine lead the way. I noticed a dark sedan in the driveway and tried to remember if that was Juliana's car. Josephine glanced at the vehicle and straightened her shoulders.

The door opened. George Shaw and Juliana Dodd waited on the porch, eyes gleaming and lips curved in big smiles. George's arm draped over her shoulders.

"Hello, Aunt. I'd wondered where you'd gone," George said.

"Aunt," I sputtered. "Aunt?"

Josephine handed her tote to Juliana and stepped into a hug from FBI agent George Shaw.

"It's good to see you, boy."

"I wouldn't have thought you felt that way scrunched down hiding in that car." His slowly spoken words had their effect. Josephine looked chastised. She kissed him on the cheek before glancing at her niece.

"I didn't want him to blow my cover," she said in her defense.

We burst into laughter at the picture of this seventy-something, beach bag toting woman in orthopedic shoes having her undercover persona "burned".

"Child, I would expect your brother to keep folks standing on the porch, but your mama raised you better."

Juliana smiled. "I know you're stalling for time, but you're also right. Excuse me for not asking you in. Please come in."

Harry smiled and shook his head. "You go ahead and enjoy what you're about to hear. We've a young man to see about."

Harry wasn't going to bring up the quilt. Fine with me. Josephine smiled at us. "Thank you for an interesting day. Thank you for everything."

"Think she'll tell them about 'everything'?" I asked once we were in the car.

"I don't think so. She rather likes to talk in layers. It's not in her nature to give you the whole story at one sitting."

"That's probably how she gathers the stories on the Underground Railroad. One person tells her something, then remembers more. Or maybe another family member reminds them of an event."

"Perhaps they check the family Bible," added Harry. "My family was never big on recording anything in our Bible.

I sat up straighter and put my hand on Harry's arm.

"What is it?"

"I'm sure Josephine said she saw a crate in the cellar filled with books, one of them a Bible, and some papers. The Klops wouldn't have kept someone else's Bible."

"Maybe it belonged to whoever sold the house to the Klops. But that's still in this century."

"What if that person moved the stuff belonging to the previous owner into the cellar? Maybe he thought some relative would pick it up. Maybe it got forgotten in the cellar. Maybe—"

"Maybe we'll continue this conversation later. Appears we have company," Harry said as he pulled into the driveway.

My brother's car was parked in the drive.

THIRTY-TWO

MARTY AND WILL spent the night "camping" in the backyard. Marty had decided to bring Will home to camp out. I hoped the great outdoors would keep those early risers in their bags past 7:00 a.m.

I slipped out from under the covers before dawn. My favorite place to wait for sunrise was either atop April in the meadow or sitting on the window seat settled in with a mug of coffee and my journal.

Within minutes I had my steaming coffee and favorite journal with me behind the heavy curtains that blocked the morning sun. My own little world. I sat sideways leaning against the curve of the wall, my legs tucked up to my chest. I rested my chin on my knees. I could sit like this for hours, thinking, planning, dreaming. I knew I didn't have hours; I had maybe one before the others woke.

I'd become involved in things I didn't understand. I didn't know why I felt and saw the spirits of crimes committed decades earlier. I did understand that each time I felt a presence, someone living had tried to stop me from learning their identity.

No threats had been made against me or anyone else so far. Was this death too old that no one involved still lived? What about the lady and the man with the gun?

Are you looking for someone to come after you?

Of course not. Don't be silly.

Then what's the problem?

Three people dead in one cellar!

Not your problem—let it go.

I sipped the hot coffee and stretched out my legs. Would *he* let me ignore him, the house, and the quilt? He wanted something to happen.

I thought back to the instances when I'd seen him. Each time he'd looked intolerably sad. Yet, at the house yesterday, he'd glared angrily at the quilt and Josephine. Could she be in danger? I didn't believe that a spirit could act in the real world. Their appearance could shock someone into heart failure or cause them to lose control of their car. Why would he be angry with her? She wanted to find the truth and record it. Maybe she wasn't recording the right truth.

The idea took hold of me and I had to follow up. While I'd pondered the message from the Waysayer, the sun had risen and flooded the alcove with light. Though it was too early to call Josephine, I could take care of the horses, then start breakfast.

I carried my mug to the kitchen and poured coffee into a travel mug. If Marty were stirring, I'd offer him coffee; if he snored on, I'd enjoy it in the barn.

April's soft whinny reached out to me. She was easy to hear because the barn door was open. Marty stood in front of Cash rubbing his nose and saying silly things that people say when talking to animals. He turned when April whinnied.

"Hey, sis. Good morning. Hope you don't mind. I don't think I woke them."

Marty looked like a kid, rumpled shirt, hair sticking up on his sleep side, and laces untied on his sneakers. He was my favorite brother, a fact I hope I successfully hid from the other three.

"Mart, it's not like they're babies you have to worry about waking."

"Yeah, that was a stupid thing to say."

I offered him the travel mug.

"Thanks, I can use this." He sipped at the coffee. "Mocha Madness?" he asked.

I shook my head. "Meadows Magic, highly caffeinated and guaranteed to kick-start your day. What's happening in Berkeley now that you're back in town?" I opened a fresh bag of horse chow and scooped out several portions for Cash. "Back up, piggy, or you won't get any," I admonished Cash as he tried to eat the nuggets from the scoop.

Marty hadn't answered. I stepped up to April's stall and gave her two portions. Ever the lady, she waited until I'd removed the scoop from her tray.

"Hand me the water can, will you?" There was no answer and I turned around. "Marty?" My brother sat on a hay brick staring into space. "Oh, sorry. Uh, what did you say?"

"Never mind, I got it. What's wrong? Where did you go?" I mixed a few drops of vitamins in the water container, sloshed it around a little, then poured equal amounts in each water pan.

"Sorry." He stood and stepped toward me. "I'm not sure what's happening between me and Eve. I want to move back home, but I think Eve is going to file for a divorce. It's been six months since she asked me to move out. She seemed different towards me when I got home from Canada. She heard what happened and I guess she thought about how she'd have felt if I'd been killed. After a while she pulled away again. I can't keep putting myself in danger just to get her affection, can I?"

Knowing my youngest brother, I sincerely prayed that was a rhetorical question.

I slipped an arm around his shoulders, no easy task from my shorter height. He rested his head atop mine and spoke into my hair. "Everyone seems to be settling down. Karen and Hannah have the kids, Dad and Jan are talking marriage, and even Ric is getting hitched from what I hear."

My arm tightened around him. I stayed quiet and he continued.

"I know Glenn's divorced and he's gone on with his life. I guess I will, too. Dad and Jan have been tiptoeing around their plans, trying not to 'rub it in'. I feel like I'm a drag on their happiness."

I removed my arm from his shoulders and punched him high on his arm.

"Oww. What'd you do that for?"

"For being a dope. Dad loves you. Don't talk like that."

He continued to rub his arm.

"Baby. Come inside and help me make breakfast."

He grinned at me. "No can do." He checked his watch. "I'm waking Will in five minutes and we're making breakfast for you and Harry. Pancakes, sausage patties, eggs, and juice. You were elected to make the coffee. We'll let you know when breakfast is ready."

We walked out of the barn arm in arm. "We can eat outdoors. I'll set the patio table for four."

Elmo sniffed at the tent flap. A corner unzipped and the orange fluff dashed in.

Marty and I laughed. "Guess he's up."

"I'll check on Harry."

Seven o'clock. Still not a decent time to call strangers. I dialed my dad.

"Hello."

"Hi, dad. It's me. Thanks for watching Will last night. I'm sorry we ran late, but the most bizarre things happened. I'd love to fill you in later. Plus, I know you've been trying to talk to me about your plans. I want to be a part of whatever you've got going."

"You always were, wweetie. Stop by this afternoon.

I'm making a strudel and I need some tasters. Next family event, when Edna shows up with her pizzelles and Baba's, I'm bringing my strudel."

I wondered about my dad's competition with my Aunt Edna's baked goods. He already made the best gravy in the family. He'd set his sights on the bakery title. This would be tough. Edna's bakery ranked the best I'd ever had anywhere.

"Okay, we'll stop over later. Then we can talk, too."

"Sure, honey. See you later."

Seven-fifteen; still too early. I fiddled with making more coffee, tidied the clutter on the counter top, pulled out plates and silverware and napkins for breakfast.

Marty called from the mudroom. "Grace, my shoes are dirty. Can you bring me the bag in the refrigerator?"

I carried the Guido's Grocery bag to the mudroom. "Glad to see you shop local." Guido's was the little grocery store that our Nonna had walked to every day. She'd bring her string shopping bag and buy only what she was preparing for that day. "Where's your string bag?"

"I'm not enough of a dork?"

"You'd probably start a trend. Oh, I talked to Dad. We're all invited this afternoon to be guinea pigs for his first strudel."

"Great. Dad's mistakes are better than most people's best. Don't let me forget to send you a copy of a picture I took of Will and Elmo. The cat was inside Will's bag up at his head tucked under Will's chin. They were asleep. The *click* woke up Elmo. Blackmail photo for sure when Will starts dating."

I remembered all the dorky, cute, embarrassing photos my dad had on each of us.

I thought about how quickly twelve-year-olds become eighteen and realized Harry's time with Will as a kid was limited. Harry stood at the sink filling the electric kettle with water. Coffee had never been his drink.

"I was about to do that when Marty came in for the breakfast food he and Will are preparing for us."

Harry's eyebrows lifted.

"Don't worry. Marty's an Eagle. He knows how to cook and he'll make sure Will does everything safely."

I grinned and lifted up on my tiptoes to kiss his cheek. "Anyway, I peeked at the food and the sausage patties are pre-cooked. No danger there."

Harry carried his tea to the nook. I sat next to him. We watched the birds feasting on the hulled sunflower seeds. Harry slipped his arm around me and kissed my temple. "Didn't say a *proper* good morning."

His euphemism made me smile. There hadn't been a lot of "proper good mornings" since Will moved in with us. We needed to set up some courtesy rules, like knock and wait for an answer before you come in, or don't even think about knocking until after 7:30. I turned my face and kissed Harry full on the lips.

"Don't make plans for later," he murmured when I pulled back.

"Too late. I told my dad we'd be his taste testers this afternoon for his first strudel. Sorry."

Harry smiled. "I'm certain we will find a way. After all, your parents had five children. They must have figured it out."

"What caused the children?" I deadpanned.

Harry burst into laughter. "I love you, Gracie Elena Morelli Marsden." He held my chin and kissed me again.

Harry's lips froze on mine and I guessed why. We casually pulled apart. Will stood in the doorway. He'd come in to announce breakfast. He kept staring at us like we'd done something awful, his eyes starting to moisten. He must have heard Harry's proclamation of love. That had to hurt the young boy who wanted nothing more than for his dad and mom to get married. He couldn't be feeling cheery. I know my stomach tightened with anxiety.

Harry's greeting wasn't what I expected. He caught Will off guard too. "Good morning. I hear you and your uncle are preparing breakfast. I know Marty prefers coffee. What's your choice, coffee or tea? I've the kettle on and Grace has some sort of odd name bean on tap."

Offering Will his choice of adult beverages rather than a justification of what he heard and saw was genius. Will puffed up, pleased to join the adult world even at this minor level.

"My odd bean for the day is Meadows Magic, loads of caffeine to jump start your day," I said.

"My tea is a capricious blend of orange spice and mango." Harry grinned. "The way I see it, you can be caffeinated or capricious."

Will looked from one cup to the other, then from me to his dad. I could tell he didn't want it to be about choosing one of us.

I offered an alternative. "Or you could start out with juice to clean out the camp morning mouth and switch over later."

He immediately ran his tongue over his teeth. "Yeah, I think the juice sounds good. For starters," he added.

He accepted his beverage and told us to hurry out before Uncle Marty burned the sausages. We quickly followed him to the patio where one of them had set the table and filled a chipped camp coffeepot with wild daisies gathered from the area adjacent to the corral.

Will cleared his throat. "Please cross your arms in reverence and say the Philmont Grace. *For food, for raiment,*

*for life, for opportunity, for friendship and fellowship, we
thank Thee, O Lord.*"

My eyes watered while I repeated the words I'd said
many times on campouts with my brothers. The words
that had bonded boys and men for the hundreds of hours
they spent in scouting and for a lifetime.

Harry had recently learned the words and I heard him
flawlessly repeat them.

"Amen," we pronounced together.

"Let's eat," Marty urged.

I CAUGHT THE phone on the fourth ring.

"Mrs. Marsden, are you all right?"

I drew in a breath to stop the panting. Sheesh! I was out
of shape. "I'm fine. Just ran for the phone." I recognized
Josephine Hossack's voice.

"I hope this is not too early to call, but I wanted to talk
to you, right away."

"Not too early. I wanted to talk to you, too. Since 6:30
this morning."

"Seems we're early risers. Would it be inconvenient for
you to drive out to Juliana's home this morning around
ten o'clock?"

I had no plans. I figured Harry would spend the day
with Will.

"I have invited my old friend Clarisse and her nephew
to join us," Josephine continued.

That would be Jack's father. The one who told all the
stories that prompted his son to investigate the cellar.

"Grace," she said, dropping her voice. "I also wanted
to tell you that I did see him at the window. Please come."

THIRTY-THREE

She hung up quickly. It took me a moment to grasp what she'd said, what that meant to me. Someone else living had seen him. Please come? Wild horses couldn't keep me from showing up.

I dashed back to the patio in time to rescue my dishes from the grey bins of soapy water and rinse water my brother had set up to show Will how he used to wash up.

"Marty, you can do the silverware, but I'll handle the dishes and mugs." Harry grabbed up the coffee mugs. "I'll be right back to set up the axe yard," he said before following me inside.

"You're setting up the axe yard?"

"Will needs to practice with a short handled axe and hatchet. Too bad council has banned long handled axes from the program. Those were fun to bring crashing down on unsuspecting logs."

Harry sounded positively giddy at the prospect. I wondered if Will would get any time in the roped off enclosure with his two mentors around.

I explained the phone call and Harry smiled.

"There was a time I'd have joined you, but being with Will is such a hoot. I love watching him, listening to his prattle about imagined injustices on the playground of his life. It is…" Harry hesitated.

"Awesome," I supplied.

He nodded his head. "Absolutely."

I reached up and kissed him. "Go, enjoy him. That's what dads do. I'll take copious notes."

I hurried through a shower and was dressed in minutes flat. I brushed my heavy hair straight back and tucked the sides behind my ears. Before any strands could escape, I pushed a black headband into place. Out of sight, out of mind, and out of reach. If I didn't see a thick strand hanging over my eye I wouldn't be tempted to twirl and tug, twirl and tug, until strands loosened.

I detoured into the yard. "Bye, guys. I'll be back in time to go to Dad's."

The roped-off area designated the only place the sharp tools could be used. Marty swung the axe against helpless logs while Harry waited, hatchet in hand, for his turn to further decimate the log. Will watched from the patio table. He whittled at small pieces of split logs to build a pile of kindling and tinder for the bonfire they'd planned for tonight.

"You be sure to rotate with Will or I'll tell Dad."

Will grinned and waved goodbye. Harry and Marty kept their heads down hiding the smiles I'm sure were there.

JOSEPHINE SAT ON the porch with two other people.

"Thank you for coming. Grace, this is my oldest friend, Clarisse Watkins, and this is her nephew Jackson Johnson. This is Grace Marsden, the lady who is helping me discover the truth about that old house."

I was surprised at the introduction but didn't contradict her. We shook hands and said our pleasantries.

"How is your son feeling, Mr. Johnson? I know he had a headache."

"If he were a mite younger, he'd a had more than a headache." Jackson's lips twisted in a sour expression. "He had no business in that there cellar."

Josephine interrupted what I suspected had been discussed before I arrived. "Can I get you some tea or lemonade? My niece is not a coffee drinker and I make do with whatever is available."

"Water is fine. I've had too much coffee already."

One could never have too much coffee, but my answer seemed to suit Josephine's hostess mode. She returned with a glass and a small pitcher of water. I filled my glass to be polite but didn't drink. Although I wanted to talk about whoever it was we saw, I didn't dare bring it up with the others around. I wondered how long they'd been there and how soon they'd leave.

"We're waiting for my nephew, George, and someone from the Oak Park police department's cold case unit."

"A cold case unit is investigating the death of the *Waysayer*?" I had taken to using the title to proffer some dignity. It was difficult to call him "slave", a foreign concept to my late-20th-century upbringing.

"No, not him; seems that death is too cold." Josephine's thinly disguised disdain brought nods of agreement from her companions. "They're coming to talk to Jackson."

Jackson fidgeted with the edge of his napkin. He folded it forward toward the glass, creating a triangle. He did this on all the corners. Watching him fiddle made my fingers itch to do something similar—create a pattern to repeat and repeat. As a kid, I loved the "Pete and Re-Pete" riddle. I loved repetition, I loved pattern, I loved symmetry. *Appears as it appears*. In that instant I knew why the *Waysayer* had been angered when the quilt rested on the porch.

"Appears as it appears!" I said excitedly. "It's not the Judas Quilt. It's Judas himself!"

THIRTY-FOUR

CLARISSE AND JACKSON appeared rightfully confused by my disjointed outburst. Josephine stared at me, a dawning expression filling her eyes. "I'd hoped I'd finally found it. My initial research indicated it could have been in this area. Further readings of journals and newspapers made me think that maybe I was wrong. I started to suspect what you somehow just confirmed for me."

She turned to Clarisse. "The person who owned that home in the 1850s wasn't a conductor on the Underground Railroad, he was a slave catcher."

Clarisse's shocked expression matched her nephew's. To be tricked so cruelly sometimes just yards from freedom tore at anyone's sense of fairness. She asked me, "How do you know? You seem sure."

I wasn't about to share, and a quick glance at Josephine assured me she was staying silent, too.

"I have a photographic memory," I said slowly. "It's not perfect, but my recall is good. My mind likes to study patterns. It automatically tries to put things in their place even when I'm not thinking about it. Then something triggers the memories"—I pointed toward the perfectly folded napkin—"and my mind points out the pattern, or what doesn't fit."

"That's amazing," she whispered.

"I can't make it happen, it just does." I sipped from my glass to buy time. I sensed more questions. Josephine filled in while I continued sipping.

"I did it the hard way," she said, smiling, "by tracking down newspaper accounts, church records, and bible entries."

"Bible," I interrupted. "You said you saw a bible in a crate with other books when you were in the basement with Clarisse." I looked for confirmation.

"What kind of stories have you been telling this child?" Clarisse aimed a frown at the grey-haired woman sitting next to her.

"Now don't fret," said Josephine with a wave of her hand. "I said nothing that wasn't the truth."

Clarisse smiled and shook her head. "Like you'd know the truth if it bit your behind. Filling your head with all them stories from all those folk whose brains been addled with fear and age." She nodded toward Jackson. "See here what storytelling done to his family."

Josephine patted her friend's hand. "Clarisse and I have never come to terms with my avocation. She thinks I should be teaching normal subjects."

"Hmmph. That is all I'm saying on the subject." Clarisse folded her arms across her chest. She tried to look cross, but her eyes gave her away. She couldn't hide her love for her nephew and her best friend.

"I remembered the Bible," Josephine continued. "When I visited the house that afternoon I sneaked down and found it. That's all I took. I suspected the Bible would belong to the original owner, Joseph Pholfer. It was in my bag the entire afternoon. My heart did beat a little faster when that detective showed up. Of course, the fact that he's an older version of Denzel could have contributed to my palpitations."

We laughed at her disarming explanation. "I just thought of the Bible. You were way ahead of me."

"Remember, I am trained and committed to searching

out information. And I'd seen it before even though I had no interest in it then."

"Hmmph, trained and committed. You are just a natural snoop. Always was, always will be." Clarisse unfolded her long arms and patted Josephine's hand.

George and a plain-clothes detective arrived during the current reign of laughter.

"Is there something funny about all this that wasn't in the report?" George's smooth voice teased. He moved quickly to Josephine's side and pecked her cheek with the obligatory gesture.

"Detective Robson, these two ladies I know—Josephine Hossack and Grace Marsden. My aunt will have to complete the introductions."

Josephine did just that while George carried two more chairs to the table. Robson declined any refreshment and removed a small notebook from his pocket. The detective looked directly at Jackson.

"Thank you for coming forward. Oak Park hired me because of my experience with cold case investigations. Our cold case division is new. Any help we can get from the public is appreciated."

Jackson Johnson cleared his throat. "Before I begin, I want you to know that I had no thought about what I'm to tell you these past fifty years. I'd pushed it out of my head what with growing up and takin' on an adult's life. I could kick myself that the stories I told about pirate's treasure and secret tunnels has come back to hurt my boy."

"Mr. Johnson, I want you to understand that your son is not in trouble," Robson said reassuringly. "I'm here to find out if you remember anything you saw when you were a boy that might identify the victim or send us in the right direction. I understand from my Captain that you called us after your son told you what happened. Our concern is for the person carrying the gun and the woman with him."

"You should be; she killed her sister."

THIRTY-FIVE

DETECTIVE ROBSON PRESSED his pen through the top sheet. "You know who the woman is? You saw the murder committed? Mr. Johnson, this interview has jumped the tracks. If you've been concealing a murder…"

"Relax, detective." George Shaw put a restraining hand on Robson's arm. "We don't need to get formal. I'm a law enforcement officer and can attest to the fact that you followed procedure here. If at any time you make the call that continued questioning of Mr. Johnson could taint a future prosecution, you can stop and advise him of his rights."

He held up his hands to ward off the jumble of protests sparking around the table. "I said 'if'. Now let the man, let the detective, do his job. Mr. Johnson, if at any time you feel beleaguered or intimidated, you can choose to stop the interview." He waited for Jackson's nod. "Good. I'd like to hear your story."

Jackson sipped his lemonade. I thought he might be hoping for something stronger as he cleared his throat nervously.

"I loved to visit my Aunt Clarisse. She lived in a big old fancy house. My momma would bring me with her when she visited her sister. First off, my momma would keep me close by so I couldn't touch anything. After a bit they'd get to talking and laughing and they'd forget about me settin' there all quiet. I'd take off to the cellar quick as I could 'cause that's where the pirate's treasure was buried." His eyes lit up with an excitement from a lifetime ago and years slipped from his face. "I'd spend hours pretending I was a pirate searching for the treasure. I opened up boxes and cabinets and that's how one time I found the tunnel."

He extended his glass to George who silently refilled it. Jackson peered at the lemonade, then swallowed half of it in one quick gulp before continuing.

"I had opened the bottom doors on a cabinet set against the wall and pulled out a small crate full of books. That weren't treasure, but I kept lookin'. When I crawled into the cabinet to search the corners, I felt a push of air against my face. Then I saw a hole in the wood. I pulled at the broken slat and it came off in my hand. There before me was the tunnel.

"I pulled out a few more slats to make an entrance and went exploring. I made sure to put the crate back inside the cabinet when I crawled out. Each time I came to the house I'd bring something to help me search the tunnel. I'd bring a flashlight, some old stuffing to set on, even a shovel with a cracked off handle that someone tossed in the alley.

"One time I carried in an old box from the Sears and Roebuck store. I told my momma that I'd brought my army men to play quiet. I always wondered why momma never thought how big that box was when she knew my army men fitted in a shoebox. I expect she was lookin' forward to her visit and paid me no mind. I was goin' to find the treasure map and dig up the gold.

"On the evenin' you're wanting to hear about, my momma and me were goin' to spend the weekend with Clarisse. Her folks went away and she'd asked ifin' her sister and boy could stay with her 'cause she ain't never stayed alone before.

"I was excited to have that old cellar to myself. I felt sure I could find that treasure ifin' I had time and no

interference from my momma. They took me to the pictures on Saturday, then out for ice cream. I think you went
with us." He nodded toward Josephine.

"Not on Saturday. That wasn't my day off."

I marveled at how Josephine had changed her life from
a spunky housemaid to a spunky college professor. Must
be the spunky part that connected the dots for her. She
was surely living the American dream.

Jackson shrugged his shoulders and continued. "Any-
wise, that night Aunt and momma wanted to step out and
visit with you."

Josephine nodded and smiled.

"They was gonna' be next door and they thought I was
asleep. I'd snuck my flashlight upstairs, and once they left
I scooted down them stairs and began rootin' through that
crate I'd found. I thought the map would be with all them
old books and papers.

"'Bout an hour later I heard low voices up at the top of
the stairs. I knew it weren't momma. I thought maybe the
owners had come home early. I didn't want to cause no
trouble. I backed into the cabinet and a little ways into the
tunnel. The light came on before I could close the doors
all the way. I stayed real still.

"I'd seen them ladies before visiting the young man who
lived there. Momma said they was society ladies and that
young Mr. Klops had no more business stepping out with
them than the man in the moon." He smiled at the joke
he'd shared with his mother.

"I didn't have to worry 'bout them seeing me. They
was talking and crying and sad; I almost cried with them.
They kept their voices hushed talkin' soft to each other.
Then Miz Dolly she says to her sister, 'It's time. Be strong
for me.' The other girl, her heart's breakin' with her sobs,
but then they do the strangest thing. Miz Dolly takes out

an oilcloth tablecloth covered with little purple flowers. I remembered thinking if they left it behind I might take it up for my momma."

Jackson's next words came in a near whisper.

"They done left it behind, but she was in it."

THIRTY-SIX

WE'D ALL LEANED forward in our chairs when Jackson lowered his voice. Now Josephine and Clarisse reached for each other's hands and Detective Robson looked quickly at George Shaw.

I rubbed at the goose bumps on my arms. Jackson and the others kept calling these women Trixie and Dolly. Did anyone know their real names? Were Karen and I the only two people who knew who they were?

"Lordy, I ain't allowed myself to think about that night, made myself think maybe I dreamed it. It was late at night. I was suppose to be asleep." Jackson rubbed his hands over his face.

"Mr. Johnson, exactly what did you see?"

Robson's words were rushed. I sensed something else in his voice—excitement. I understood enough about police work to know they always kept something, some bit of information, out of the newspaper. Could it be they'd neglected to tell the reporters about the remnants of oil-cloth decorated with tiny purple flowers?

Jackson sighed and bowed his head. His words dropped slowly and without feeling. "I saw Miz Trixie close up Miz Dolly in that cupboard."

"Just like that, one sister forces the other into a hole in the wall, and there's no struggle? It's been fifty years and you said yourself you were supposed to be asleep. Maybe you did dream this."

Jackson's head snapped up when he heard George's skeptical tone. He stared at the agent.

"You don't know how many times I hoped it was a dream." He shook his head slowly. "Weren't no dream, Detective. Weren't no struggle either. Miz Dolly drank something from a real pretty silver flask she took from her purse. She got sleepy after that, real sleepy, so much that my eyes was closing watching her.

"She gave her purse to Miz Trixie who was sobbing and looking like she wanted to bolt right out of there. Miz Dolly kept saying, 'Be strong for me, I need you' and things like that, giving her sister comfort. After a bit, Miz Dolly climbs into the cupboard.

"I can't see her no more, but I can hear her settlin' and rustlin' that oilskin around her. Then Miz Trixie gets up close and they talk a mite but I can't make out nothin' 'cept when Miz Trixie cries out, 'It's not better for me'. Then they is quiet again.

"Pretty soon I don't hear any more rustlin', only Miz Trixie crying soft. I watch her slide a piece of the wall till you can't see the cupboard no more. Then I hear her make a funny noise in her throat. I saw her bend down and pick up a sparkly pin about this size." He held his thumb and forefinger two inches apart.

"I thought for a minute it coulda' come from pirate treasure. She stared at the pin for a bit, then she looked over at the wall. She kinda' stepped toward it, then she turned back around, jammed that pin in her purse, and ran up the stairs. I didn't hear the door open. She musta' stopped near the top. Maybe my momma and aunt were home. I think now she couldn't make herself leave."

Jackson threw his head back, drew a deep breath, and blew it out slowly. The action seemed to settle him and he went on with his story.

"My heart thumped hard and I thought it'd come out my chest. I was scared to walk past that wall and scared to go up the stairs. I lay real still waiting to hear her leave. I musta' fallen asleep 'cause the next thing I hear is momma and Aunt Clarisse callin' my name all scared like.

"I called up to them and they came rushin' down them steps like the soldiers in them Indian movies. I wasn't goin' to walk past that wall alone. They hauled me up the steps threatening all kinds of things." He stopped and smiled at Clarisse. "You and momma never knew I was happy to see you I didn't care what you did to me."

"You never told anyone what happened?" asked George.

"No, sir, I did not."

"Why?" Robson sounded incredulous.

Jackson shrugged. "I was a twelve-year-old colored boy spending the night in a white man's house where my aunt worked. I didn't want to cause her trouble. I didn't want to get in trouble. When I heard they was puttin' in a floor over the cellar, I got scared that somebody found out. But nothin' happened. Mostly, I thought if I kept it to myself, I could pretend it never happened. Worked pretty good all these years till that newspaper story came out and my boy done what he did."

He straightened his shoulders. "Feels good to tell somebody. Shoulda' done it years back, but things was different then. Colored boy tellin' the police he knew where a white woman was buried? No way they'd believe me."

No one argued his point.

Jackson peered into Robson's eyes. "Do I need to come to the station with you?"

"Yes, sir. You'll have to explain more to the unit and sign your statement after it's been approved by you. I hope you can do this as soon as possible." The detective swung his gaze towards Clarisse and Josephine. "Who were these sisters? We haven't been able to identify the remains." He poised his pen over a new page.

The two long-ago friends stared at each other, disappointment filling their faces. Josephine broke the silence.

"We never knew their real names. We called them Trixie and Dolly. It's not like the family would have introduced them to us. Gertrude might remember, though. They used to visit her brother."

Clarisse nodded. "They was always getting Mister Kurt in trouble with his papa."

"How so?" Robson asked.

Clarisse grinned. "People talked in front of servants like we wasn't there. Mr. Klops, he never held with spending money on silly things. He weren't a drinking man neither. I'd hear them two arguing about Mister Kurt's new clothes or the clubs he'd go to with them two 'floozies', he'd call them. Mr. Klops could not abide being in the same room with them girls and he'd stomp out when they arrived all smilin' and simperin' at Mister Kurt. I don't think the girls meant any harm. They was raised different and they was American girls."

Robson returned his notebook and pen to his pocket. "I really thought I'd solve this case quickly with an eye witness report."

I struggled with my conscience. Would I get Hannah and her contact in incredible trouble for having those crime photos? If this were a murder investigation I'd be in trouble for not telling what I knew. It didn't sound like a murder. I decided to wait.

"Excuse me, Detective Robson," I said. "Do they know the cause of death for any of the, um, people?"

He shook his head. "Not yet. Current homicides take precedent over three cold cases. Until we found the man's body, we were working with two victims that died eighty years apart. Negates the idea of a serial killer. We have to wait for the State lab and they are backlogged."

"Maybe the FBI could help out." Josephine smiled at her nephew. "We know the black man in the cupboard wasn't a local resident. He came across state lines. Doesn't that mean it could be your jurisdiction?"

"Aunt Jo, you watch too much television." George folded his arms across his chest and leaned back in his chair. "I can't request three autopsies to satisfy your curiosity."

"Not three, just the one, the first one they found." Josephine stared sternly at her nephew. "It could have been a hate crime. Someone could have hidden him in there, but then left him to die."

No one spoke. I knew Josephine didn't really believe what she said. She knew how profitable returning a slave for the reward could be. If he'd been left to die, it hadn't been planned.

George slowly unfolded himself from the chair. "No promises," he said before bending over to whisper in Josephine's ear, "I'll see what I can do."

Robson stood also. He handed Jackson his card. "Please call me within a day or two to set up an appointment." He motioned towards Josephine and Clarisse. "I'd like the three of you to sit down with a sketch artist. Maybe we can identify this woman by how she looked fifty years ago if Ms. Klops can't give me a name." He turned to leave, then hesitated, shifting from foot to foot before saying, "Is Juliana expected home soon?"

Josephine eyed him. "Do you know my niece?"

Robson grinned. "I'd like to get to know her better. We met last time George was in town."

"I'll tell her you asked after her." Josephine's frigid tone effectively ended the conversation.

George headed down the porch steps as George detoured

to his aunt's side. He kissed her cheek and gave her shoulders a light squeeze. "Stay out of trouble."

She grinned. "I hoped you wouldn't forget to give me my sugar, all grown up and important now."

George's sheepish grin showed how much he cared for his aunt. He caught up to Robson and didn't look back.

I still wanted to talk to Josephine, but her company wasn't leaving and I had to straighten out a few things. I thanked her for including me and thanked Jackson for sharing his incredible story. I wanted to get to Gertrude before the police did, call Hannah before I said anything about the photos, and speak with Karen to confirm what we'd found.

I DIDN'T NOTICE the unmarked police car behind me until the light on the roof went on.

I hadn't been speeding. Daydreaming maybe, but not speeding. Maybe the speed limit was lower on this stretch of road and I hadn't notice. I slowed down and pulled over, putting the car in park.

Great! A speeding ticket. What else?

THIRTY-SEVEN

A TALL, THIN, dark-haired man emerged from the car and walked slowly toward me favoring his right leg as he moved over the uneven edge. His awkward gait caused his short jacket to gap. A gun grip stuck out from his waistband.

Every alarm in my head went off and the hair on my neck scraped against my collar. That was enough for me. I put the car in gear and pulled off the shoulder. I hadn't checked for traffic and by luck didn't collide with anyone. I did catch the look of surprise on his face, then anger. He turned and hobbled back to his car, but didn't rush to follow. Why not? Was he calling ahead for assistance? I sped around a slight bend and lost sight of him in my rear view mirror.

Traffic picked up and I felt comfortable mixing into the heavier flow. By the time I reached my dad's house in Berkeley I had convinced myself that I'd run from a traffic stop. I'd spill my guts to whoever was assembled and wait for a consensus on my course of action.

Cars crowded the street and driveway. My dad gathered quite a group when "food call" went out. The front door opened and Harry sauntered toward me stuffing the last bit of pastry in his mouth. He chewed and swallowed quickly.

"You missed the first cut, but there's more…" He stopped abruptly and frowned at me. "What's wrong? You're as pale as a sheet."

I threw myself against him and wrapped my arms

around his waist. "I took off after a policeman pulled me over." His arms tightened around me.

"You're shivering. Come inside, where we can talk." He walked me towards the door, then suddenly halted, apparently realizing the Morelli home filled with Morellis and friends wasn't conducive to quiet talk.

"There you are." My dad appeared in the doorway. "We started without you, but there's plenty…" His eyes narrowed as his gaze shifted from my face to Harry's. "What's wrong? Is someone hurt?"

I rushed to assure him. "No, dad. No one's hurt or sick or dead or anything like that. A policeman stopped me. When he got out and I saw his gun…I don't know; I got scared and I, um, pulled away."

"Honey, all policemen carry guns." Dad cocked his head to one side. "What spooked you?"

"He didn't have a squad car, only one of those lights on top. And he didn't have a uniform. When he walked toward me his jacket gaped and I saw the gun in his waistband…"

"Waistband!" both men shouted. I jumped at the tone of their voices.

"You did the right thing," Dad said. "No detective carries his gun in the waistband of his trousers."

Harry looked over his shoulder and glanced quickly up and down the block. "Let's go inside."

Hellos greeted me when I entered, but the discerning one in the bunch, Karen, spotted my distress. She handed me a plate with strudel. "I had to fight off three people for this. Sit over here and I'll run interference." Laughter greeted her quip and she guided me to a chair in the corner away from the strudel-laden table.

Karen pulled a cup of coffee from the table and placed it in front of me. "Eat first, talk later." After years of hanging with us she'd learned the *Morelli Mantra*. I smiled in spite of my fears.

I wasn't a bit hungry. I needed to ask her questions. I took a tiny bite and sipped at the lukewarm coffee.

Harry sat down beside me and asked quietly, "Where did he pull you over?"

I described the stretch of Rte. 30 where I'd been stopped as best I could. I wasn't sure.

"I'll make some calls and find out if by chance Eola or Aurora or Montgomery has an unmarked squad. Any chance you noticed the make of the car?"

I shook my head. "Sorry, just that it was dark gray."

Harry and my dad walked to the bedroom dad used as an office. They'd have some privacy there. Karen sat down across from me. Her short, curly, dark blonde hair bounced cheerily around her face as she settled into the high-back chair. She leaned forward resting her forearms on her thighs.

"What's going on?"

"In a minute. First, did you make copies of the pages we marked in those books?"

Her quizzical expression answered me.

"Oh, damn!" I said in exasperation. "Those were the papers you gave me. I didn't even look at them, just stuffed them in my bag. I've got to get home and check something."

Harry hadn't returned. I caught my brother's eye and he started towards me. I had to get home and check those photos.

"Karen, tell Harry and my dad I had to leave. Bye!"

I rushed past Marty with a quick, "Gotta' go. I'll call you. Thanks for watching Will."

I DROVE THE limit, but chaffed at every driver who waited an extra second when the light changed from red to green.

All the way home I kept changing my plan. If the photo of Mrs. Coe showed her wearing a necklace similar to the shoe clip in the evidence photo, could I hand over the copy and say my sister-in-law obtained crime-scene photos from a friend? How could I get the name of the sisters to the police without getting Hannah or myself in trouble?

I pressed the garage door opener and nosed into my parking space next to Harry's Jaguar. He'd driven in with Marty expecting that he and Will would drive home with me. Reasonable expectation if he weren't married to a nutcase.

Hey, go easy on yourself.

Yeah, easy. It's never easy around me.

He knows that. Don't see him dashing off, do you?

Not yet.

Don't go borrowing trouble.

I pictured the thought of stepping up to a neighbor with a measuring cup in my hand and asking to borrow "a cup of trouble, if you can spare it please."

I turned the knob on the kitchen door. My forward momentum carried me one step before I realized too late that the normally locked door opened under my hand.

THIRTY-EIGHT

THE DARK HAIRED man motioned me into the kitchen. The gun in his hand pointed down at his side. I forced my feet forward, staring at the gun and praying it wouldn't rise.

"I'm sorry it's come to this."

The female voice startled me. I'd been focused on the man and hadn't noticed the woman with him. She sat in the nook staring out the window, her back to me. She turned and faced sideways but remained seated.

I rolled my tongue in my mouth trying to produce enough saliva to speak. Dry as cotton I croaked, "Come to what?"

The man moved behind me and closed the door. He motioned for me to join the woman. He hadn't spoken yet; I wondered if he was incapable of speech or simply not motivated enough to talk.

"Interesting, Mrs. Marsden, that you didn't ask who I was. But that's because you already know."

I stood a few feet away. "What does that matter?"

Her hollow laugh chilled me. "It matters, my dear, because your interference has caused me to revisit a time and place in my life that caused me great sorrow."

"The cellar in Oak Park where your sister's remains were found?"

There it was, *in for a penny, in for a pound*, Harry always said. I watched her face. Her eyes flashed with anger, then a sorrow so deep and drawn appeared that my jaw dropped. In spite of my fear my throat tightened at the pain I saw sweep across her face.

The man stepped toward me, raising the gun to waist height, his elbow tucked to his side.

Lydia Coe held up her hand and spoke softly, "Put that away, for now. We have much to talk about."

The "for now" wasn't lost on me.

"Please, sit down."

I slid into the seat across from her and she shifted to face me.

"I must implore you to stop snooping into affairs that don't concern you. You don't know what you're setting in motion."

"That's it. I don't know and I don't want to know. And I'm not the only one. Why did you single me out? Why not everyone else who has been in that house since the first body was discovered?"

The frustration and appeal for the truth rang clear in my voice. Her eyebrows arched in surprise. I pressed my point, feeling it was to my advantage to do so.

"Why me?"

"Your reputation precedes you, Mrs. Marsden. A clever woman who happens to become involved in cold cases. Who happens to solve those cases. You're a bit of a celebrity in certain circles."

My stunned expression urged her to continue.

"Several of my friends belong to the 19th Century Club in Oak Park. Your biggest fan also belongs."

"Gertrude." It wasn't a question. I knew Gertrude and her friend Gloria Oinstuk never missed a meeting.

"Ms. Klops has kept the ladies apprised of your adventures. As recent as last week's meeting, she assured everyone that you would solve the mystery. She's quite fond of you and unusually vocal where you are concerned."

I clasped my hands on the table. "What do you want? I'm not the only person who is interested. I'm really not interested. I was drawn to the 'mystery' as you call it by the discovery of the first remains. My sis…someone I know showed me a photo of that shoe clip." I pointed to her necklace.

Her hand covered the piece, then slowly retreated until only her fingertips stroked the surface.

"This is a brooch refashioned as a necklace when the pin could not be repaired."

"It's the twin of the one found with your sister. It's a fancy piece to wear everyday unless it has great sentimental value. I'm not the only person who knows that. You would have to kill at least three other people." My last words quivered in the air. I dug my nails into the palms of my hands to keep from shaking.

"Kill you? You think I'm here to kill you?"

I don't know which one of us was more surprised. I nodded toward the man who stood behind her, his gun down at his side again.

"I don't think it shall come to that." She twisted around to look up at him. She reached out for his hand and he immediately lifted it to hold hers. Adoration and concern flashed across his face. "He has killed once, but that was necessary."

He killed for her? Did he kill her sister? Did Jackson have it wrong?

He leaned down and said softly, *"Leibchen, sagen sie nichts."*

His admonishment to say nothing surprised me; not the words, but the language. Her protector spoke German.

She leaned her cheek against his hand. The simple gesture revealed her feelings.

"Mrs. Marsden, I am not here to kill anyone. I wanted

to plead with you to persuade others to stop further investigations. I realize now that it has gone beyond that point."

She slumped with the weight of failure. "We will leave
you." Her head bobbled on thin shoulders when she stood.
I hadn't noticed the prominent blue veins in her hands, the
thinly stretched skin across her nose and cheeks.

"Please," I spoke softly, "will you tell me what happened?"

"*Nein, Leibchen,*" the man pleaded.

I saw her eyes and knew she wanted to tell this story.
She removed a small leather-bound book from her purse.
The cover showed signs of years of careful use.

"*Ist kluges dieses?*"

"I don't know if it's wise to trust her, but I am tired and
someone must know the story. It is necessary now."

Her companion seemed to become increasingly agi-
tated, shifting from foot to foot, ducking his head in a
nervous gesture. I'd seen that gesture before, but my mind
couldn't pin it down. I stared at his face. Had I noticed him
somewhere before today?

I heard the remorse in her voice. Another sound reached
my ears. The garage door was opening. The man heard
it too. He backed away from the door and raised the gun.
Maybe she had decided not to kill anyone, but he hadn't
agreed. I heard the car door slam hard and I knew Will
was coming through the door.

THIRTY-NINE

I LAUNCHED MY body at the man, knocking him off balance and slamming him into the counter. The force of my blow pinned the arm holding the gun between his body and the cabinets.

In the split second when I collided with him I heard, "Kurt, no!" and Harry shouting my name. Then came the gunshot.

The man grabbed at me to regain his balance, and in that moment, he realized what had happened. Lydia Coe lay on the floor struck by the fired bullet. He sank to his knees, crawled to her side, and lifted her head into his lap. Her eyes fluttered open. She tried to lift her hand. The effort proved too much. She tilted her head toward his chest.

He mumbled low fast words that I couldn't catch as close as I stood. His face streaming with tears, he bent close to kiss her forehead.

Harry lifted the gun from the floor, called 9-1-1, and asked for the police and an ambulance. He turned to me. "I sent Will to Barbara's and told him to call the police and stay there. If they weren't home, he was to wait in the back yard out of sight. Are you okay?"

I heard the dilemma in his voice.

"Go check on Will. There's nothing going to happen now."

He kissed my cheek and left through the mudroom. Before he was out the door I heard the sirens. Barbara must have been home and called first.

Only moments later I let two policemen in through the front door. One officer pushed the door further open, then stood with his back against it and faced the room. He kept his eyes on the rooms behind me. The other officer asked the questions.

"Are you the homeowner? What is your name?"

"I live here. My name is Grace Marsden. Please, a woman is hurt, in the kitchen."

"Have you called for an ambulance?"

I nodded as another set of sirens broke the silence.

"Did the intruder leave your house?"

I realized they didn't know about the shooting. I shook my head. We'd reached the kitchen. "They're here."

The policeman's face reflected confusion until he saw the woman apparently shot in the chest cradled by a sobbing man.

His partner pulled his gun. "Sir, put her down and stand up."

Kurt held her tighter. "*Nein, nein. Ich lasse sie nicht.*"

No translation needed; he wasn't leaving her.

"Is he the shooter?" the one pointing the gun asked.

"Yes, but it was an accident. I mean, he wasn't aiming at her. I mean, the gun went off when I ran into him." My face flushed, the heat from my neck causing a sheen of perspiration on my upper lip.

"Do you know his name?"

"She called him Kurt."

"Kurt, you have to put her down. Do you hear the sirens? They are here to help her. Stand up, Kurt."

The officer doing the talking turned to his partner and mouthed that he couldn't see a weapon.

"He doesn't have the gun anymore," I said quietly.

The officer holding the gun kept his eyes on Kurt when he asked, "Where is it?"

Before I could answer the sirens grew louder, then stopped.

"I'm not letting anyone else in here until I know it's secure," said the first officer. "Sir, if you want help for this lady, you're going to have to stand up and put your hands behind your head."

Kurt slowly, painfully understood and gently laid Lydia's head on the cold floor. He stood, but never moved an inch from her body.

The officer pulled Kurt's hands down in front of him and snapped handcuffs around his wrists. He quickly patted the man's pockets and pants to make sure there were no weapons. "He's clean."

The other policeman holstered his gun. "I'll stay here. You bring the others inside."

Kurt sank to his knees and sat back on his heels, his thigh touching Lydia's shoulder. His awkward attempt to hold her brought pity to my heart.

Two paramedics guiding a gurney followed the officer to the kitchen. Two other policemen arrived and they moved from room to room making sure I hadn't been coerced into lying about other intruders. I heard the calls of "clear" throughout the house. With the final "clear", the original responders visibly relaxed.

I moved to the nook to get out of the way. The leather journal lay on the floor near the bench where Lydia must have dropped it in her haste to stop Kurt. I sat on the edge of the bench and used the heel of my shoe to slowly push the book out of sight.

The EMTs had their hands full trying to pry Kurt's hands and upper body from Lydia's shoulders. He'd hunched down over her as though to protect her or infuse her with his warmth.

One paramedic crouched down next to him. "We can help her, but you have to give us room to work. Please, let us help her."

The reassuring tone worked. Kurt gently released Lydia and allowed himself to be pulled away from his *Leibchen*. His tears had stopped and his eyes filled with intense sorrow for what he'd done.

You feel sorry for him? He pointed a gun at you.

I don't think he would have used it. I caused this when I rammed him.

He was unraveling. You don't know what he would have done.

"Ma'am? Are you okay?" asked one of the paramedics. "We've got to roll, but I can call another unit to the scene."

"No, I'm fine. Shook up is all."

He nodded and helped his partner guide the occupied gurney through the door.

Lydia's pale face was a close match to the sheeting covering her. She looked frail and unresponsive.

"*Bitte*, please, may I be allowed to travel with her. She is my wife." Kurt's voice shook with emotion. I was shocked to hear his perfect English.

The officer started to shake his head, but Kurt held out his hands. His wrists and the cuffs of his jacket were stained with blood.

"I am manacled, I will cause no harm." His eyes pleaded for compassion. The officer motioned him ahead and they left to catch up to the ambulance. The other officer stayed behind.

"Will he go to jail?"

"Absolutely." The policeman looked at me in an odd

way. Maybe my tone of compassion for the "shooter" bothered him.

"Mrs. Marsden, your kitchen is a crime scene and we
have technicians on their way. You need to move to another room and stay out of this one. I have questions to
ask, but let's take it out of the kitchen."

He turned and started for the door assuming I'd follow.
I kept my eyes on his shoulders and reached down for the
book. When I stood, I stuffed the journal in my waistband
and resettled my sweater over the slight bulge.

I followed him out of the kitchen. "We can go in there."
I pointed to the living room and watched as he settled himself on the couch.

"Aren't you going to sit down?"

I hadn't thought about that. Standing with a book tucked
in my waistline was one thing. Sitting was another.

"Uh, I'm too wound up. If fact, I have to use the bathroom."

I hurried to the powder room to hide the journal. They
wouldn't be searching the bathroom. I tucked the book
under a pile of hand towels. For good measure I took the
old soap dish filled with decorative marbles from the small
shelf and balanced it atop the towels. Some people are
bathroom snoops, maybe cops too. I remembered to flush
and wash my hands. I didn't know what he could hear, but
I wanted to cover my bases. I walked out and headed toward him making a show of rubbing moisturizer into my
hands. If the guy were married or even dating, he'd know
girls take longer then men.

I sat down across from him.

"Mrs. Marsden, a Barbara Atwater placed the call to
9-1-1. Do you know her?"

"She's my neighbor." I hooked a thumb over my shoulder. "My husband sent his son to her to call the police."

"Where's your husband now?"

"He went to check on his son."

"We got a call that there was a second 9-1-1 request."

"My husband called when he saw Lydia. He wasn't sure the Atwaters were home, if the first call had been made. He took the gun with him."

The officer's head shot up from his note taking. "He took the gun?"

"Yes, he didn't want to leave it here. I mean, shooting Lydia was an accident, but we didn't know how else Kurt might react."

Harry came in through the mudroom and stopped abruptly when he saw us. He lifted his hands away from his side.

"Officer, my name is Harry Marsden. I live here. I have a gun in my waistband. I can raise my hands and you can take it from my back, or I can remove it and hand it to you butt first. Your call."

I couldn't believe my eyes. Harry acted like a criminal waiting with his hands lifted waist high.

"Harry, for heaven's sake, it's not—" A stern voice cut me off.

"Turn around, Mr. Marsden." The officer stepped forward and removed the gun from Harry's waistband. "Thank you, sir. I appreciate your behavior."

Harry nodded and sat down next to me. "I placed the second call to 9-1-1." He glanced toward the kitchen. "How is she?"

"She was too pale, Harry. I don't think it's good."

"I have a few more questions…"

The police presence continued for two hours. Technicians arrived and processed the crime scene. More questions came from a supervisor who'd been called before Detective Robson finally arrived. He'd been alerted that a name from the list of persons of interest in his cold case investigation—mine—had popped up.

With Detective Robson came George Shaw, and with him came Marisol who brought Ric along. It was like the old children's rhyme, *The Farmer Takes a Wife*, almost down to the last line, *the mouse takes the cheese*.

Would I be the cheese left standing all alone when this was over?

FORTY

ONLY THE NEWCOMERS remained. The police had completed their work and left a messy kitchen behind. I had blood and other extraneous compounds to clean up.

Harry had called Jan to ask her for a Hazmat referral. She'd recommended a company that did this type of clean-up work and a young man from "All Clear Cleaning" was now in my kitchen scrubbing and disinfecting everything.

Alerting Jan brought my dad, my brother Marty, and my cousin Nick rushing to the scene. George Shaw confessed that he'd told Juliana where he was going. We're weren't surprised when a short time later she and Josephine rang the bell.

I counted nine people besides Harry and me. When the doorbell rang again we glanced round at each other like actors in a B movie. "Who could that be?" someone asked in an exaggerated tone.

"I'm taking bets it's Walter," my brother said.

"Or my nosey sister," Ric added.

Walter and Gertrude walked into the living room. Marty high-fived Nick. "I should have known they go together," he smiled.

I had to talk to Gertrude alone, or at least with only Walter and Harry around. How could I cut her out of the herd browsing around the coffee and pastries I'd managed to hustle out of the kitchen between the technicians leaving and the cleaning guy's arrival?

Fate tapped me on the shoulder. Really it was Walter, but close enough. He motioned me toward the hallway.

"Missus Grace, I am giving a hard time to you *mit* Gertrude's problems. I am sorry to always bringing you trouble."

"Walter, you and Gertrude aren't bringing me trouble. Neither of you had anything to do with the bodies in the cellar. I have to talk to you and Gertrude about something. It's important, but I don't want to talk in front of everyone. It's personal for Gertrude."

Walter nodded. "*Ja,* her brother. I am helping to make the way for his funeral. She has comfort after many years to know his fate."

Oh, boy, this wasn't going to be easy. Was I absolutely sure of what I was going to tell her? Should I wait? What if I'm wrong? What if I'm right? I'm going to tell her, By the way, Gertrude, you brother isn't dead. He's alive and well and married to Trixie or Dolly, and oh yeah, he shot one sister and killed the other one.

I swallowed hard. *In for a penny, in for a pound.* "Can you get Gertrude and meet me in the library? I think everyone else is putting their pieces in the pot."

My metaphor went wide.

"No, Missus Grace, no one *ist* making food. You want I should go pick up?"

"I meant… No, I don't want pick up. Please, meet me in the library."

I stopped in the powder room and retrieved the journal. I wanted it with me.

Walter and Gertrude settled side-by-side on the small couch in the room. I remained standing, then felt I should deliver the news at eye level and pulled a chair closer to them.

"Gertrude, what I'm going to tell you is a shock. I can't sugar coat it."

My food metaphors were confusing Walter. Gertrude smiled and patted his hand. *"Wenn Sie einem Kind einen Bonbon geben, um die Medizin zu nehmen."*

I caught the "give a child a sweet" and "medicine" so I knew she understood.

Walter nodded and we were on the same page again.

"Gertrude, I don't believe the body in the basement is your brother."

She stiffened and Walter's arm encircled her shoulders.

"I think the part about him disappearing was true and that he is alive. I think the reason he disappeared is not what you were told. Your brother Kurt stood in my kitchen less than two hours ago and shot his wife, Lydia Coe."

I didn't know what to expect. Would she hate me? Be angry with me?

Gertrude slumped back against Walter's arm, then shot forward reaching for my hands. "Where he is now? I must see this man. I *vil* know."

Her eyes brimmed with tears. "I *vil* know," she repeated softly.

Harry entered the room. "There's some wild speculation going on out there that I thought you'd want to…" He looked at Gertrude, then Walter. "What's wrong? Are the police continuing to question her?"

I explained quickly and saw the disapproval on Harry's face.

"Grace, we should have checked further. You could be wrong. This isn't fair to Gertrude."

He was right. Had I built up an unreasonable hope in her heart? At that moment I wished I had waited. Would I have wanted this turn of events if it'd been one of my brothers? I decided I would. Did that give me the right to hold out sketchy truth to her?

She thought so. She lifted her hand to stop further discussion. "I am thanking you for telling me. How do I find him?"

"We tell the police our theory and let them open the doors," said Harry. "As it were, we have an assortment of them in our living room. Shall we?"

He stood at the door and let Walter and Gertrude pass first. When I attempted to flit past him he turned and blocked the doorway.

"Gracie, this could be one of the most irresponsible things you've done."

"Just one?" I said, trying to diffuse his disapproval.

"Another would be not turning over that book in your waistband." He reached out and tapped my abdomen. "I'm sure any one of our assortment should have that in their custody. Please tell me you found it after the police left and that your intention was to call."

"Took the words right out of my mouth."

He let me pass.

More like put them in.

Well, I don't have much choice, do I?

I removed the journal and walked briskly into the living room intending to toss the book to the first cop who made eye contact.

Marisol and Ric were leaving with Walter and Gertrude. Ric had won the coin toss since he was local and apparently wherever Ric went, Marisol followed.

Robson made eye contact with me. And the winner is…

I walked toward him, my hand outstretched. "I found this on the kitchen floor." I glanced at Harry. "I was going to call the police when you all started showing up. I guess I'll give this to you."

The detective accepted the book.

"Thank you, Mrs. Marsden." He glanced at Harry. "I'll make sure the local police know what your intentions were."

My intentions are the last thing I'd want the police to know. A hint of a smile played around Robson's mouth. He knew; that's the look he shot at Harry.

"Do you think it's important?" I asked, hoping he'd open it to check if it were a diary or a fancy "honey do" list.

He tapped the cover. "We'll have to see."

"Can't we see tonight?" Josephine's clear voice asked.

He looked startled at her impertinence. He hadn't been around her long enough to catch her style.

"You are the lawful representative," she continued. "Can't you make a cursory examination of the contents on site and offer a succinct opinion to its value in this case?"

Man, she was good. Her vocabulary and tone was *tough teacher* all the way. I stood up straighter and noticed some other shoulders snapping back. Good teachers had that effect on all of us.

Juliana and I added our encouraging comments, much to the disapproval of at least one man in the room.

"Hey, don't pressure the guy. He's only doing his job." My dad held up his hands. "Josephine, you gotta' appreciate his position. He just got this case. He's gotta' take everything back and let his superiors make the call."

If my dad wanted to rankle Robson, he'd found a small chink. But only a tiny one. Robson turned the tables on us.

"I'd like to hear what happened this afternoon. How this book even came to be here."

That did it. All eyes turned on me and I knew he'd put off making his decision on whether he'd include us.

I went through the events, explaining how I'd rushed home to look at the photos I'd left there. I repeated the bizarre conversation with Lydia and the fact that Kurt spoke only German with her. No one interrupted until I recounted my decision to tackle the gunman.

"Mother of God, Gracie, you could have been killed." My father's emotional outburst tore at my heart.

"I couldn't take a chance, Dad. Will always rushes through that door like a tornado. I couldn't take a chance."

Harry's eyes were moist and his emotion caused me to choke up. I didn't trust my voice to continue.

Robson assessed each of us, then finally decided. "I'll take notes." He stood up and slipped the journal into his pocket.

George Shaw left with Robson. Juliana wanted to leave, but Josephine tinkered with her coffee cup and spoon, stirring and tapping once, stirring and tapping… The pattern mesmerized me. I drew closer to her.

"Grace, I'm going to pop over and collect Will," said Harry. "The cleaning man is finished and things look normal again."

"Mr. Marsden, I could use some air," Juliana said with a smile. "Could I 'pop over' with you?"

Harry motioned for her to precede him through the room. "I'd be delighted. I'll give you the Queen's tour."

"OKAY, JOSEPHINE. WE'RE alone." I made show of checking over my shoulder and beyond hers. "He's not here, and you know who I mean. Why did you lie to the police about who you saw? By the way, how did you describe Jack's brother without seeing him at that door?"

Josephine settled the spoon next to the cup. "I had seen him walking past the house twice while we were inside. When the police asked for a description I just plugged him in. I had no idea he was still in the area, that he was Jack's brother."

"Why lie?"

"I've never seen a spirit before. I didn't want to share the experience with them; I wanted to talk to you."

I didn't know if I should be flattered.

"As for him not being here, I don't suspect he'll leave that house until he's ready."

"I've never seen him in the house, only outside. I thought maybe even as a spirit he couldn't tolerate being in that cellar. We know about him now, that he most likely was a *Waysayer* and that he died when John Coe was jailed and couldn't get back to him. But why is he still here, and what is his connection to the quilt? You don't think it's the Judas Quilt."

"John Coe may have been jailed, but I'm suspecting that he didn't mind the charade. If he were a *conductor* he could have found a way to get word to someone about the frail old man trapped in the cupboard. He was a member of the community and would be allowed visitors.

"No, I think he kept to himself and waited to be released. A few days wouldn't kill the old man, just weaken him and make him easier to return for bounty."

"According to the papers you checked, he was killed on his way home. No one knew about the *Waysayer*…" I couldn't complete the thought.

Josephine nodded. "Horrible, slow death." She swallowed hard and dabbed at her eyes with her napkin. "His house stood empty till his people from Fullersburg, the area around Graue Mill and York Tavern, claimed it. That house next to the mill was a station like the mill itself."

"If he was a slave catcher masquerading as an abolitionist, did the Fullersburg Coes know? Were they legit?"

Josephine nodded quickly. "The Coe family fought against slavery, risking their fortune and freedom at times.

There has never been a doubt about their commitment to the cause.

"According to the deeds that Juliana found, the property passed to John Coe's brother who was the great grandfather of Lydia and Lucy Coe. Their grandfather owned it before Mr. Klops purchased it."

"The girls might have known the secrets of the cellar from playing there as children."

"More likely, they learned the secrets from Kurt Klops, a young man who would be inclined to explore new surroundings."

"Both Coe girls spent time with Kurt."

"Too much according to his parents. They never liked the influence those girls exerted over their son. Mr. Klops wanted to present the correct appearance in his new country."

"It's all about appearances. I'm getting a headache thinking about the deceit and false appearances." I rolled my shoulders and tilted my neck side to side. An idea began to form in my mind. "Do you think the Fullersburg Coes found out afterwards and covered up the deceit? After all, they were well respected, trusted in the community. News that Coe's brother was a slave catcher would make him and his family a pariah."

Josephine leaned toward me. "Maybe the *Waysayer* wants us to make this public, to set the record straight."

That felt right. John Coe wasn't written up as a conductor and the house was never mentioned as a *station*. For good reason; it wasn't a safe house, it was a trap.

Harry, Juliana, and Will came into the living room. Will came straight for me and locked a hug around my shoulders. He didn't speak. He released me and turned his attention to the remains on the coffee table.

"Can I have those?" He pointed to the different pastries on several plates.

"One, you can have one."

"One plate?"

The laughter eased the tightness in my thoughts and banished long dead stories to the corners of the room. They'd be there for later.

FORTY-ONE

"ENOUGH EXCITEMENT for one day, wouldn't you say?" Harry slung his arm around Will's shoulders. "When you explain this to your mum you may want to give her the minimalist version."

Will craned his neck to look up at his dad. "Huh?"

"He means don't tell your mom the scary stuff, just the facts."

Will grinned at Harry. "Why didn't you just say so?"

"I thought I had." Harry's deadpan answer cracked us up. I suspected he really did think he had.

"Enough poking fun at my superior vocabulary. It's time for you to be in bed. Is that plain enough for you?" Harry squeezed Will and ruffled the top of his head.

"Dad, I'm not tired."

"You don't have to sleep, just have a lie down."

"A what?"

"Am I the only person who speaks English in this house?" My husband's exasperated tone caused more laughter.

"He means wash up, put on your pajamas, and relax on your bed. Listen to music, read, watch some TV."

"Why didn't you—"

Harry shifted his arm and lifted Will upside down by his waist. "If you say, 'say so' again, I'm going to bounce you up the stairs on your head."

Will shouted and squirmed, delighted to be roughhousing with his dad.

"Care to finish your sentence?" Harry's bad guy tone made Will laugh harder.

This type of scene had played out at the Morelli home hundreds of times. My mom would stand off to the side and watch, occasionally warning my dad to be gentle. As we grew bigger, the warning would be for us to be gentle with Dad.

The phone rang and I left father and son to negotiate the stairs one bump at a time.

Walter was calling to give us an update. He spoke quickly, his accent so strong, that I could catch only every few words. I understood that Lydia Coe had died after surgery. I heard the word *bruder* several times. I must have been right about Kurt.

I had to ask him to repeat things many times. I could hear the frustration in his voice.

"Walter, maybe this would be better in person. Harry could come to the hospital, or you and Gertrude could come here."

"*Nein, nein.* We must are going *mit* Gertrude's *bruder* to police."

That part I understood. "Do you want Harry to meet you at the police station?"

"*Ja, ist gut. Ja, danke*, Missus."

HARRY LEFT WITHIN minutes of my conversation with Walter. He promised to call as soon as he knew anything.

I picked up empty plates and crumpled napkins from the table. Will worked with me to clear the living room of extraneous glasses. We didn't speak, but the silence wasn't strained.

I filled the sink with hot soapy water and snapped on my gloves. The sound of squeaky clean soon filled the silence.

"Dish towels are in the second drawer over. You can dry if you want."

Will pulled out a cotton towel and carefully removed a plate from the drainer.

"Why do you do that the same way each time?" He motioned toward the sink.

Hmmm. How much information makes this disease interesting and how much makes it terrifying?

Haven't figured it out yet. Depends on the person.

"I do repetitive motions, patterns, because there is a part of my brain that demands it and won't let me relax until I finish something just so." I glanced at him to get his reaction.

"Dad says you're 'extremely' neat. He calls it a compulsion to be neat."

I hadn't realized Harry had been trying to explain me to Will.

"It's a little beyond neat; closer to the extremely part. Do you know the meaning of the word compulsion?"

"Yeah, like you have to do it. Lots of people do that, don't they?"

"When someone always goes back to their front door to check the knob to make sure it's locked before they leave, that could be considered compulsive. When a person goes back many times to check the knob, even though one time should tell them it's locked, that's the obsessive part. And that's what I do, repeat patterns in order to feel I can leave or finish something."

His eyes lost interest and I knew I'd said enough.

"Could be worse. You could pick your nose and put the boogers in your milk at lunch time like Dan Fogarty does."

I swallowed hard to keep the pastry I'd had from coming up my throat.

"Argh, that's sick."

"Yeah, nobody likes him. You're okay compared to him. I'm going up to my room." He turned at the doorway. "But not to have a 'lie down'."

I smiled and called out to his back, "Thanks for drying."

So, I'm okay compared to Dan Fogarty.

High praise, Gracie girl.

I take what I can get.

The phone rang. Harry's tense voice filled me with dread.

"Things have gone terribly wrong. Gertrude's brother attempted suicide. He's back at hospital. I don't know how long I'll be. Walter is trying to convince Gertrude to let him take her home. She won't leave."

"Is he really her brother? Is Gertrude positive, or is she hoping it's him?"

"She believes him to be Kurt. The police took his fingerprints, but that will take days. Meanwhile, Gertrude's not going to budge."

"I guess none of us would, given the same circumstances. I wish I could be there for her."

"I've Walter's house key. Would you pop in and pick up a few things for Gertrude? I'll stay with Will."

"Of course I will. I'll call Jan, too. I think they've become close, and Jan is good in a crisis."

"Good thought. See you in a bit."

I knew I had a twenty-minute window. My hands picked up the photos I'd come home to look at hours ago. I had a half-hour of light before I'd need to turn on the track lights above the island. I spread the photos out on the island and lit a small scented candle. The shoe clip in the crime scene photo was a match to the necklace I'd seen around Lydia's neck.

The other photo showed the slave tag in clear relief. This tag had belonged to a house slave. That would make sense. If the remains belonged to a *Waysayer* he most likely would be closer to the family, near enough to perhaps over-hear conversations about the slave catchers. A field slave would have had precious little time to meet with other slaves and even less energy after the long grueling days spent under the hot sun and a brutal master's stick.

I sat on a stool at the island and put my head down on my arms. My forearms covered the photos. My brain had to relax. The whirling sensation in my head would mani-fest itself in my fingers if I couldn't calm my thoughts. The darkening room, the tiny pinpoint of light, the sooth-ing scent would all help me relax.

The questions paraded briskly through my conscious-ness: Did Lydia kill her sister? Why would she do that? Whose remains were in the more recent grave? Is Kurt Gertrude's brother? Did he know about the tunnel? Who used it? Why use it once slavery had ended?

Slowly, without prodding the answers came: we had an eyewitness who claimed Lydia closed her sister in the wall. Maybe the motive was Kurt or money. Gertrude's sure it's her brother. Kurt must have known about the tunnel. He lived there during prohibition. A cellar would be the absolute best place to hide illegal booze. A secret tunnel would be the best way to sneak it in and out of Oak Park.

I heard the garage door and lifted my head. No need to alarm Harry with my thinking posture.

The door opened slowly, too slowly for Harry.

I blew out the candle and held my breath.

FORTY-TWO

A WHITE RECTANGLE hovered in the open doorway.

I screamed and pushed away from the island, intending on running into the living room. Instead, my leg slipped through the rung of the stool, toppling it and me to the floor. I broke my fall with my hands and left knee. I heard the *pop* in my trapped right knee.

Lights came on in the kitchen and Harry knelt next to me.

"Don't move. Your leg's twisted."

"I felt it pop; it hurts." I clenched my teeth to keep from crying. In my peripheral vision I spotted the cleaning bag Harry had tossed aside. A pair of laundered shirts had done me in.

Will raced into the room. "What's wrong? I heard you scream."

Harry stood at the fridge popping ice cubes out of the trays, then dumping them into a towel. I hoped he didn't think he would be touching my knee with those boulders.

"Peas," I said and pointed to the fridge.

"Please what, darling? Give me a minute and I'll have this…"

"Peas, Dad not please. She wants you to use the frozen peas." He turned to me. "Right?"

I nodded. "Smaller, won't push," I managed between breaths.

Two small packages replaced the gargantuan compress.

"Gracie, I have to straighten your leg to untangle you from the stool."

I nodded my head and closed my eyes.

"Will, when I straighten her leg, you gently and slowly pull the stool away. Can you do that?"

I opened my eyes to see Will nod. He looked flustered but focused and I knew I was in good hands—all four of them.

The pain was all that I had expected, but the upside was that when Harry straightened my leg I felt a small *pop* and immediate relief from the sharp pain. He slid a towel folded lengthwise under my leg, and while Will held the peas on either side of my knee, Harry pulled up the ends of the towel.

"Son, can we borrow your belt?"

Will understood immediately and pulled his belt from the loops. Harry used the belt to secure the ice packs.

I reached for his hand. "Help me stand."

"You can't stand. Those peas will be around your ankle with too much vertical movement. Put your arms around my neck."

Harry squatted next to me, his legs braced to do the lifting. My fear of staggering my husband returned. I could see him collapsing under my weight.

"Harry, it's too awkward. Really, I can stand."

"Grace, will you please stop arguing and put your arms around my neck."

From his tone I was certain there would have been a "bloody hell" in there if not for Will's presence. I locked my hands behind his neck and tried to think light thoughts—butterflies, fluffy clouds, marshmallows. Harry's arms slid under my thighs and shoulders. Gossamer wings, dandelion puffs.

He stood easily and carried me to the couch. "Will, put that pillow under her knee when I drop her."

Will's eyebrow arched in mock surprise.

"It shall be my honor to carry you over any and all thresholds for as long as we live and love," he whispered. I snuggled closer, thrilled to be in his arms.

"Yuck!"

Harry laughed so hard there was a moment when he might have dropped me. He settled me on the couch and Will tucked the pillow under my knee.

"Let's see how you feel in thirty minutes. We'll take the ice off in ten minutes, wait fifteen, and reapply for another ten. Does that sound right to you, Will?"

Will beamed. "Yep, that's what I would do."

He sat on the floor next to the couch and with simple candor asked, "How did you fall off the stool?"

Harry added, "What made you scream?"

How could I tell them I was spooked by laundry? How could I tell them I'd been in a half daze somewhere in the 1930s?

The phone rang.

Will jumped up. "I'll get it."

He returned quickly. "Dad, its Uncle Ric. He says it's important."

Harry and I exchanged a worried glance. I scooted up into a sitting position while Harry took the call. His voice was too low for me to catch the words. Will returned to the floor.

"Is Uncle Ric going to marry that lady FBI person?"

"That's the plan." I heard my voice and almost recognized it. If Will thought I sounded odd he didn't comment. I could chalk it up to my knee.

"Which one of them will be boss?"

I wasn't up to a lesson on give and take and working together to create and maintain a strong marriage.

"I mean, who has more power?"

Power? What the heck was Lily teaching him about relationships?

"Like does she outrank him?"

I felt relieved at my obvious misinterpretation. Sometimes a question is just a question. "They're different agencies. I don't think he has to salute her or anything."

My good humor vanished when I saw the expression on Harry's face as he reentered the room. He sat down in the chair opposite me and motioned Will to his side.

Will saw the change, too. "What's wrong?"

Harry put his arm around him. "Your mum and Aunt Hannah were on a bus with some of mum's photography crew. There was an accident—"

"Is Mom okay? Is she?"

Harry hugged him closer. "We don't know yet. The bus went off road in a remote area and it has taken time for the rescue workers to get to them. One of the crew was thrown clear of the accident. He managed to get up to the road and stop another motorist."

Will burst into tears and barreled into his father's chest. His sobs tore at my heart. I could only imagine what Harry felt. Tears streamed down his cheeks moistening the top of Will's blond head.

I knew he was holding something back, a scenario that was too scary to share with Will unless absolutely necessary. Will's sobs slowed and stopped. He lifted a tear stained face to his dad's. "Are we going there to help mom?"

Harry took a deep breath. "There's nothing we can do

but wait. It's morning there now and they can continue to help the people, your mum included."

His voice gave his son solace.

I noticed that he was in his pajamas. "Will, would you like to grab a blanket and sleep down here tonight? We'll be up late."

He looked at his dad who nodded. "Yeah, thanks."

Harry didn't speak until Will had rushed upstairs. "Ric said he'd ring us every hour with whatever they knew. Apparently, the crewman had some contact numbers in a notebook he carried. If he didn't, we'd not know about the accident."

"You're not telling us something." I held my breath, waiting for Harry's answer.

He lowered his voice. "There was an explosion."

I gasped and clamped a hand over my mouth.

"Miraculously, the bus landed upright after going off road. According to the crewmember, it exploded minutes after stopping. Nevertheless, he said there was plenty of time to get clear. The accident happened in a remote area. They don't have portable lights and emergency crews."

Will returned with the comforter from his bed, the small framed photo of his mom from his nightstand, and Valentino, the red bear his aunt had given him when she first met him. All bases covered.

Harry tucked the comforter around Will. He turned out the overhead light and moved the chair closer to the couch. Sometime during this crisis the ice pack had worked its way off my knee. I pulled it off my leg and swung around to a sitting position. The dull ache continued, but there was no sharp pain. Some ibuprofen would take the edge off. I needed to be focused for my men.

"Help me into the kitchen, Harry. We can talk and you can make me tea."

I wanted to give Will some quiet to fall asleep and Harry something to do. He helped me up and guided my hopping.

I sat sideways in the nook with my back against the wall to support my leg. Harry sat across from me stirring more milk into his already ecru-colored tea. He sipped it and pulled a face. I pushed my untouched cup across to him.

"I know Hanns is okay. I would feel it, know it, if she was—gone." He swallowed the hot liquid. I didn't know if his eyes teared from emotion or pain.

"I wish I had a sense about his mum. How can this be happening to him?"

I slipped my hand over his. "If this is how it plays out, think about how lucky he is to have you. A year ago he wouldn't have known you."

A small voice asked from the doorway, "Why don't you know about mom like you do about Aunt Hannah?" Will's accusatory tone wasn't angry, just sad.

"Son, it's different with twins. Aunt Hannah and I have been connected in the closest way since before we were born. We just get feelings about each other. It's different with people you meet when you're grown."

"Not if you love them. You told me on the island that you just knew in your heart that Grace was in trouble." He flung that at his father like he was daring him to deny it. Before Harry could answer Will broke eye contact. "You don't love Mom," he mumbled.

Harry slid out of the nook and took Will's hand before he could leave. "I'll always love your mum because we managed to have you. I'll always want what's best for her."

Will slipped his arms around Harry's waist. "But it's not the way you love Grace." No question, only statement.

Harry hugged him and that was answer enough.

The phone rang. It hadn't been an hour. Did that mean good news?

Walter wondered if I was coming to sit with Gertrude. He didn't know about the accident. Harry quietly explained the situation, choosing his words carefully.

He poured more tea and the three of us sat waiting again for Ric's call.

"Walter said he called your dad's house to ask for Jan's number. She was there and is on her way to hospital to shore up Gertrude."

I nodded. "What about Karen? Who's with her? Where was Ric when he called? I hope she's not alone."

"Call Tracy and ask her if she can pop over and be with her."

"Great idea, only could you call?" The cord wouldn't reach me and I hated to wiggle out of my perch. Harry lifted the receiver and waited. "834-1515, same area code."

"Tracy, it's Harry."

Once again he chose his words to paint a picture not nearly as fraught with despair as the reality of the situation. He answered a question or two before saying goodbye.

"She's on her way."

"I feel helpless. Seems like we should be circling the wagons." In past crises, everyone gravitated to a central spot like a magnet pulling in metal shavings. Karen couldn't leave because of the twins, we couldn't leave Will alone, and Gertrude wasn't going to leave her brother. I felt disconnected and on my own.

The phone rang again, right on schedule.

"Hello."

"Marsden, nothing's changed."

"Kramer, I'm putting you on speaker phone. Will and Grace are with me.

"They can't get to the area until morning. Too dangerous. The only good thing is that dawn in that region is in
thirty minutes. My source tells me they're ready to move
with daylight."

"Thanks, Kramer."

"Will, they're doing everything they can. You've got
to hang tough, okay?"

Will's eyes filled with tears. He swallowed hard, but
couldn't speak.

"He heard you. We'll get through this." Harry pulled
Will into him. "We called Tracy and asked her to be with
Karen. She's on her way."

"Thanks, Marsden. I appreciate that. I'm headed to the
hospital now in hopes of getting a statement—death bed,
I'm afraid."

"Jan Pauli is on her way to sit with Gertrude. Everyone
seems to be two deep."

"I'll check back in an hour."

Ric hung up and Harry replaced the receiver.

"Let's get you settled on the couch again, shall we?"

Will kept hold of Harry's hand as they walked from the
kitchen. I heard Harry assuring Will in a low voice that everything would be all right. What else could he tell his son?

HARRY RETURNED WITHIN thirty minutes, dawn on the other
side of the world. I shifted my legs to sit upright and Harry
slid in next to me. He put his arm around my shoulders. I
leaned into his chest, hearing the steady beat of his heart.
We sat and spoke quietly, then just sat and kept our own
thoughts. Eventually I dozed off against Harry's warm
body. The jangle of the ringing phone ripped me from a
dreamless sleep. I pulled away from Harry to let him answer the call. His conversation was low and hurried and
over in less than a minute.

"A storm broke out right before dawn. It's a bad one and they can't risk a helicopter or the heavier equipment on the unstable hillside. They have to go in using ropes and carrying stretchers down to the injured. That's all Kramer knew."

The frustration in his voice mirrored my thoughts. We can put a man on the moon, but we can't get a helicopter through a storm. My knee throbbed and I shifted to lift my legs onto the bench seat.

Harry stared at the bulge midway down my pant leg. I'd meant to change into sweats, but with everything happening I forgot. "That not good."

My knee had puffed out against the material, filling a spot normally baggy.

I waved him away. "It's sore, but that'll be gone by tomorrow.

"Maybe, maybe not. We should take you to Emergency."

"Harry, with everything going on, this is really nothing."

Harry gritted his teeth. His jaw muscles bulged as he took a deep breath and blew it out through his mouth. "I can't do a bloody thing to help my sister and Will's mom. Let me at least help my wife." His measured words and his tone left no room for rational discussion. "I'll get Will; he's had a good nap. I've not learned much as a new dad except that kids rejuvenate a lot faster than we do." He smiled and went into the living room.

Truth be told, I was okay with the plan. I wanted to be near Gertrude in her time of need. If I knew my dad, he'd driven Jan to the hospital, but not before he loaded the car with fixings for sandwiches and snacks. It would be better to wait for news with a larger support group.

Harry returned with a wide-awake Will who'd dressed

in jeans and a sweatshirt in under two minutes. I pointed at my purse on the counter. Will snagged it.

"You carry that and I'll carry her," Harry joked.

"I can walk. Help me stand. I'll hold your arm while I hop."

Harry swept me up into his arms. "This is faster." He nodded toward Will. "Get the door and mind that it doesn't hit me in the arse or you're in trouble."

Will grinned. "If you weren't holding Grace, you'd be in trouble."

Harry's attempt to keep Will lighthearted worked for now. How long could he keep the dismal truth from him?

FORTY-THREE

I HAD INSISTED on limping into Emergency under my own steam with Harry and Will's arms to steady me to avoid the appearance of a body being carried in. My decision proved sound as my dad hailed us before we'd moved far enough to find a wheelchair. He rushed toward us yelling, "Nurse, my daughter needs help." I can only imagine the scene had I entered in Harry's arms.

"What happened?" He moved next to Will. "Thanks for helping her, big guy. I've got her now." He gave Will a side hug when they switched positions. Will beamed with the praise but a little disappointed to be "let go" from his job. I smiled at him.

"It looks worse than it is. I'm sure it's only slightly sprained."

"I recall that your degree was in English, not medicine."

I rolled my eyes and felt fourteen years old again. He continued, "So, Dr. Gracie, what happened?"

His voice held no sarcasm, only concern.

"I fell off the stool in the kitchen and twisted my leg in the rungs."

"Your Uncle Jimmy nose dived off of bar stools all the time and never got hurt. 'Course, he was probably as loose as a strand of linguine." My dad leaned toward me and I puffed in his face, then started laughing.

"Dad, I wasn't drinking anything stronger than Mocha Madness. I dozed off at the island, and when I heard the door open I jumped up in surprise, lost my balance, and got tangled in the stool."

My dad glared at Harry. "Why'd you make her walk? She shouldn't be on it."

Seems I was off the hook.

My husband stutter-stepped with surprise and threw off the pace. I winced as I put more weight on my leg.

Harry spoke calmly over my head. "You ever have any success forcing her to do anything? Have you, Mike?"

"You should have picked her up. She couldn't do much off her feet."

"After the first two times I swept her up, she was prepared for my third attempt."

Now my dad altered his pace and I readjusted, in pain, again. "Oh." He readjusted his gaze and his pique, aiming them at me. "Can't you just let people help you, sweetie?"

"Guys?"

We stopped walking/hobbling and turned around. Will stood behind us with a wheelchair. He pushed down the brake and bowed slightly, waving his hand at the chair. "Your carriage awaits."

We burst into laughter, drawing a few stares and sour looks. I grinned at Harry. "Oh, he's your kid, all right. What a smooth line."

Harry's face flushed. "I want to know where he learned that phrase, hardly a twelve-year-old's fare."

My dad grinned. "We've been watching cable. A few old Cary Grant movies and some of those English comedies."

"Well done, son." Harry helped me into the chair and let Will push me to the triage desk. I could only imagine Harry's anguish knowing what could change for Will in a few hours.

Jan Pauli rushed toward us. "Oh my gosh, Grace. What's wrong?"

My dad waved his hand around. "I got the story, shaky as it sounds."

I rolled my neck and smiled at Jan.

"Mike, she's not a teenager. Her story is the story."

For all my apprehension about their relationship, I felt a surge of connection to this woman. A millisecond thought about what it would have been like to be her daughter popped into my head. It left just as quickly, but the damage was done. I felt the flush of shame creep up my neck; I'd betrayed my mother's memory.

Jan glanced at me and her expression changed. I think she read my mind.

"Of course, my kids will tell you I never believed a single story of theirs. Rightfully so when years later they 'confessed' that they really had done those things." She spoke only to me but drew laughter from the guys. She turned to Will. "Remember that, buster," she said with a huge grin and hug for him.

"Mike, I'm headed to the car for more sandwiches. Karen and Tracy and the twins are in the main lobby. They didn't want to wait at home."

My dad understood. "Will, c'mon with us and help carry the supplies. Your Dad needs to check in the 'gimp', which is a boring process."

Will looked for approval to his dad. Harry nodded.

"Thanks for the chair, Will," I said. "Those two palookas would have dragged me the rest of the way."

He waved, then caught up with Jan and my dad.

Harry shook his head. "Your father is amazing. Who would think to pack a picnic hamper? Smart idea though. I am a bit hungry. Wonder if he brought that prosciutto and melon balls appetizer."

The nurse retrieved the paperwork I'd filled out and made a copy of my insurance card. Now I was duly processed and someone came to wheel me into a curtained cubicle.

Getting my pants down over my swollen knee was the biggest hurdle and most painful part of the examination. The young doc on rotation worked quickly and pleasantly.

I reappeared in the waiting room in record time. They'd replaced the wheelchair with a cane. The choice pleased me; I hated crutches. Growing up with four brothers had exposed me to crutches on many occasions. Those of us who were ambulatory would always take turns using the crutches, leaving the injured sibling to hop around clutching the furniture.

Harry sat alone cradling a small plate in his hand while he dipped a tea bag in a mug. Dad must have brought the dishes; I recognized the pink melamine picnic ware that we'd used for years. Harry spotted me and put down his plate. He stood to help me, but I waved him off.

"I don't want to sit. Where is everyone else?"

"They made them leave the main lobby. I'll show you where they ended up." Harry picked up his plate and mug. "Want one?" He reached for a prosciutto-wrapped melon ball and held it up."

"No, go ahead. I know you love them."

Harry grinned and popped it in his mouth. "Let's go. You sure you want to use that? I'll get your chair back."

"Harry, over there. Isn't that Detective Robson and Juliana? What are they doing here?"

"Good question. I don't believe it's a coincidence." Harry stepped away from the sitting area. Robson spotted him and came over to us.

"Mr. Marsden, I didn't expect to see you." He noticed me. "What happened to you?"

"Long, unimportant story. Why are you here?"

"I thought I'd wait until the prisoner reached the station to question him, but I heard about the suicide attempt and came here instead."

"He's been admitted to a room in the main wing," said Harry. "We were headed there. Had to stop off and take care of her knee."

"Why?" Robson asked, then immediately added, "Why are you headed there?"

Before Harry could answer Juliana asked, "Do they serve food here?" She nodded toward Harry's dish. "Is that melamine?"

Robson rolled his eyes. "What was it you promised? You'd be so quiet I wouldn't know you were here except for your great smelling perfume?"

Juliana grinned. "Sorry, I'm a little hungry, and I collect melamine and Bakelite."

"The food and the answers are in the same place." Harry motioned us forward. "There are other issues involved, and somehow the hospital became a central location." Harry quickly explained about the bus wreck halfway around the world that had drawn us together. "My father-in-law can't gather with more than three people and not bring food."

Harry led us down the corridor that connected the Emergency Department to the main hospital, but turned before entering the spacious lobby area. The cheery painted geometric wall designs gave way to one shade of sage green. Harry pointed to a door marked *Volunteer Lounge*.

Gertrude is a volunteer; she must have suggested this room. I noticed a small hand-printed sign *EB Assignment Planning* and hoped we weren't displacing or interrupting anything.

Harry pushed open the door and heads turned. My dad popped up first and pulled a chair out for me.

"Here, honey. Sit down. What'd the doc say?"

I eased into the chair, surprised to find such comfy furniture in a lounge. Must be castoffs from grateful and generous former patients. Good Samaritan Hospital served several affluent suburbs.

"Keep off it a couple of days, take the anti-inflammatory pills, ice it, and so forth." I rolled my hand accentuating the "and so forth."

Tracy moved a smaller chair in front of me and lifted my leg onto it. "Nice sweats," she said, commenting on my hospital issued, Good Sam stenciled across the butt, sweatpants. My jeans were folded in a plastic bag that hung from my wrist.

Harry made introductions and Juliana found a salami and provolone sandwich with her name on it. She'd never had the combination before and seemed to enjoy every bite.

Robson and Harry stood away from the group talking in low tones. I noticed immediately that Gertrude, Walter, and Ric were not present. Karen had scooted over for a hug, then returned to the twin bouncy seats, each occupied by a sleeping baby. Marisol had waved but stayed put near the babies, sneaking glances at their sleeping faces.

Wonder if she's thinking of a family?

Most people do when they get married.

Yeah, I know. Most people.

The pain of being childless caught me unawares at times. My eyes filled with tears before I could harden my heart. She would have beautiful babies with Ric. Ric, who'd offered me that same scenario. Ric, who'd waited for years after I rebuffed him.

Ric, who'd said he'd always love me. Always is a long time.

"Grace, are you all right?" Jan asked in a low voice.

I cleared my throat and accepted the napkin she laid in

my hand. "I guess everything caught up to me." I swallowed hard to stop a wave of tears I felt mounting.

Tracy stepped closer. "What's up?"

"I think she's coming down from the excitement, and her knee is probably giving her more pain than she expected," said Jan.

"That's a fair assessment from someone who's non-medical personnel. I just happen to have two little beauties that I take when any combination of stress and pain gets to be too much." Tracy held two blue pills in her palm and a glass of water in her other hand. "I offer them only to friends, people I feel worthy—"

"Give me the darn things already." I reached for the pills and the glass.

Jan and Tracy watched while I swallowed and drained the water. I blew my nose and cleared my throat again. "Thanks."

Jan patted my hand and moved back to sit next to my dad who was explaining to Juliana the ingredients of the calzone he'd pulled from the seemingly inexhaustible cooler.

"Grace, I'm thinking of heading home," said Tracy. "Why don't I take Will with me? He can hang with my guys and goof off until they pass out. I'm working tomorrow, but William is home. One more monkey won't matter to him."

"That sounds great to me, and I'm sure Will would agree." I glanced at my stepson who sat quietly at the moment devouring a huge slice of chocolate cake. "It's not my call, though. Harry may want him close. I don't know." My sigh and tear-streaked face must have attracted Harry's attention. He broke away from Robson.

"He's got something fascinating to tell us. I'm not sure

if now is a good time." He motioned toward Will. "Some of what he's got to say could be rough."

"Then I have the perfect solution." Tracy repeated her offer ending with, "When you get the news, whatever it is, morning will be time enough to hear it."

Harry hugged Tracy. "Thank you. You are one in million."

Harry motioned Will over and asked if he like to spend the night at Tracy's.

"What about finding out about Mom?" Will's thin voice cracked. I saw Harry swallow and take a breath. My throat tightened.

"Your dad can come right over when he knows something," I said. "Or he can come in the morning when you guys get up."

I could see the struggle on his face.

"Is it okay to wait until morning?" he asked Harry. His eyes pleaded for absolution.

"Of course it is. Absolutely." Harry's voice thickened. He cleared his throat. "Mum would want you in bed at a decent hour. You know that."

The reference to Lily as 'mum' rather than 'your mum' meant the world to Will. His shoulders lifted and he smiled.

I really wanted Lily to be alive. Her near death experience might change Harry's perspective of what's important. Whatever he decided, I still wanted her alive.

Harry opened his arms and Will rushed in for a hug.

"Mind Aunt Tracy and Uncle William. I want to hear how you made your bed, cleaned up after yourself, mowed the lawn, washed the car—"

Will, who had mindlessly nodded to the tasks, caught on and interrupted. "Daaad, stop it already."

"Yeah, stop it already," Tracy mimicked.

"See you in the morning, pal."

Will hugged my dad and Jan good-bye. No one else got hugs, just a wave. I guess in the scheme of things you always cover your bets and hug grandparents.

The atmosphere changed after they left. Robson stepped toward the center of the room and held up the journal he'd taken from me hours earlier. The grim expression on his face chilled me.

"I promised someone I'd read this before I turned it in as evidence in a cold case. I've come to question a dying man on the contents of this book to determine the veracity of this most bizarre story."

He sat across from my dad. Harry sat down next to me. You could have heard that proverbial pin crash to the floor.

FORTY-FOUR

WALTER BURST THROUGH the door, sweeping his gaze across the room until it settled on Robson.

"Inspector Kramer say *kommen* now. Kurt *ist* waking.

Robson responded immediately, slipping the book back into his pocket. "Sorry, I'll be back."

The door shut behind them and several voices and a thin *waaaaa* filled the room. Of course everyone quieted when they realized they'd awakened one or perhaps both babies.

Marisol pointed to the bouncy seat on the other side of Karen. Conner voiced his opinion of being awakened a little louder. Granny Jan swooped in and lifted him from his chair, laying him in her arms. She moved away from the center of the room and rocked and crooned until he settled down.

"He's quiet now, but wide awake," she said. "If you have a bottle I'm sure he'll take one, then be out again."

I thought, *yep, just like Uncle Jimmy.* I caught my dad's eye and I knew he'd had the same thought. It was scary how much alike we were.

"Harry, you were in a huddle with him for a while. Care to share?" Karen asked. Her strained high tone belied her attempt to be breezy. The lines drew tight around her mouth and eyes, eyes too bright with anxiety.

"I don't have the particulars. He told me either Kurt and Lydia were mastermind criminals, or they were victims of a type unbelievable by today's standards. He hoped to get the answer from Kurt."

"Tell us what you have and maybe we can piece it together with the little we know." I sounded confident that we knew something.

"The book is a diary started by Lydia Coe in 1932. The entries are sporadic, recounting parties she attended, outings with her Hinsdale area friends. After she meets Kurt, the entries become more frequent. She and her sister, Lucy, are each attracted to the handsome young man. Apparently both set out to claim him. Lydia writes that she is losing him because her sister is more charming and outgoing. Lucy is only 18 months older, but to her sister, she seems worldly and sophisticated beyond Lydia's reach.

"Kurt won't choose. He prefers to be seen at the trendy clubs and sleazy gin mills with two beauties on his arms. Lydia is convinced he only asks her along to make her sister jealous. She doesn't care. She enjoys the clandestine trips to the speakeasy. She believes Kurt to be the sexiest man in the world. And the most adventuresome. He is the one who shows them the secret of the tunnel. It's still Prohibition and Oak Park is parched."

Harry paused and reached for the mug he'd abandoned earlier. He pulled a face at the cold contents. My dad took it from him and popped it in the microwave. My mind spun like the turntable in the microwave. When it beeped would I have cohesive thought? I'd bet on hot tea.

"Harry, Gertrude's account of her dad is that he was strict with rules and tight with his money. They'd spent every penny to get to the States and buy the house. Where'd Kurt get the cash to wine and dine his ladies? No loans, no plastic, no allowance." I ticked them off my fingers.

"Exactly. These ladies were accustomed to a fancy, not frugal, lifestyle. Kurt needed money. He's the one who showed them the secret of the tunnel. He used the tunnel to transport what I believe was called 'hooch' in those days. He'd take delivery of cases of illegal alcohol and either hold it in the cellar or take it out through the tunnel to grateful bar owners. He'd always arrive early and his customers never saw anything except Kurt standing next to an old Reo. They assumed he'd driven the contraband to that location. He told his father he'd been given the car in trade for some work he did at one of the local establishments. The car needed work, but Kurt knew someone who understood these new machines. He kept it at his friend's house where they could work on it. He told his father that he might study mechanics. Mr. Klops never suspected. Kurt kept clothes in the armoire in the cellar."

"The same one that young Jackson hid in that night?" I asked.

Harry nodded.

"What about that night?" my dad asked. "They knew about the cupboards?"

Harry nodded again. "According to Lydia, who it seems felt honor bound to record all of Kurt's daring deeds, they knew about the two cupboards on that side of the cellar. They never suspected there was one more on the other side. Kurt thought that since that was an interior wall, there'd be no way to carve out a space. Kurt hid the cases in those two cupboards just in case anyone in the family ventured down. He knew his mother and sisters hated the dank, smelly cellar. His mother had refused to put up her preserves and pickles in the cellar, preferring instead to build a small pantry in a corner of the big kitchen. His father had bad lungs and knees from serving in the trenches during WWI. The steep stairs and dank air kept him on the upper level.

"There is a mention of Jackson liking to play in the cellar. Lydia records one comment that Kurt made about planning to scare the little boy to keep him from wanting to play there."

Juliana spoke up. "That was some plan, killing someone."

We looked at one another, each with our own thoughts about what really happened that night.

Harry shrugged. "That's about it. Robson left before he could tell me more. I know Lydia recorded something that night."

"We've got to get him back here." Jan's outburst made us smile.

The door opened and Robson entered followed by Walter. Each of us stared at the detective, perhaps wondering if he'd been "summoned" by Jan who paled when she saw him.

Jan recovered and asked Walter, "Is Gertrude alone?"

Walter's frustration came out in his tone and syntax. "*Ja.* Kurt *ist* saying how he come to be not dead. Only Gertrude would Inspector let in the room stay."

"Walter come and sit. I have coffee." My dad pointed to the chair next to Marisol. "Detective, you too." Dad held up the carafe, looking at both men for guidance.

"*Danke*, Mr. Mike. I am liking *ein koffee.*"

"Ditto with the *danke*," Robson said with a grin. "I couldn't have said it better."

"Detective Robson, I've told them the part of the story from the diary that I knew. Can you tell us what happened that night?"

A collected shift in body language seconded Harry's request. He looked around the circle and toward the door. A quizzical expression came over his face. He pointed at the door. "This is the volunteer lounge. Why hasn't anyone come in here?"

Now that he mentioned it, it did seem odd that no volunteer felt the need to relax a bit or at the least have a snack or beverage. We looked at each other with equally puzzled expressions. Except for Walter. He squirmed and ran his fingers inside his collar.

"Missus Tracy says she is making sure nobody *kommen*. She put sign on door. Nobody here *ist* not us."

"Whatever *EB Assignment Planning* means it worked. Volunteers have avoided this room." I shook my head. "Totally Tracy."

Juliana poked Robson. "You were about to say…"

The detective looked at her with more than a professional interest. He nodded. "Mr. Klops—I'm calling him that for ease of identification—is awake and lucid. He has confirmed the events of that night with the diary's entry. This is the most bizarre cold case I've encountered. If Mr. Marsden has filled you in, you know both women were in love with Kurt. Lydia's own admissions recount arguments between herself and her sister over him. At that part of the diary I thought I was reading about a murder-for-love plot." He accepted a cup of coffee from my dad and took a cautious sip. "These sisters were devoted to each other despite their competition for the young man. Tragedy struck the girls in the form of an incurable, devastating disease. Lucy Coe was diagnosed with leprosy."

The gasps and accompanying grimaces from most of us showed just how intimidating and horrible that disease resonated with us.

Jan clamped a hand over her mouth and Karen's face turned a mottled shade of pale. Juliana stared at a spot on the floor while I swallowed hard, regretting eating the prosciutto. Marisol seemed the most calm of all of us; maybe her FBI training had kicked into gear.

Robson continued. "They were horrified. Lucy's fear of the disfiguring, painful death she faced prompted the suicide plan. There is no doubt that Lucy Coe committed suicide assisted by her sister." He paused to sip his coffee.

"I understand Lucy's desire to die rather than suffer from the disease, but why go missing? Why didn't she take the drug and die in her bed?" Harry's calm voice asked.

Several of us nodded in agreement.

"Because of the terms of their family will. Lucy was the oldest and would receive her trust fund at twenty-five. According to these dates she had only fifteen months until she reached her twenty-fifth birthday. She wasn't going to suffer that long. But she didn't want Lydia to lose her trust. They concocted this plan to make it appear that headstrong, impulsive Lucy ran off with some no-good musician or gambler. There certainly were enough of them hanging around her according to her sister's entries."

Marisol spoke up. "Were the terms of the trust not clear?"

Robson smiled at her. "You're on the money. It's not that the terms weren't clear, but they were written to appease two sides of the same family. The girls' grandfather settled two huge trusts on each of his son's children as a unit. I'll have to pull the original paperwork to substantiate this, but it appears that if Lucy died before her twenty-fifth birthday the trust swung to the other Coe side and her cousin who was next oldest. If Lucy were only missing, but not declared dead until after Lydia turned twenty-five, the trust would stay on her side and pass to her.

"I've never seen anything like this. In order for Lydia to receive her trust they had to make it appear that Lucy left home for brighter prospects and fully intended on collecting her trust. Lucy wrote postcards that Lydia would mail from different locations after Lucy's death. They even had a letter ready to be sent to the family attorney a few months before her birthday asking him to settle the trust in a certain bank account and another letter to the bank president asking for her sister Lydia to be assigned as co-signer on the account.

"The night she died, the girls had planned to be at two different parties to establish the beginning of the ploy. It was not unheard of for Lucy to stay out one or two nights before returning home. No one would be concerned until the third or possibly fourth day.

"Mr. Johnson's description of what he saw matches what Lydia wrote. They were devoted to each other in life and death wasn't going to change that. I don't know if Lydia Coe would have told me this story in person, but her diary clears her and Klops of any murder charges."

"For Lucy Coe's death. But if Klops is alive, whose remains are in the morgue?" Harry asked.

Robson shrugged. "That's the Inspector's case. Mine is pretty much wrapped up unless he can't get answers from Klops." He scratched his cheek. "Kurt has been cleared of two homicides, Lydia's and Lucy's," he ticked off his fingers. "Will he get off with number three?"

If Kurt Klops lived, would he be facing murder charges? If he died without confessing, would the identity of the man in the grave go unknown just like the identity of the man in the cupboard? Beyond *Waysayer*, Josephine couldn't trace him to a plantation, to a family.

"Is he really dying?" I asked. "I mean, it would seem unfair and senseless for Gertrude to find out her brother was alive only to watch him die. At least if you get to spend some time with someone—"

"Stop. Don't say that." Karen's voice became shrill. "You've had a lifetime, me a few years." She rushed to Harry, reaching for his hands. "I want Lily to be all right, but not if it means Hannah doesn't make it. Am I a monster?"

Harry pulled her into his arms and patted her back as sobs she'd held in escaped in heaving shudders. He rocked from side to side and spoke softly. "You're no monster, dear girl. You're human and hurting. It will be okay. We don't have to choose; they can both make it. They'll be as right as rain." He stroked her hair and held her until the sobbing stopped. She pulled away and stared into his eyes.

"Can one family be that lucky, Harry? Can we?"

I'd been thinking the same thing. What were the chances that Hannah and Lily could survive? Why not? If they sat in the same section they could have made it to safety. What about the stories of one person surviving and the person next to them not? I shook my head to drive the "what ifs" out of my mind. Instead, I reached my short arms around them trying to add my comfort to theirs.

It became immediately apparent that my willing arms would not make the circle. Jan stepped to the other side and stretched her arms around touching my wrists with her fingers. She had comforted Hannah's son and now Hannah's partner. Juliana and Marisol sat next to each other drawing some compassion from each other. Only my dad stood alone staring into space, perhaps thinking of how it ended with my mom.

That's how Ric found us when he entered the room. With our heads bowed only Juliana and Marisol saw him. They stood quickly. Jan saw him next. We felt her arms stiffen, then drop from the circle. We separated.

"Ric!" Karen cried, then stopped. Her brother's face held no professional distance. The pain at what he must tell us etched deep around his eyes.

Harry guided Karen to a chair and gently pushed her to sit. He stood behind her with his hands on her shoulders. Harry squeezed her shoulders, then lifted her head.

Ric couldn't look at Karen; he kept his eyes focused on

Harry. "The storm subsided enough for rescue teams to go in two hours ago. They learned that the bus broke in half when it rolled and that the explosion reported burned only a small part of the bus. The wreckage is spread out over a larger area than first anticipated."

"Ric, stop talking like a cop," Karen pleaded.

He squared his shoulders. "The search is ongoing, but they're fighting against time. Another storm is hovering and they are pulling out with the people they have found; eleven survivors and five bodies." Ric raised his hand to stop questions. "There are several women who survived. My source tells me he thinks a few are American, but no one is stopping to check IDs. They're getting them out of there before the storm makes them part of someone else's rescue efforts." Ric hesitated. "That's what we've got."

Harry's hands were gripping the back of Karen's chair. "You're not telling us everything." It wasn't a question.

Ric's gaze locked on Harry's.

"No, I'm not. There's no way to verify anything at this point. There's no sense in…" Ric crouched in front of his sister and took her hand. "They think one of the deceased women was American or British. She had long blonde hair."

The bombshell exploded, hurtling emotional shrapnel in every direction. Karen's eyes went blank, then filled with comprehension and finally pain. Ric stayed at his sister's knee holding her hand and rubbing her forearm.

Harry had turned away from Karen and leaned straight-armed against the wall. I slipped my arm around his waist.

"It doesn't have to be one of them. We don't know how many American or British women were on the bus."

He spoke without lifting his head. "What are the odds it's not one of them?" His voice shook with emotion. "My

God, Grace, I'm praying it's not Hannah. Does that mean I don't care—"

I placed my fingers on his lips. "Shhh. It means no such thing."

He pulled me into his arms his voice low; I could barely hear him as close as he was to my ear. "I can't give her up, even if it means Will won't have his mum."

I pulled back a little and looked into his eyes. "You are not making the choice. It's done. It is what it is and praying or wishing won't change it." The pinch at the back of my throat signaled I had maybe a moment before my tears joined his. "We don't know for sure. Pray on that." My voice broke and I buried my head in his chest. I cried for the pain I saw on his face and for the torment he was feeling.

His protective instinct kicked in and I felt his hand patting my back. I rested my cheek against his chest and looked at Karen. Ric sat next to her still holding her hand and talking softly to her. I couldn't hear the words only the tone.

My dad's face reflected the sorrow in the room. Jan had her arm around his waist, her head tipped against his shoulder. Tears traced a path down her cheeks.

Marisol had moved closer to Ric and Karen, but kept her distance, ready to be there but not overstepping. She was a good fit for him, his personality.

Harry stood straighter. "What?"

He whispered, "It's not Hanns. I've been trying to feel her loss and I can't. It's not her." His voice bore the edge of hysteria. He turned toward Karen, but I pulled him round to face me.

"You have no proper identification. You can't know for sure. Don't build her hopes without proof."

He looked calmly at me, then smiled. He touched his chest. "I know here." He turned again toward Karen.

I don't know if Ric guessed his intent. He stood quickly and approached us. "A word with you, Marsden?" He nodded toward the door. Harry followed him out.

I slipped into the chair next to Karen and held her hand, still warm from Ric's grip. Years before we had sat together, she comforting me, when I thought Harry had been killed. I knew from that experience how friendship could ease the anguish. It was shortly after that ordeal that Karen met Hannah who'd come to see personally that her brother had survived. We were full circle. Suddenly, without any more information than Harry had, I felt that this vigil would turn out joyously as it had for me. Hannah was alive!

Karen stirred. I must have squeezed her hand or somehow sent a signal through my body language and she responded. I rubbed her arm and whispered. "Keep a strong thought that she's alive. You told me that years ago and it worked. It'll work again."

She lifted her head and looked straight into my eyes. "They're purple." She smiled and grasped my hand.

We stayed that way until Harry and Ric returned. Harry motioned me over to the door.

"Kramer thinks I should go to Brazil and help with the identification and arrangements to get them home. For once I agree with his idea." He glanced at his watch. "I can leave in a few hours." He put his arms around me. "I hate to leave you and Will."

"I know. Is Ric telling Karen the plan?"

Karen had pulled her hand out of Ric's grasp.

"I have every right to go," she said loudly.

"Don't be unreasonable. He can travel in a few hours.

You have two kids who need you especially if..." Ric hesitated. "Karen, please think of them if not yourself and me."

His plea hit home and as much as I knew she wanted to go, her eyes moved across the room at the bouncy seats and knew she had to stay. She turned to Harry. Her voice cracked as she enjoined him to bring Hannah home. He nodded and pulled me behind him. I whirled to say goodbye. Before the door closed I glimpsed a tableau of concern etched on the faces of those inside.

Walter all but barreled into us in his haste to bring us the news. Kurt had rallied. It seemed he would cheat death after all. Walter decided to bring food to Gertrude since she wouldn't budge. They weren't exactly chatting, but they were exchanging some words.

Harry explained his mission to Walter. The older man's face filled with concern.

"*Dat ist* no place *gut* for you."

"Walter, *Stoppen Sie zu sprechen.*"

"*Nicht werde Ich nicht.*" He turned to me with a fire and fear in his eyes.

"Missus Grace, they are making trouble if he go back."

"Walter, enough," said Harry. "If you want to help me, please keep an eye on Grace and Will. I will be back in a few days and I will have Hannah and Lily with me. I swear before God."

Harry hustled me out to the parking lot.

"What did he mean? What trouble?"

I hobbled along as fast as I could to keep the pace of his long legs. He saw my dilemma and slowed down.

"Who would cause trouble? Why shouldn't—"

"Bloody hell, Grace, stop! Please stop talking, asking. I have to do this." We'd reached the car and he opened my door. I grabbed the edge and leaned against it.

"I want to know how dangerous it is for you to go back."

Harry covered his eyes with his hand, then ran it back through his hair leaving his normally smooth strands sticking about his head.

"Grace, life is about choices. This is my choice. Please understand."

"What about me? Don't I get a choice? To chose that you stay and let someone who is not a marked man do this job."

"If there were someone else, don't you think I'd let them take the risk?" Harry's low matter-of-fact tone didn't fool me.

"No, you wouldn't. You'd go."

I eased my grip on the door and slid into the seat. Harry closed the door and quickly joined me in the car. The engine burst to life before his door had closed.

We didn't speak. I bit my lip to keep back the tears.

Someone else could do this, you know that don't you?

I don't know that.

Yes, you do, Grace. C'mon, he's rushing into danger for his sister and his son's mother.

So? That's admirable. Foolhardy, but admirable.

So who is he rushing to, really?

"Stop it," I screamed.

Harry swerved and righted the car. "Grace, what is it?" He looked out my window, then half turned and glanced in the back seat. "What is it?"

I couldn't believe I'd yelled and out loud to boot.

"I'm sorry, I was thinking and got…I'm sorry." What could I say?

"Good Lord, Grace, I about lost control." He glanced at me and covered my hand with his. "Please think more quietly when I'm driving." He pulled my hand up to his lips and kissed it. "I'm coming back, darling. Don't doubt that for a moment." He released my hand and pulled the car into the garage.

We entered the darkened kitchen, Harry in the lead. "Let's get you upstairs. You need to get off that leg." Harry took the cane from my hand. "You don't need that." He lifted me into his arms and carried me in the dark through the living room to the staircase.

He set me gently on the side of our bed and knelt to ease off my shoes. His hands reached for the buttons on my shirt while his mouth found my lips. His mouth felt warm and firm and wonderful. Without breaking contact he shifted over me onto the bed and rolled me with him.

We lay side by side hurrying our fingers through buttons, sweeping aside our clothing. I thought only of Harry and only in the moment. I refused to allow thoughts of "sorry to inform you" to enter my mind. Tonight was what we had, forever, for always.

FORTY-FIVE

HARRY HAD LEFT three hours after we arrived home. I'd dozed and awakened to the noise of the shower. The scent of soap and his aftershave followed him out of the bathroom. I could see his outline in the low light. He moved quickly and easily in the dark pulling clothes on and sliding items from his bureau top into his pockets. He had no need to pack. My husband belonged to an elite group of people who trained to be ready to leave home in minutes. He'd had hours. The duffle, always packed and stored in our closet, lay in the doorway.

I shifted to a sitting position searching for my sweats and shirt in the tangle of linens. Harry came to me.

"Good morning, darling." He kissed me full on the lips. "Hmmm. You are delicious." He pulled the covers up and held them aloft. "Scoot back under there. No need for you to come down."

I knew he wanted to make this easier. I had a few minutes before my heart would dictate my emotions. "You mean you'd rather remember me laying naked in the dark on a love-stained bed?"

"I love it when you talk that way. Haven't I always told you that you should write romance, not children's books?

I held my injured knee and rolled back into bed. Harry pulled the covers over me and settled them around my shoulders. I lifted my arms over the cover and reached for his neck, pulling him down to my mouth. At the last second I tilted his head sideways to whisper, "Fine, but you're coming home to a gimpy gal wearing sweats and a barn shirt."

His laughter and proclamation of "I love you, Gracie Elena Morelli Marsden" still lingered in my head and gave me comfort now hours after Ric Kramer had arrived to drive him to the airport.

My dad had called an hour ago asking if he and Jan could stop by. I knew he wanted to check up on me, how I was doing. I'm sure Walter had expressed his concern about Harry's safety.

It'd had been only six hours—Harry was still in the air—but words like *interminable* popped into my head.

I'd showered and dressed in a Rosary College sweatshirt and a pair of cut-offs. My knee throbbed less, which amazed me. Of course, I had been off my leg. A slow smile spread across my face and settled in my heart.

My dad explained when he called that when Tracy found out what was happening, she offered to keep Will all day, then bring him out tonight when she finished work. He had countered with, "Bring the boys and we'll cook out."

"That's all right by you, honey, isn't it?" he'd asked an hour ago, promising to be here with all the fixings.

Good to his word, my dad now stood in the kitchen unpacking the provisions. He'd not only brought food for the cook out to which now my brother Marty was short listed, but he'd also brought a few "extras" for the Marsden larder.

"Here's a package of Uncle Pete's homemade sausage, fresh ground the other day. I bought a jar of Sicilian olives at the market last week. Caputo's has everything. I know Harry likes these."

"Dad, we can buy olives." I appealed to Jan who merely shrugged and grinned.

"The way I heard the story the cats got the olives."

I burst into laughter at his deadpan delivery. "Okay,

okay, I give." I placed the olives in the cabinet. "What's in the white bag?"

"Aunt Edna's pizzelles and Easter braid."

I raised my eyebrows. "Easter braid? I didn't think she'd have leftovers."

"They're not. She makes these every month. She's not a seasonal baker."

I glanced at my dad's waistline. "Apparently not."

Jan hooted and immediately coughed to cover the lapse.

My father had decided to make my home his base of operations today. While I brewed coffee and arranged non-seasonal bakery on a serving plate he outlined his plan.

"We've decided to stay in Berkeley for a few more years. We're redoing the kitchen, cabinets, floor, the whole shebang. Jan likes this island thing, but I think the kitchen is too small."

"So we're compromising on a peninsula," she finished.

"Yeah, like the Yucatan."

More laughter filled the room. I beamed my gratitude at my dad. Boy, did he know me or what?

We sat at the island. "When we left last night Walter was excited about Kurt's apparent recovery. What else did he say?"

My dad looked surprised. "That's right, you didn't hear about his confession."

"Walter's confession?"

"Not Walter, Kurt. Have more coffee, honey, you're not focused." He lifted the carafe and topped off my mug.

"This story is as bizarre as the other two. Kurt was using the cellar as a *safe house* for his hooch. He was making a nice piece of change, enjoying swinging with the Coe girls, when a monkey wrench by the name of Jimmy 'Bags' Murphy hooks up with him. Murphy sees

the sweet deal and wants to deal himself in for an unreasonable piece of the action.

"Kurt's had some wise guys try this before and he's
been able to use his supplier like a guardian angel to persuade the thugs to be reasonable. The glitch this time is
that Murphy plays the one card Kurt can't afford to ignore.
Murphy threatens Kurt's father with, get this, exposing
him as a Nazi sympathizer."

My jaw dropped. "Could that really have done any damage? I mean, he wasn't a Nazi. Right?"

"Didn't matter back then. Germany had smashed
through Poland and France. People were scrutinizing all
Germans even those born in this country. That's when
Braun became *Brown* and *Schmidt and Schneider* changed
to *Smith and Snyder.* Sauerkraut became cabbage." He
shook his head. "Not a good climate in which to be accused of Nazi connections. Kurt said his dad was proud to
be in America it would kill him if his neighbors shunned
him, or worse, if the government decided to deport him."

"This was 1939 or 1940. Why was Kurt still hiding li-
quor? They'd repealed Prohibition."

"Several towns remained dry, including Oak Park. Kurt
serviced the towns that were voted dry. His routes took
him up to Evanston and out west to Wheaton. There were
still speakeasies only they called them clubs."

"Kurt killed him when he threatened his father?"

"He described the fight, explaining that Murphy died
when Kurt threw him down on a rusted out fireplace grate.
The noise attracted the older man. When Kurt explained
the threat, his father's face crumbled with the knowledge
that his son had killed a man to protect his dream, his
new life.

"Mr. Klops helped Kurt bury the body. Kurt worried
about retribution against him or his family from Murphy's

brother. In those moments of panic and confusion the two
men planned their argument and story. Kurt did write the
letter that Gertrude mentioned her father had read, then
burned. Kurt had enough money to get to Canada. He
kept in touch with Lydia. She'd always been the one. He
adored her.

"He almost came home when his mother died, but Mr.
Klops warned him off. He'd seen two strangers on the
block and feared they were part of Murphy's gang. Time
passed and Lydia came into her trust and moved to De-
troit. Eventually she and Kurt were married. Kurt did return for his father's funeral, but in disguise. It pained him
to pass within feet of his sisters and not reach out to them,
to comfort them".

"Couldn't he have come back? I mean, how powerful
was this Murphy guy that Kurt would stay away?" I asked.

My dad shrugged. "I don't know if that was the whole
reason. If any of it came out, especially after his father
died, he'd still be facing murder charges. I think he felt at
that point that the girls had gotten on with their lives and
his return would only bring them shame and possible danger. If those men hanging around were part of Murphy's
gang, it could spell trouble for the family."

"Gertrude must be devastated. To know he was close
by all those years. What brought them back to Illinois?"

"They tried to buy the house when Gertrude sold to
Karen and Hannah. The sale went through quickly and
they lost that opportunity. He said they believed they had
to move back to follow the plans for the house. They panicked when the first body was discovered, fearful the other
would be found, too.

"Lydia and Lucy had chosen the cellar for Lucy's resting place because it was in a home. During Lydia's sub-

sequent visits to the family she'd always find a reason to visit the cellar.

"Mr. Klops put in the floor to hide Murphy's grave. With the renovation in full swing it was bound to happen. When they heard the remains were of a black man they were stunned; they hoped that would be it."

"It was Will who suggested to Ric that there might be more cupboards," I said feeling a swell of pride.

My dad nodded. "Yeah, his comment turned the tide and put Kurt and Lydia in the trick bag."

The phone rang.

Harry's voice sounded firm and clear like he should walk in from the next room.

"Good morning, darling. I wanted you to know I've landed and I'm waiting for my guide and transportation."

"You have a guide? I mean, do you know him?"

Harry's low chuckle filled my heart. "Yes, dear. I know I mustn't talk to strangers. I called ahead to someone whose friend knows the area. It will take about three hours to get there. I'll call you as soon as I have news."

"Please be careful. Please."

"You know nothing can keep me from you. Take heart, Gracie. I love you."

My throat tightened and all I could muster was, "Me too."

"Later, darling." The connection broke and my tears followed.

Jan had her arms around me guiding me to the nook and the bench seat. I used her arm instead of my cane to hobble across the tile.

"Gracie, you know Harry. He'll be safe, he'll be back."

I gulped air and nodded. "Just why back there?" I managed to jerk out.

"That's what Walter was fuming about. You should have

seen him tear into Kramer. He accused him of manipulat-
ing Harry at a vulnerable time, encouraging him to go to
the one place in the world he should avoid."

My father's words chilled me because I'd only thought
them, not heard them out loud. The blood drained from
my face leaving me light-headed and unfocused.

"For heaven's sake, Mike, shut up!" Jan's voice reached
me through the fog. Some part of me registered humor that
my dad had been told off. Most of me concentrated on the
horror of what I'd heard.

I felt the cool glass pushed against my hand, then Jan's
dry hand on mine coaxing it around the glass. "Take a sip,
honey. You'll feel better."

As if that's all it would take to stop the joy draining
from my being. I lifted the glass to my lips and sipped,
then gulped the liquid. No matter; I felt empty.

FORTY-SIX

ONE BY ONE the people involved began to appear on my doorstep. Walter and Gertrude arrived before Tracy and the boys. Jan had told them Harry would be calling in the evening and suggested they stop by.

Gertrude had been with Karen whenever she wasn't at Kurt's bedside, so Karen knew to come. When Karen told Ric that Harry had called and would call again that evening and that she had to be there, he offered to help her tote the babies, since all her babysitters would be in Pine Marsh.

Marisol called Ric about their dinner plans and he invited her. When Marisol told George Shaw who told Detective Robson who blabbed to Juliana who immediately told Josephine... You see how the house filled up.

Earlier in the day I'd recovered from my dark thoughts when my dad and Jan shared their wedding plans. They wanted a fall wedding with the ceremony in the backyard, officiated by my brother Joseph of course, and the reception at the Pine Marsh Golf Club. I listened to their prattle about guest lists and decorations, realizing they were sharing the details, not only the high points, to keep me engaged in positive, jubilant thoughts.

When even my romantic nature couldn't absorb one more "darling" or "sweet" detail I begged to be excused to look after the horses. They nodded and beamed at each other. I'm sure they felt their ploy went beautifully, and had it been their generation, they would have bumped fists.

I avoided the arrival of several people by spending the

next few hours working in the barn, cleaning out stalls, grooming the horses, straightening the tack, in general, hiding in the barn.

"I thought I'd find you here."

Ric's voice startled me, yet I had expected him to seek me out. I turned and faced him.

"No matter what, they need attention." I had bits of straw in my hair and on my jacket. In the past, Ric would have moved in too close for comfort and brushed the straw from my clothes. I braced to step back. No need. He stood rooted in the doorway.

"I know, you taught me that. I remember you wouldn't let me ride until I knew all the body parts and how to care for them. Sheesh, I thought you'd never let me ride." His dazzling smile failed to light up the room for me.

"Your dad wanted you to know that he put some lunch together."

"Thanks, but I'm not hungry." I turned back to my task hoping he wouldn't step up behind me and offer to help. That would have been his obvious approach to get closer to me. No footsteps across the ground, no movement of air or smell of Colours. He'd left; my shoulders relaxed. I thought to lash out at him for suggesting Harry's involvement, but Harry would have come to the same conclusion without Ric. Wasting energy on negative recriminations wouldn't bring Harry home any sooner.

I knew I'd have to leave the comfort of the barn and face the gathering. April and even Cash sensed my unease and tossed their heads. "It's okay. It's okay," I repeated in a singsong tone to them, wondering how it would be okay if Connor or Will lost their moms. I was an adult when my mother died; the pain and loss so devastating, it has taken years not to cry just thinking about her absence in my life.

Connor wouldn't remember Hannah, but Will... My

heart ached for the little boy whose life had turned topsy-turvy with the introduction to his dad. How would he cope without his mom? Would he turn to me, allow me a place in his life without rancor or what ifs? That was asking a lot from a kid; it took me awhile to accept Jan in my dad's life.

"Grace," Will shouted. "Grace." His voice grew louder as he zeroed in on the barn. Harry's son rushed through the door raising dust as he skidded to a stop.

"Everyone is inside. Uncle Ric said you were out here an hour ago. Aren't you coming in?"

An hour! I'd lost all track of time. I stared at Will, seeing all the grown up parts of Harry in his face, and resisted the urge to hug him to me. Unbidden, the thought that Will might be all I'd have of Harry sprang to my mind. I swallowed hard to fight the tears that accompanied the awful thought. I nodded and followed him out of the barn.

People spilled out of the house following my dad and my brother. One carried the snacks, another the beverages. Most everyone carried a drink already; guess they wanted to stay close to the source.

I washed up in the mudroom and used the back stairs to avoid anyone coming through the living room to the back. I'd perfected hopping up the stairs. The quiet of my bedroom welcomed me and thoughts of playing truant took hold. They wouldn't miss me. They each had stories to tell. We all were waiting for the same phone call. I could slip into bed and avoid…

Life. You could avoid life.

Don't do it, Gracie. This is how it starts.

I don't want to face them.

You don't want to face yourself. This way isn't for you. Mom hid. We loved her.

Did Mom love herself?

The door slammed downstairs; the boys must have

come inside. They might be coming up to Will's room. I closed my bedroom door and waited. They hustled past my room, all three talking at once about the newest Nintendo game. The door to Will's room closed.

I showered, dressed in fresh barn-scent-free clothes and combed my hair in some semblance of smooth. I gripped the edge of the vanity. My mind needed to rest. *Grip, inhale. Grip, exhale. Grip, inhale.*

Seven more and I could leave. I tracked my progress by visualizing lifting a finger for each sequence.

My eyes opened after number ten. Same violet eyes and pale face. Somehow my hair had managed to frizz up at the crown. I searched through my closet and found a baseball cap that sort of matched my outfit. I could at least look pulled together even if my heart and mind had fragmented with fear and worry.

I heard the boys thump down the stairs. I used the back stairs, again reaching the ground floor two steps behind their rushing figures. I smiled, remembering how as children my brothers had never walked. It was some kind of power walk ready to break into a trot, almost a sprint, if someone yelled "last one to get there is a rotten egg."

"It's good to see you smile." Marisol said. She had walked through from the living room.

I waved my hand at the back door. "It's the kids; hard not to smile at them."

She nodded. "How is it working out with Will? Must be difficult at times."

I wondered why she'd ask. Then I remembered what she'd said when she left to return to her post last year. She'd told me I'd be raising a son.

"Oh, yeah, your prediction. I guess it is tougher when you don't start out with an infant. We won't be dealing with that stage."

She stared at me. "Don't be too sure about that."

"Sure about what?" My brother had barged in from the mudroom.

I felt myself blushing. Marisol moved in front of me to face Marty, effectively blocking me from his view. "Your sister is sure we won't run out of food. I think we might." Her seamless lie fooled Marty.

"Of course she knows we won't run out of food. We're Italian. It's better than fishes and loaves."

"Nonna Santa would have washed out your mouth with soap for that."

"Only if you translated what I said, tattletale." He play punched my arm. "C'mon, foods ready. I'm supposed to clear the house and get everyone outside. Anyone else in here?"

Marisol and I shook our heads. We headed for the door, Marty in the lead.

"Wait. Let me get the phone from Harry's office. We can plug it in outside."

Marty caught my arm before I turned. "Already done. We sent Will up to get it before you came in."

No reason not to go out there and face the crowd. Marisol stepped aside, motioning for me to pass her.

Was she being polite or cutting off my escape?

FORTY-SEVEN

BURGERS, BRATS, CHICKEN—the works! I didn't think I could possibly eat a bite and couldn't fathom how I'd eaten the chicken, brat, potato salad, cucumber salad and three-bean salad someone had heaped on my plate. I smiled at the picnic plates. The sprig of pink daisies up the side reminded me of happy times except for last night at the ER. Would this afternoon erase the sad memory or would more sadness associate with the plastic plates?

As though in a macabre version of *The 1001 Arabian Nights*, each person with a story to tell about the house on Grove Street came forward.

"I have searched through records of the day and I cannot find anything more on Mr. Coe of Oak Park. He died and his house passed to his brother, Lydia and Lucy's grandfather, who let the house sit empty for years arranging with neighbors to care for the property. At the turn of the century when the grandfather died, his son decided to sell the house. The man who bought it lived there for fifteen years until he enlisted in WWI. He was killed in Flanders and the house passed on to his younger brother who had no interest in the property. After the war, the brother hired an estate agent to sell the house. Post-war years were difficult and the house sat empty again until 1925 when an immigrant family from Germany," Josephine paused and smiled at Gertrude, "made the deal of their lifetime and bought the house. It needed extensive repairs and the house had developed an odor. The estate agent told the brother to get what he could and the deal with the Klops family was struck.

"Mr. Klops, an excellent chef, knew that he'd find work in the large city of Chicago, knew that people would find the money to escape to an elegant supper club to forget their troubles."

Gertrude smiled wistfully, remembering happier times. She ducked her head in short bursts affirming Josephine's story. I'd never known her father was a chef. Is that who taught her how to make that fabulous strudel? Stupid me, I guess I thought all Germans could make strudel. Like all Italians could make gravy? All the ones I knew could. I shook my head to get back on track.

"Missus Grace, *Sind Sie wohl?*"

"I'm fine. Just didn't know your father was a chef."

She smiled proudly. "*Ja.* He *vas* a chef for Berghoff Restaurant. Mister Herman take him in for work right away. He work very much hours. Sometimes after he *vas* finished cooking he change his clothes and go be waiter. *Mein vater* never afraid to work hard."

Josephine resumed the story. "Mr. Klops did well at Berghoff's. Berghoff's did well surviving prohibition by serving near beer and Bergo Soda Pop and expanding their food service. He provided for his family even hiring help for his wife whose health was frail. You know the rest of the story from mine and Clarisse's experiences."

She shook her head. "How strange that my avocation has brought me back to my roots and the biggest mystery I've encountered in my forty years of research about the Underground Railroad."

"Bizarre is more like it," Marty mumbled.

Marisol asked the question that had developed in my mind. "If you can't find the *Waysayer's* family, what happens to him?"

Josephine smiled. "That bothers me, too. I'd hate to think of his remains in a hermetically sealed box on a shelf. I've decided I'll tell his story in the book I'm finishing now. I think he'd want someone to know about the treachery and duplicity he encountered.

"You think so, Grace?"

I smiled at her, feeling a piece of my turmoil subside. "I know he would."

She nodded. "Me, too. Once the morgue releases his remains I'm taking them to Ottawa to be buried with my grandfather, Julien. I think he'd like to meet him. I'm adding *Waysayer* to the headstone with the epitaph, 'Home to the Lord 1852, at Peace 1994'. I know it sounds chilling, but it's the truth. His story will be told."

Silence followed her explanation.

"I don't suppose it matters much to the Coe family," Karen said. "I've been reading up on the family. They were prominent during the Underground Railroad and genuinely helpful. They were instrumental in helping several slaves escape after hiding them in their home while they waited for dark and a boat or wagon to take them on their next leg to freedom. The Coes were friends with Pierce Downer and related by marriage to Frederick Graue, the mill owner.

"Their support was documented and collaborative. The Coe who owned Gertrude's house worked alone. Even the report of his arrest had conflicting information."

Josephine perked up. "I read only one newspaper account in my research."

Karen grinned. "Well, if you give a librarian a cookie…" She stopped and smiled at the confused faces.

Benny piped up and finished, "He's going to ask for a glass of milk. Only it's a mouse, Aunt Karen, not a *liber-ryan*."

We burst into laughter as his correction. He grinned

from ear to ear, thrilled to be the center on adult attention and not be in trouble.

Not to be outdone, Matt chimed in with, "Yeah, and if you give a moose a muffin he'll want some jam to go with it."

Josephine held up her hands. "So what did your librarian friend ask for when you gave her the puzzle?"

Karen grinned. "She asked if I wanted to see the 19th Century Club's minutes and reports from that era and if I wanted to read the Cicero Life News."

"Why the Cicero newspapers?"

"Because Oak Park didn't vote to secede from Cicero until 1902. That particular paper held a different account of Coe's arrest and subsequent death. That account stated that Coe was arrested for *chicanery*, their word not mine, with the deeds and cash deposits from three area farmers who used him as their agent. This paper felt sure enough of his death to print the name of the farmer who was later arrested for killing Coe."

"I thought he'd been killed by a horse's kick," I said.

"He was, but I guess someone was controlling the horse that kicked him."

"How did anyone get the idea that Coe was a conductor on the Underground Railroad?" Josephine asked.

"Another man, J.A. Coles from Maywood, shows up in the First Baptist Church's records as having been arrested on the same day as John Coe. Mr. Coles lived in the '10 mile house', a house that functioned as a tavern, a post office, a gathering place for farmers and more importantly, a station on the Underground Railroad."

"Gee, maybe we can go there with my troop." Will said. His eyes gleamed with adventure—another gene he'd received from his dad's pool.

Josephine spoke. "Will, it was razed in 1927. You know what's there now?" She waited a beat. "A McDonald's."

"Seems a shame no one knew about it in time to save it and restore it," my brother said. "So the account of Mr. Coles was confused with the arrest of Mr. Coe?"

Karen shrugged. "It would appear that's exactly what happened."

Marty continued. "Is there anyone left in the Coe family to care if this story comes out?"

We all turned to Gertrude and her new-found connection to the Coe family.

She shook her head. "*Nein*. Because of her sister's sickness, my *bruder und* Lydia never have babies." Her wistful tone tugged at my heart.

"The cousin died in war. Never married, no children. Lydia *vas* last one."

Walter slipped his arm around her shoulders.

Each body had a story and now we knew each story. I felt a sense of closure for those long dead. But instead of bringing me an anticipated peace, the fact that the mystery of the cellar on Grove had been explained left my mind less encumbered and more open to fretting and fearing the present.

Everyone claimed to be stuffed, even the offer of strudel tempting only the boys and Marty. Will took Ben and Matt and Marty to the coach house to have their dessert. "Me and Dad are going to turn it into a clubhouse," Will'd said as the other boys trailed behind him across the yard.

Marisol, Karen and Ric wandered toward the greenhouse. Dad and Jan talked quietly about where they'd set up the arch under which they'd be married.

The twins slept away tucked in their carriers in the shade. Gertrude and Walter sat near them.

The phone rang. Time moved in slow waves emanating from the phone rolling towards me.

I snatched up the receiver. "Hello."

"Darling, I haven't much time. Another storm is moving in and we're losing light. Tell Will his mum is alive. For your ears only, she's bad off. They're airlifting her to hospital in Sao Paulo. I'll join her there after, after..." his voice thickened.

"Harry, what is it?" I forced myself to ask. "Hannah?"

"People saw her after the crash, but we can't find her. She's gone. I won't leave without her, without Lily. Darling, I don't know any more except that I will come back to you. I'll call as soon as I can. I love you, Grace."

Those were the last words he spoke before the overseas connection was severed. I slumped in my chair and dropped the useless receiver to my lap.

The ringing phone had alerted those nearby to return. The short conversation gave them little time to reach me before it was over. A sea of faces stared at me, begging me for news. Karen leaned closest.

"Gracie?"

I lifted my tear-streaked face, staring momentarily at each worried face. What would the next hours and days mean to us? Would Lily survive? Would Hannah be found? Could Harry stay longer in that country without endangering his life? My voice croaked.

"Lily is alive. Hannah is missing. Harry is staying."

No one moved; no one spoke. I closed my eyes and heard him in my head. *I will come back to you.*

* * * * *

REQUEST YOUR FREE BOOKS!
2 FREE NOVELS PLUS 2 FREE GIFTS!

◆HARLEQUIN®

INTRIGUE®

BREATHTAKING ROMANTIC SUSPENSE

YES! Please send me 2 FREE Harlequin Intrigue® novels and my 2 FREE gifts (gifts are worth about $10). After receiving them, if I don't wish to receive any more books, I can return the shipping statement marked "cancel." If I don't cancel, I will receive 6 brand-new novels every month and be billed just $4.74 per book in the U.S. or $5.24 per book in Canada. That's a savings of at least 14% off the cover price! It's quite a bargain! Shipping and handling is just 50¢ per book in the U.S. and 75¢ per book in Canada.* I understand that accepting the 2 free books and gifts places me under no obligation to buy anything. I can always return a shipment and cancel at any time. Even if I never buy another book, the two free books and gifts are mine to keep forever.

182/382 HDN F42N

Name	(PLEASE PRINT)	

Address		Apt. #

City	State/Prov.	Zip/Postal Code

Signature (if under 18, a parent or guardian must sign)

Mail to the Harlequin® Reader Service:
IN U.S.A.: P.O. Box 1867, Buffalo, NY 14240-1867
IN CANADA: P.O. Box 609, Fort Erie, Ontario L2A 5X3
**Are you a subscriber to Harlequin Intrigue books
and want to receive the larger-print edition?
Call 1-800-873-8635 or visit www.ReaderService.com.**

* Terms and prices subject to change without notice. Prices do not include applicable taxes. Sales tax applicable in N.Y. Canadian residents will be charged applicable taxes. Offer not valid in Quebec. This offer is limited to one order per household. Not valid for current subscribers to Harlequin Intrigue books. All orders subject to credit approval. Credit or debit balances in a customer's account(s) may be offset by any other outstanding balance owed by or to the customer. Please allow 4 to 6 weeks for delivery. Offer available while quantities last.

Your Privacy—The Harlequin® Reader Service is committed to protecting your privacy. Our Privacy Policy is available online at www.ReaderService.com or upon request from the Harlequin Reader Service.

We make a portion of our mailing list available to reputable third parties that offer products we believe may interest you. If you prefer that we not exchange your name with third parties, or if you wish to clarify or modify your communication preferences, please visit us at www.ReaderService.com/consumerschoice or write to us at Harlequin Reader Service Preference Service, P.O. Box 9062, Buffalo, NY 14269. Include your complete name and address.

HII3R

Reader Service.com

Manage your account online!

- Review your order history
- Manage your payments
- Update your address

> **We've designed
> the Harlequin® Reader Service
> website just for you.**

Enjoy all the features!

- Reader excerpts from any series
- Respond to mailings and special monthly offers
- Discover new series available to you
- Browse the Bonus Bucks catalog
- Share your feedback

Visit us at:

ReaderService.com